HALO

John Loveday

HALO

A HARVEST ORIGINAL

HARCOURT BRACE & COMPANY

San Diego   New York   London

Requests for permission to make copies of
any part of the work should be mailed to:
Permissions Department, Harcourt Brace & Company,
6277 Sea Harbor Drive, Orlando, Florida 32887-6777.

First published in Great Britain
in 1992 by Fourth Estate Limited

Photograph on part openers by the Douglas Brothers.

Library of Congress Cataloging-in-Publication Data
Loveday, John.
Halo / John Loveday.
p.   cm.
"A Harvest original."
ISBN 0-15-600113-6
1. Frontier and pioneer life — West (U.S.) — Fiction.   2. Mothers
and daughters — West (U.S.) — Fiction.   3. Overland journeys
to the Pacific — Fiction.   4. Photographers — West (U.S.) — Fiction.
I. Title.
PR6062.079H34   1994
823'.914 — dc20   94-35930

The text was set in Cochin
Designed by Camilla Filancia

Printed in the United States of America
First U.S. edition 1994   B C D E

To Evelyn, Sharon, Marina,
and Julian

Author's Note

The place called Halo in this novel does not exist; it never existed, though I like to imagine the last edifices of a ghost town steadily collapsing, unregarded.

The quotations from Walt Whitman's *Leaves of Grass* are from the 1855 first edition. Issued by Whitman himself, this version remained little known until its publication in 1959 by The Viking Press.

This hour I tell things in confidence,
I might not tell everybody but I will tell you.

I am the poet of the woman the same as the man. . . .

Walt Whitman,
Leaves of Grass

Part One

Justly Wading

1

Justly was wading, holding up her skirt, in speckling sunlight and shadow under the trees. I had stopped fishing when she came, though she had wanted to watch. She had come against the fallen tree, where I sat among torn roots. It was where the stream widened into a pool and the water was still and you could see fish moving in the brown depths when the light was right. We had not had much to say, and she had slipped into the pool suddenly, without a word, and waded out. When the water was above her knees, she stood there, facing away across the stream and up the slope, her dark gold hair touched with disks of brightness.

Her shoulders were skinny, and her arms and body looked smaller than usual, against the dazzle. The skirt was one of her mother's which she had recently started to wear, too long and tucked at the waist. It made her seem like a smaller version of her mother, though she was not so pretty.

"Scrag?"

"What?"

"Can I go any further?"

"No!"

I imagined her dropping into a dip, calling out in alarm, the skirt spreading wide on the surface, then seeing her slip down and the waters close, myself swashing into the pool to save her.

"No, it's deep out there."

"How do you know?"

"I swum there."

I thought she would know I was lying but she did not answer.

She stood there for a while and I watched her. We were two months out from Independence and it seemed like six or maybe longer. This was the only long stop in over a week, and the wagons were gathered a little way downstream behind the trees, at another pool, with lower banks where the horses could water. I had known this girl for as long as I could remember, but my memories of her in Scrimshaw — little pictures of her by a gate, or in a doorway, or turning a corner in snow last winter — were already fading and blurring, as if from very long ago. It was as if she had become somebody different.

When she turned, she came toward me very slowly, hardly stirring the water, veering a little downstream, so she came in on a curve to the right of my place among the tree roots. It was deeper there than on the other side, where she had entered, and the water was halfway up her thighs. She would have disturbed the spot where the fish waited.

She had gathered her skirt now in one hand only, the other grasping one of the roots that tapered out toward her, leaning back a little, letting it take her weight, humming quietly. I saw that the water reflected the underside of her skirt, the pale glimmer of flesh. "What are you staring at?" She had not

said it anywhere but in my head. She had closed her eyes
against the sun, and was humming. I looked back at the thing
in the water and watched the motes of surface dust drift over
it, and the minutest of ripples make it waver in its darkness,
and felt a rush of guilt. The image scattered as Justly strode
in toward me, clambering over roots and bank, her skirt falling
and clinging.

"Mind if I set a bit?" Then, "You gonna fish?"

"Be gone."

"They'll be back." She looked at me, touching the rod. "I
have a go?"

I took the worm tin out of the hollow and held it to her.

"Put one on the hook."

"Jesus," she said.

There were three or four worms only, squirming weakly
in the rusty bottom of the tobacco tin. She took one out and
held it dangling.

I offered her the hook.

"Put it on."

"Jesus."

She took the hook, brought it close to the worm.

"Whereabouts?"

"Stick it in the middle and push it on a bit."

The hook went in and the worm writhed wildly. Justly
screeched.

"Push it on. Like a concertina."

She held it at arm's length and made the hook go well
along.

"Sorry I scritched."

I took the rod and cast for her, out to the right, beyond
where she had waded, then let her hold it. We sat for an hour

and she caught nothing. We talked about Scrimshaw. At moments it seemed very real, and I could smell the drain behind Rodd's Store or someplace, and see the sharp-angled shadows and white-painted walls, or hear familiar voices, but then, almost immediately, it would become remote, blurred, soundless. Several times, when our voices as they were then came back momentarily, I wanted to say, as I would have done in Scrimshaw, "You got no drawers on," but the voice in my head sounded oddly foolish, and my heart thumped in alarm.

"I got things to do," I said at last, lying. I wanted to be away from her, to soap a harness, or split firewood, to look busy. When I took the rod and swung the line in, the worm was lifeless. I made her take it off so she would know the feel of the whole business without the pleasure of the catch. She flung it away, high and far, and it plipped into the water.

As I got up she dropped into the pool again on the shallow side of the tree and washed her hand, then gathered up her skirt and waded out a bit.

2

Justly's mother was leaning against the wagon, smoking her pipe. It was a clay, with the longest and slenderest stem I had ever seen. She kept tilting her face up, so her coppery curls touched back against the cover, half closed her eyes, and let the smoke out in gentle meanderings.

"Scrag, I'm showing off to you." She looked at me. "You," she said, pointing the stem at me, "should be giving ear to Thou-Wert." She took a draw. "Just listen to that old ranter."

From inside the circle of wagons there was the sound of Thou-Wert in full voice.

"Let us listen to the Lord of Hosts, let us listen to the Savior of Souls, let us listen to the Comforter of the Sorrowful, the Upholder of the Oppressed, let us listen to the Guide in the Desert, the Mover of Mountains —"

"Let us listen to Thou-Wert," said Lorelei. She held the pipe out. "Like a draw?"

I took the pipe. The stem was damp from her mouth. I did not wipe it, but found it gave me an odd excitement to purse my lips around where hers had just been. The fire was low in the bowl and the smoke was too hot now. I took several draws, shallow and timid, but pretended to enjoy them before handing the pipe back.

"Lead us not into temptation," she said. "Let's go and listen."

She put the pipe in the wagon, and we went across the circle toward Thou-Wert. There were a dozen wagons in the circle, and most of the people from them were gathered in the center, where Thou-Wert was standing on an upturned tub. A few of the smaller children were scattered in the grassy space around.

"And who can say," Thou-Wert was going on, "and who can say he came without some fear in his heart, at the prospect of prairie, and desert, and mountain? Thou wert fearful! But cast thy fear upon the Lord, and fear not, for He will uphold thee. And who can say he came without shame, without shame for things done and things not done, for the secret in the heart and for the public sin? In shame thou wert, and He walked with thee."

He was a burly, dark-haired man in black garb, his face ruddy. He noticed us coming up behind the group.

"And who has come without hope, without hope — hope of finding, like Scrag" — he waved his arm across their heads, which turned or half turned to follow — "the comforts one day of a family bosom, or the hope of Lorelei and Justly for the smile of His Countenance upon them, or, oh, the hopes of any one of us — George and Will for fine timber smoothing under their planes, Clement and Martha for the fine herds swinging now in the pods of their bull, hopes of Sylvester, dreaming pictures and poems by the waters of the Willamette, of Clancy and Jane, asking, Lord, no more than a simple plot on which to turn Thy soil?"

Thou-Wert went on, naming them all. Sometimes heads turned, but mostly they were still after the first few names. Sometimes someone said "Amen" or "Praise be, yes," and once or twice there was a giggle of embarrassment or amusement at a turn of phrase. His words were warm and seemed heartfelt, but everybody knew that to Thou-Wert words came easily.

Sylvester, a tall man in a shapely gray suit and with a broad-brimmed black hat in his hand, stood in front of us. When Thou-Wert named Justly's mother, he turned, touched his hat to his forehead, and moved aside a little, allowing her to see past him. When the preacher had finished and people were moving apart, he looked at me with a smile.

"Spurious," he said. "Spurious, don't you think, Scrag?"

I would look the word up in my grandmother's old dictionary as soon as I got back to the wagon, but I thought I had guessed the right meaning and said, "Could be."

Justly had come around from the side of the group and joined her mother. They walked ahead.

"Now, there's a pretty woman, Scrag, don't you think? Well, I know you do."

I felt an impulse to affirm, not to let the moment for declaration pass.

"She is."

"And if I were going to love a woman for more than apple pie, I could find something fascinating there, Scrag."

Lorelei turned and smiled, as if she guessed we were looking at her.

"I'll lend you a book, Scrag," Sylvester said. "*Leaves of Grass*. Something unusual."

Sylvester's conversation often made me feel uncomfortable, because he seemed to want to treat me as if I could understand his meaning. He must have known that I would be thinking it out long afterward.

"I'll bring it along sometime."

He went off. I followed Justly and her mother through the space between our wagons. When Lorelei fetched her pipe, the three of us played the game of passing it over. They both passed it to me rather than to each other, and I found that the odd feeling of excitement came with it from Lorelei, and she seemed to know about that and to laugh because of it.

3

By candlelight, I looked in the dictionary for "spurious." The first meaning it gave was "not genuine," then, from the last line of the entry, "not legitimate" and "bastard" leaped up. Thou-Wert's face and voice changed from what I had seen and heard that afternoon, and I saw a gloomy cobbled street, which I thought to be in London, in which pale children, whose voices I could not quite hear, stood near doorsteps or moved away downhill or turned toward me, as if looking curiously at a stranger. Thou-Wert seemed to belong in this place, a child of uncertain origins, quite unlike the tanned and ruddy man whose image instantly returned. The momentary vision made me wonder for a while about his earlier days, about the beginnings of others in this band of people crouched or lying under their wagon covers, ready to move west again in the early light.

"Not genuine; not proceeding from the true source, or from the source pretended; counterfeit, false, adulterate": I read and reread the words, brief pictures and sensations flitting up from them. Was this what Sylvester meant? Did he mean that Thou-Wert was himself not genuine? Everybody knew that he was not a real minister, but he did not need to be, surely, did he? Or was it that the words themselves, the ideas that Thou-Wert spoke and lived by, were deceptions? Did Sylvester mean that Thou-Wert was deceiving himself or those who listened? Or both? Did he deceive others knowingly?

From the next wagon there was laughter, a pause, more laughter. I wondered what Justly and her mother might be saying, and listened, but no words came. I opened the cover and listened again, but their voices were low, rising only intermittently to laughter, sometimes separately, sometimes together. It seemed to be some game they were playing. I looked at the moon and stars awhile, thinking how they must be looking the same from Scrimshaw. When I went down and peed against the wagon wheel before turning in, I looked up over the ridge of the cover at the spaces between those glimmering specks and wondered if anyone out there was watching.

4

On a command from Axel, we halted. There was suddenly silence, broken only by the slight creak of harnesses or the snuffle of a horse. We were in open grassland, slightly undulating, with sparse groups of wiry trees and slopes away toward blue distances. I felt my first fear of the journey. I looked slowly around, slope by slope, hummock by hummock, from moving cloud shadow or tree shadow to brightness, and saw nothing that seemed to betray a figure, or more movement than grasses swaying slightly in currents of air. In places there was a shimmer of heat haze. Nearby, a few bees moved over purple clover.

A long time seemed to pass before anyone moved or spoke. By then the horses had started to graze, occasionally shaking heads or swishing tails. One by one, the men dropped down and went forward. As I came near, Axel pushed over the body of a young Indian with his foot. It suddenly turned on the small incline, an arm flinging limply outward, the legs going wide, so that he lay spread-eagle, a host of flies buzzing up in agitation but immediately settling again. Even while he was being turned, someone said, "God, they've cut his parts off!"

The man had a throat wound, from which blood had poured and was still seeping. His upper body was bare, and his hide trousers had been slashed apart in the act of mutilation.

"Holy Father," Thou-Wert said loudly. "Holy Father."

Axel looked back at the line of wagons and flung a gesture toward them.

"No vimen! Vimen keep avay."

Axel set his feet apart, stuck thumbs in his wide belt, and stood there solidly, his open shirt showing blond chest hair. He would be obeyed.

Some of the men went back to the women; others stood exclaiming in disgust or pity.

"Not dead long," said Axel. He tilted back the brim of his old slouch hat and brushed sweat away. "Not an hour, maybe."

"What kind of bastards done that?" said Clancy.

There was opinion that this was a tribal punishment, the body left for scavengers on unsacred ground, but Axel said the killing could have been done by white men. In the last two days, since leaving the side of the stream, we had seen, in the evidence of ashes, that another small company was not far ahead. If we were gaining ground on them, as appeared to be the case, it would not be long before we caught up. Axel was worried. If Indians found the body, we would be in danger. Two choices were open, to catch up with the other company and face any attack with greater numbers or stay on our own and strike off on a different trail, leaving pursuers with two ways to follow. After some discussion he said we should stay separate, even if we had to take an unmarked trail.

"Holy Providence will protect us," said Thou-Wert. "Let us bury this poor creature and be on our way."

Unnoticed, Justly and her mother had come up on the

other side of the wagons. They now crossed through and came beside me.

"Aw, who would do that?" Lorelei held my arm, at the same time drawing Justly to her.

"No vimen," Axel said sharply. "Go."

The men who had retreated to the wagons were coming back again, women craning over the boards to see what they could. There was a babble of discussion about the direction to take, the need to move quickly, and whether the body should be buried. I backed away a bit with Justly and her mother. Thou-Wert said the body must be buried, some men said that burial was against tribal custom, some said that a buried body might not be found, others that Indians would hardly miss the signal of newly turned soil. Clement said he would make a cross from some bars of a spare hen coop, so the grave would be taken for a wagoner's.

"Ve bury him," said Axel. "But damn quick."

Shovels and spades were fetched and the grave was being dug. Most people got up on the wagons again to be on the lookout.

"Vot's that man doink?" Axel called.

Sylvester had come out of his wagon with his tripod and camera. Beside me, he set out the legs of the tripod, regardless of Axel's words, and humped the polished wood-and-brass box of the camera onto it. Axel strode over.

"Vot you tink you doink?"

"It's obvious what I'm doing." Sylvester hardly gave him attention. "Would you stand aside a little, so I can see?" he asked Thou-Wert.

"I will not," said Thou-Wert. "This is a vile thing you are about."

"How is it that?"

"Obscene. An abomination."

"I'm recording. This is part of the story."

"A vile part. I say you should put that apparatus away."

"And *I* say," said Axel, "I tell you put that avay."

"You tell me what you like." Sylvester continued to adjust the camera.

"I am paid to lead," said Axel. "I am chosen by all, and I lead. I give orders."

Sylvester turned.

"You give me no orders on this. You lead the wagons. I'll lead my life."

"You lead funny life," said Axel.

"For what purpose might such a record be made?" asked Thou-Wert.

"Truth." Sylvester smiled. "The truth, part of your stock-in-trade. I apologize, I do not mean that offensively. But truth. The record of how it was. Here, under this particular bit of God's Heaven, at this particular moment."

"But this is a vile thing, an outrage, an offense to God."

"So was the Crucifixion," said Sylvester lightly, "but think of all those paintings of it."

"I find the comparison blasphemous," said Thou-Wert. "I know you intend no blasphemy."

"All these people will talk of what they saw here," said Sylvester.

"Ah, they will that."

"Would you condemn that?"

"I could not. Verily, I could not."

"Some will write of it. In letters, in diaries."

"I shall myself."

"Why should a picture be more offensive?"

Thou-Wert hesitated.

"I know not why. But it is. Perhaps because it lacks moderation."

"Perhaps because it tells truth more starkly," Sylvester said.

"Ve vaste time," said Axel.

Thou-Wert turned to him.

"Sylvester should make his picture."

Axel shrugged and turned away to inspect the grave.

"Would you not want him partially covered, at least?" Thou-Wert asked.

But Sylvester was already seeing to the camera's work. When he was finished, the grave was ready. The body was rolled into an old blanket and dropped down. Axel ordered the bloodstained grass and soil to be cut away and put in the grave, too. Most of the company who had not already been drawn forward by the argument or by the spectacle of the photograph-taking came now to hear Thou-Wert's graveside words, which were surprisingly brief.

"Thou wert wounded in such a way that the Holy Scriptures do specifically debar thee from the Kingdom of Heaven, and thou wert a sad heathen, anyway, but the Lord of Hosts have mercy on thee, poor man, and succor thee on thy journey. Amen." He looked up at the company and raised his hand. "And the Lord be with us on ours."

"For we might need thee," said Sylvester, aside to me, "with Axel in charge." He turned to Lorelei and Justly. "Perhaps one day I could make some pictures of you 'vimen'?"

Lorelei seemed pleased.

"Partially covered, at least."

I knew that she was quoting the words Thou-Wert had used a few minutes earlier, as a joke, and I felt the need for some lightness to break the horror of the scene, but in that moment I also felt the foolishness of being young, aware of implications, in words or tones of voice, that were not quite graspable. In that moment, looking away in confusion, my eyes met Justly's and read in them a similar feeling, though she immediately linked arms with her mother and joined in her smile.

"Part of my true record," said Sylvester.

"Up on vagons," called Axel. "Ve start."

The grave was strewn with grass, the rough cross standing just clear of it, and we moved off, Clement's bull, Tickler, bellowing at the rear of the train, at being dragged from good clover.

5

JOURNAL, 1859

Saturday, June 11
A short while after the burial yesterday we lit out across a low hill into unknown country.

Wednesday, June 15
The danger has gone, but we are far from where we should be, following a shallow but fast stream, looking for a place to ford.

Saturday, June 18
Two days' rest before we go over.

6

Axel was standing in midstream, stripped to his britches, his blond hair and pale body gleaming. Some of the company were watching, others in wagons or working around them.

"Scrag! Clancy! You come help. Just two." He lifted a leg and indicated: "Keep boots on."

He had decided to move some of the small boulders, about which the waters were swirling, to make a clearer passage for the wagon wheels. For about twenty minutes he had been surveying what needed to be done, trying places with a foot to find holes into which a boulder might be rolled, putting both arms into the water to test a rock's resistance, measuring depths from one bank to the other.

I threw off my shirt and ran into the water. In spite of the sun and the shallowness, it felt icy. Clancy, a little, very dark-haired man with gray at the temples, kept his collarless white shirt on, to the amusement of onlookers, who made comments like "Decent-dressed at all times, Clancy," imitating his voice, while Clancy strode in, rolling his sleeves.

We followed Axel's lead, struggling with the boulders he indicated, working close and in harmony. Clancy's breathing was bad, his chest wheezing, but his strength was tremendous, and he sometimes shifted quite easily a boulder over which Axel labored in vain.

"If he like that wiz shirt on, what he like puttink it off, I vant to know, hey, Scrag?"

"Tell him ask Jinny, Scrag." Clancy wheezed at his joke.

I had felt pride at being chosen by Axel for the task and now felt, in spite of not being able to respond in their manner, pleasure at the connivance of both in drawing me into their jokes. I knew that I was pleasing Axel in following his instructions and sensed his surprise at the way I could manage. Occasionally we had to get out of the water for a while, to warm our legs in the sun. Then, it was a new experience to sense the shape of my body in relation to Axel's, which was handsome but beginning to fatten. Sylvester came with his camera to the water's edge and had us stand for him, a bit forward of midstream, Axel between his helpers, an arm across the shoulders of each.

When we had finished, Clancy went back to his wagon while Axel and I sat on the bank. I wanted not to break the bond the task had made. After a while Lorelei called.

"Scrag, you come an' change them britches."

Axel laughed. "You go let her change them britches, Scrag." To Lorelei he called, "I come, you change mine ma'am?"

Justly and her mother were combing and pinning each other's hair near their wagon.

"You got dry things?" Lorelei asked.

"Plenty," I said. There was one dry pair in the tin trunk.

"You come an' have tea with us when you're fit," she said.

I closed the flap and then stared at the right-hand side of

the canvas with fascination. We were drawn up a little way
back from the stream, and my wagon was a few yards off from
some young birches. On the side near them, a small round
hole I had tested that morning with my finger, intending to
patch it later, was letting in a line of light, which was hitting
a spot on the other side, somehow carrying with it a perfectly
formed, upside-down image of a tree. How could this be? I
walked across the beam, and the picture disappeared, moved
aside, and it came back. I fluttered a hand across, and it
flickered.

I felt in the trunk and found my other britches. Then it
occurred to me to hold a clean white shirt into the line of light
and catch the image upon it, then to move the shirt backward
and forward, to watch the effect. I was doing this when Lorelei
came up the step and tapped at the cover. I called her in to
see the picture.

"Why's it upside-down?" she asked. "Can I tell Justly
come see?"

Justly came, and we played with the image awhile, check-
ing outside to see which tree it was, making the picture sharpen
or blur, wondering how it should be there, until the interest
was exhausted.

"Go an' make tea, Justly," Lorelei said. When Justly had
gone, she said, "Them britches."

"I'll change," I said.

"Go on, then."

I unbuckled my belt, taking time, waiting for her to go.

"Go on, then. Change y' britches, boy."

Regardless of the surge of embarrassment, I wanted to
obey her. Carefully, deliberately, trying not to scramble and
betray my nervousness, I pushed off the wet things, dried

myself, and put the fresh clothes on, not once looking at her. We did not speak. As I finished, she picked up my belt, put it around me, and buckled it.

"Let's get some tea," she said.

I held the cover open for her and then jumped down and held my arm to her as she came down the step. She smiled and gave me a playful punch above the belt buckle.

"You're some man now, Scrag." She linked her arm into mine, leading me to the wagon. "Come an' meet my beautiful daughter."

As she caught up her skirt to climb the steps, and I saw her own shapeliness as I followed her, I could think of nobody being more exciting than Lorelei herself.

7

We forded the stream in the early light. The sun was over our left shoulders, catching the top, left side, and rear of each wagon, as the train staggered and swayed, dipped and skewed its way toward the low gap in pink-gleaming rocks on the other side, against a sky so clean and pale blue that it seemed like the first dawn sky in the world. The horses whinnied in alarm, and whips cracked to keep them nerved for the effort, while Tickler bellowed his protests from the rear.

In a few minutes we were all across, except for Lorelei and Justly. Despite Lorelei's spirited insistence that she could manage to cross without a man at her reins, Axel had said, "Do like I say, or stay in damn vater if you git stuck." While kindling was collected, and breakfast fires started to crackle, Axel waded back to fetch Lorelei's wagon. They were only a few yards into the stream when Prancer, with no sense of other horses leading to give him confidence, reared and plunged in panic. Axel shouted and whipped the horse forward, but it immediately reared again, this time skewing aside, so that the wagon pitched dangerously, and the partner horse, quiet Nancy, whinnied in terror.

I watched with Sylvester as Lorelei took the whip and reins from Axel, put the whip in its holder, and tried to coax the horses forward. When no progress was made, Axel got down into the stream and was holding up his arms to persuade Lorelei to let him carry her across. She was telling him no, when it obviously occurred to her to send Justly. She gestured Justly down, and Axel took her as if she had no weight at all and came toward us, looking embarrassed, one arm beneath her shoulders, the other under her thighs, carrying her like a small child. He set her down near us.

"Lucky she don't git vet petticoats," he said. "Now I go lead over stupid horse an' stubborn voman."

He strode away, but as he approached her Lorelei waved him off and dropped down into the water, her skirt swirling, and staggered to the horse's head. At first, Prancer resisted, but, as she soothed and calmed him, his head came down and he was still. Slowly, patting and stroking, she eased him forward, then kept him moving toward us. Axel stood and watched, then followed stupid horse and stubborn woman out of the stream. As he plodded up the slope behind the wagon, his heavy haunches bulging, he reminded me of Tickler. There was no bellow, but as he passed us he said to Justly, "You know, your mama deserve git vet ass." He looked back over his shoulder and added, "I like that, though. I like that."

"He means he likes her stubbornness," said Sylvester. "Ambiguity, Scrag. Sweet ambiguity."

Justly went, and Sylvester asked me to join him for breakfast. We shared a fire with Clancy and Jane, and cooked fresh eggs from Sylvester's two hens. While I sat waiting, I thought of Lorelei taking off her dripping skirt in the shadowy wagon.

8

The thin book had a dark green cloth cover, with *Leaves of Grass* printed in gold, the letters growing into leaves above and roots below. There was no author's name, but Sylvester said it was by Walt Whitman, who stared out from his picture inside, opposite the title page. He was a roughish-looking man, bearded, and with a black hat, worn tilted, as Sylvester often wore his. His shirt was open at the collar, with a dark undershirt showing. He had one hand in a pocket of his trousers, the other on his hip, with a thumb in his belt, perhaps. He held his head a little to one side, looking as if he might be sizing me up. He looked like a man who might have just stepped down from a wagon. At the foot of the title page was "Brooklyn, New York: 1855."

As I drove along that morning the book agitated me from my tin trunk, where Sylvester had told me to keep it safe when not reading. He had handed it to me just after breakfast, saying there was no book like it.

"The first poem, that's the one. And don't worry about what you don't understand. Let lines pick themselves out and float around in your head."

Two or three were already doing that. I had flicked over pages while I was sitting at the reins, waiting to move off.

> *I mind how we lay in June, such a transparent summer morning.*
> *You settled your head athwart my hips and gently turned over upon me. . . .*

> *I saw the marriage of a trapper in the open air in the far west . . . the bride was a red girl. . . .*

Sylvester was right. I wanted the words to float in my head, to repeat themselves, in part and all together, to come together and drift apart, with their pictures, now sharp, now fading. I wanted to think about meaning only if meanings were clear, not to puzzle, to let the words be in my mind and say themselves over, without connections.

This was June. I was driving through such a transparent summer morning. Already I felt that the thin green book in my trunk would be important to me in some way that Sylvester understood. When, at mid-morning, we halted to make coffee over a shared fire that Daniel quickly set with brushwood, I took the chance to turn the pages again while my mug cooled on the grass beside me in the wagon shade.

"Scrag." It was Justly. "Scrag, I look up in your dictionary?"

I closed the book. It was the first time Justly had ever asked for the dictionary.

"What word?"

"What's 'ambiguity' mean? I asked Mama an' she don't know."

I fetched the dictionary and helped her to find the word, pleased to be finding it for myself. She said, "Ow," and went off. Soon she came back with her mug, Lorelei following.

"What you reading, Scrag?" Justly asked.

"Words," I said.

I wanted for a while to be alone with the book, but they sat down with me.

"Pretty book, Scrag," Lorelei said. "Gold letters an' all. Hey, that's good, leaves an' roots. *Leaves of Grass* — what sort of book is that, Scrag?"

"Poem book. Sylvester's."

"Sylvester *write* them?"

"No. Fella called Whitman."

"I see?" She put out her hand and I gave her the book. She turned pages. "I don't read good, but I read," she said. "Your granny taught you, Scrag?"

I said yes, and for an instant I smelled the scent of my grandmother's clothes, her black skirt and white blouse, and saw the little terrier, Pip, licking a plate at her feet as I looked at the book with large print on her sloping lap.

Lorelei stopped on a page, absorbed in it for a while, then read aloud:

"Twenty-eight young men bathe by the shore,
Twenty-eight young men, and all so friendly,
Twenty-eight years of womanly life, and all so lonesome."

She was reading slowly, carefully, as if she had not read for some time. The sound of her voice was suddenly beautiful, as if I had hardly heard it before.

"She owns the fine house by the rise of the bank,
She hides handsome and richly drest aft the blinds of the
window."

Lorelei smiled.

"You like this, Justly? Can you just see her there, watchin'
them?"

"Peekin'," said Justly.

"No, she ain't just peekin'. I can tell that." She looked at
the page silently for a moment, then said, "She's thinkin' which
one does she like best."

"Which one does she?" asked Justly.

Lorelei closed the book and gave it back to me.

"You read us that sometime, Scrag?"

"I liked listenin' to you," I said.

"I want to hear you," she said. "You come in one night
with us."

"Maybe." I wanted to say yes, but wondered if Sylvester
would mind if I took his book to others. It seemed, in some
odd way, a bond between us, as the task in the stream with
Axel had made a bond. Anyway, would I dare to read, even
if Sylvester said I should?

It was time to move again. We were on a plain covered
with small pink flowers that merged toward a distant range
of hills in a flat pink mistiness, above which the hills blurred
in a dark mauve line against a sky that was now deep blue.

9

Under a low yellow moon, Daniel told me a story. We sat on a barrel beside his wagon, the tethered horses shifting occasionally nearby, Daniel's pipe glowing and gurgling, his weathered face lit up from time to time by a match flame.

He had been west before, in '43. Nobody in the company knew that, not even Henrietta. It seemed a long time ago, another life. He had not wanted to talk of it. Henrietta was not one he could tell things that mattered, even before her deafness. He could sit across the table from her and feel "hellish lonesome."

He had been with his first wife, with a big wagon train on the Oregon Trail. The train had split up, and he had gone off with a small company, following a valley north.

"In this moonlight I think on it," he said. "We come to this place in a valley. An' the first night we was there was moonlight, with a great halo around the moon, an' we said, 'Here we stay,' an' we called the place Halo. 'This could be Halo City one day,' she said. 'Call this place Halo,' she said, an' we all agreed."

They had taken the halo for a good sign.

"But it wun't a good sign," Daniel said. His young wife had taken a fever and, with no doctor, had died in three days. He had turned and come back on his own. They had said he was mad, traveling in a wagon through that country alone.

"And I was, too, Scrag, mad of grievin'. An' there was Indians watched, an' they never touched me or stood in my path. I swore they had some understandin', an' I never feared an Indian that day to this."

Daniel was silent. When I said that he was coming west again, he said he had taken a sudden feeling that he wanted to face the way the sun goes down, and just go on traveling. No, he was not looking for Halo, and we were, maybe, too far north, anyway.

"But," he said, "I wouldn't rule out that I'll jest sidetrack a bit when the time come, an' go down there an' stand a while by the stone I set."

Back in the wagon, I tried *Leaves of Grass* again, having found earlier that it was possible to read only a small amount at one time, because the book was strange, unlike anything I had ever tried, and the pictures that rose from the page started my thoughts away from them to things that came from my own mind. There was also much that I could not understand, the pictures that leaped up spaced often between wide stretches of words that stayed where they were, seeming no more than the letters they were made of. I had gone out into the moonlight and the heavy scent of flowers to be free of them.

It was Axel's rule that we should not walk on the outside of the circle at night, to avoid being taken for intruders. I had felt restless and had wanted to wander off a bit into the field of flowers, and had been glad of the luring glow of Daniel's pipe.

Now, I went back to Walt Whitman. Earlier, I had tried to read from the beginning. Now, I searched till I found the lines Lorelei had read in the morning, and read on.

Which of the young men does she like the best?
Ah, the homeliest of them is beautiful to her.

Where are you off to, lady? for I see you,
You splash in the water there, yet stay stock still in your room.

Dancing and laughing along the beach came the twenty-ninth bather,
The rest did not see her, but she saw them and loved them.

As I read and reread the lines, the lady's face, which had been vague and shadowy as she hid behind the blinds, became Lorelei's. I tried to dismiss it, but it refused to go.

The beards of the young men glistened with wet, it ran from their long hair,
Little streams passed over their bodies.

Faces of some young soldiers who had stayed a few days in Scrimshaw, red-cheeked from riding in the sun, served for the twenty-eight.

An unseen hand also passed over their bodies,
It descended tremblingly from their temples and ribs.

The hand was Lorelei's. The hand on my belt as she buckled
it. Then I willed it to be some other, and a vague, pale-bodied
woman, too vague for recognition, stood, not by a shore but
in a stream, with the soldiers, who also became vague, and
the stream filled my mind, and was then the pool in which
Justly had waded, and the pool became its brown depths
where Justly had stood by the tree roots, and the brown depths
dwindled to the motes and surface dust and the faintest ripples
passing over a dark reflection.

I closed the book. I sat for a time, thinking of the stages
of our journey, letting places sharpen, blur, and mix in my
mind, and said the names of places, real names and the names
I had invented, like Justly Wading for the place of the pool
and Pink Plain for where we had traveled that day and were
now camped, and wondered about the journey ahead, which
somehow seemed to become part of the darkness outside, a
great yellow moon swinging above, the strange name of Halo
City repeating itself silently.

10

"That one's a honeypot," said Daniel.

We were coming with our coffee mugs at mid-morning to where Lorelei was leaning on a wagon wheel, smoking her pipe, with Justly, Axel, and Clancy looking on.

"You don't need vorry about gittin' vet ass no more, 'cause I dry you," Axel was saying as Justly giggled and Clancy wheezed. He chafed his hands together vigorously. "I give goot rubdown."

It was two days after the fording, and Axel seemed intent on making some further mileage out of it.

"Go an' rub Prancer or Nancy," said Lorelei. "I got Scrag here."

Clancy bent over, wheezing and spluttering. Justly's glance at me seemed to say that she thought her mother was serious.

"Sure," I said quickly, trying to rise to the banter, not to fail as I had with Axel and Clancy joking in the stream. The pretense seemed somehow provoked by Justly's glance.

"That's it, boy," Daniel said.

"Goot voman need man, not boy," said Axel. "Need organ-grinder, not monkey."

Lorelei's manner changed.

"I reckon that's right rude, an' you apologize to Scrag."

Axel's grin went.

"Scrag know I joke."

"Sure," I said. But I resented "monkey."

"Apologize," said Lorelei.

In the moment of Axel's reply, it was clear that all his joking with Lorelei had been a cover, the awkwardness through which he blundered toward a serious intent.

"I apologize to Scrag," he said, looking foolish.

"An' Scrag ain't no boy," said Lorelei.

"Ve roll them vagons," said Axel. As we turned to go, his jauntiness came back. "But don't forgit, ma'am, if you git vet . . ."

He hurried past us to the head of the train.

"An' that kid's a honeypot with the lid on," said Daniel.

11

J O U R N A L , 1 8 5 9

Friday, June 24
After an hour following the edge of the range yesterday, we came to a wide way in. We're going west again.

Saturday, June 25
The valleys are winding but generally wide. Axel said that we soon may not be able to make the circle at night as valleys get narrower, so he wants the order of wagons always to be the same. It usually is, anyway. Axel — Thou-Wert — Sylvester — George Abbott and Dora, 2 children, 2 spare mules — the Abbott timber wagon — Will Abbott, Emmy, 2 children, two spare mules — Daniel, Henrietta — me — Lorelei and Justly — Clancy, Jane, a cow, and a spare horse — Traven, Jeanie, 2 children, a pony, and 2 spare mules — Clement, Martha, 3 children, two cows, two spare horses, and Tickler.

Sunday, June 26
Thou-Wert preached about our Good Providence. We crossed the Great Plains without sickness and with everyone in good spirits. Most trains lose somebody, and there are many

deaths for every mile of that journey. He said it was the Hand of God. Axel said afterward that he helped God somewhat with the difficult things. Thou-Wert agreed with Axel that we should travel today even though it was Sunday, because we need to use the good weather. There will be bad days in the mountains. After service there was a court (Axel, Thou-Wert, George, and Clancy) because Traven and Jeanie's son Dick stole rabbit bits from Martha for his dog. Dick said the dog took the bits himself, but Clement said it was the boy. The court decided (but Clancy disagreed) the boy had done it. Axel said he should be larruped by his father. Traven said Thou-Wert should do it and Thou-Wert cut a stick from a bush and thwacked him over a barrel while Traven whipped the dog. The boy was blubbering behind Traven's wagon, and then, when we were moving off, he was nowhere to be found, nor his younger brother nor the dog. There was a search and they were found way back down the trail, up in the woods. This time Traven larruped them all with his belt and we went on after a long delay, with the boys hollering in the wagon, Jeanie shouting at Traven, and the dog barking.

12

We sat by candlelight waiting for Sylvester to come. Lo-relei had told Justly to put a second candle for him to read by. They had both put on pretty dresses I had never seen before, and smelled slightly of lavender. When Justly stood lighting the second candle, in a high candlestick, the first, which was lower, made light through the fine dress stuff and showed the shape of her small breasts. I thought of the lady "aft the blinds of the window" secretly watching the young bathers, and of how Justly was like them, unaware. Lorelei seemed to know what I had noticed, smiled at me across the table, and put her hand out, covering mine with a light stroking touch.

From the darkness behind, there was the good smell of new cakes they had managed somehow to bake, on an open fire, in the short time between our halt and nightfall. Thou-Wert had said yesterday that everyone in the company had helped Providence by keeping to the ways of home. "Home": the word stayed a moment in my mind, and a place called Scrimshaw seemed an immense distance off, the girl with small breasts seemed a skinny-chested child again, and the woman whose hand touched mine was momentarily the pretty lady it once pleased me just to be noticed by.

I felt anxious. I had told Sylvester how Lorelei had asked me to read from *Leaves of Grass*. Sylvester had said that was a fine idea, but, seeing my nervousness about reading aloud, had offered to read to us himself. Lorelei had been pleased at the thought of entertaining Sylvester, but I felt now a gnawing of jealousy that I was trying to disregard. The distance between Sylvester's assurance and my own seemed to be so great. How did people ever acquire their huge competence at this or that? During the afternoon, as I drove the trail, I had dreamed myself in Sylvester's place, words falling from my voice with power to hold Lorelei's attention. Sentences or bits of sentences had said themselves over to the sound of creaking harness and grinding wheels.

There were two taps on the wagon side and then Sylvester was at the flap. Lorelei told Justly to open it, and when she did so, Sylvester took off his hat and made a little bow of greeting. He was wearing his best suit and carried a polished wooden box under his arm.

"Good evening, ma'am. Good evening, Justly, Scrag."

The touch of stiffness in his courtesy seemed something to envy. It seemed something more than just good manners, a quality in himself. I was pleased that he should bring to Lorelei and Justly a quality so unlike the rudeness of Axel.

Lorelei showed Sylvester where to sit, opposite me on a bench at the little table, which had been moved out from its usual place close to the side. Justly would sit beside him, Lorelei beside me; but for the moment they were busy, Justly unwrapping glasses from napkins in which she had taken them from storage, Lorelei uncorking a bottle she had taken from somewhere in the shadows.

"This I was keepin' for Oregon," she said, "but there's another bottle for then."

"We're honored, ma'am. Isn't that so, Scrag?"

I said I was honored. I was not sure what I was honored for, but I felt a leap forward in assurance when the words came out as firmly as if I had framed them myself.

"Cherry wine I made from my own tree."

With surprise, I saw tears brim to her eyes. As she poured the dark red wine, which ran smoothly into Sylvester's glass, caught by the candlelight, they welled over and stood on her cheeks. We all noticed, but nobody said anything.

"Thank you, ma'am," said Sylvester quietly when all the glasses were full. "Will you propose a toast for us?"

"I'd be pleased if you'd say 'Lorelei' — and if you'd say the toast."

"I'll say both." He looked at his glass silently for a moment, then held it up so the candlelight shone through it. "Lorelei — may what we all find somewhere be moments as sweet and civilized as this."

After we had tried the wine and said how good it was, Lorelei brought over the cakes. As we ate and drank we talked of small things. Sylvester took from his box some photographs, mostly showing various members of the company at moments in the first weeks of the trail. Among these there was one that had no people in it at all, a view of Scrimshaw as it became part of the horizon, an empty foreground, a few blurry buildings beneath a steep, cloud-banked sky. Suddenly that picture seemed to stand for the Scrimshaw in my mind, and would always be an image that returned when I thought of the place.

Lorelei refilled the glasses, and then Sylvester opened *Leaves of Grass*.

How long he read before he paused for wine to be poured, I do not know. We were lost to time. His clear, deepish voice, the sounds of the words themselves, the pictures they made, the merging of picture into picture, the abrupt changes from one kind of picture to another, Sylvester's pauses to explain something or to tell us of parts he was leaving out—all held us, as a story holds children. I knew I was understanding only a small part of what I heard, and that Justly would be understanding less, but this seemed of no importance. Sylvester's voice, Walt Whitman's words, were opening a way into somewhere I had never been, somewhere it was strangely disturbing to be but to which I would return.

> *"I follow you, whoever you are from the present hour;*
> *My words itch at your ears till you understand them."*

I knew that would be true from the moment I heard it, and the words stood in my head immediately. When Sylvester reached the story of the lady watching the bathers, Lorelei touched my hip and then kept her arm lightly across my waist, tightening her hand sometimes when she wanted to show me that something pleased her or, perhaps, that she guessed something would be pleasing to me.

> *"This is the press of a bashful hand . . . this is the float and*
> *odor of hair. . . ."*

When Sylvester stopped, seeing that Lorelei would pour more wine, he said he had gone on too long and that he feared he had bored us, but we asked him to continue.

"That pleases me more than you know," he said. "For a short while, then, when we've had a pause."

"You know what our name means?" Justly asked. "Campion?" Without waiting for us to reply, she said, "Little white flowers. Ain't that nice?"

"I've seen them," said Sylvester. "Pretty things."

"You knew, then."

"I suppose I did."

"How?"

Lorelei said Justly had taken too much wine. Justly held out her glass to the candle.

"Ain't that lovely red?"

"When I was in England," said Sylvester.

He told us about Europe, when he was young. He had always longed to return, perhaps to stay, until reading *Leaves of Grass* had made him think of America in a new way.

"I'd still like to go and see Europe again, but I'd come back."

Lorelei asked why he was coming west.

"These," he said. He touched the box of photographs. "These are my *Leaves of Grass*. There are so many pictures waiting to be made. The record of how it was."

"That day we found the dead Indian boy," said Lorelei. "That's what you said then. I wasn't sure what you meant then."

"You'd like to see the picture?"

He opened the box again.

"Jesus," said Justly.

We looked at it in silence. The slightly banked grass, the Indian's body, the blood, were reduced to a range of brownish tones that somehow, instantly, took over from true memory the power to appall.

"I would like," said Sylvester after a few moments, "people who see the picture to feel as we felt, who were there."

"I liked the way you stood up to Thou-Wert," said Lorelei. "That old ranter."

"Spurious," I thought, and wished I had the nerve to say it.

"When people write of such a sight," said Sylvester, "they may exaggerate or be too reticent, according to their feelings. But the camera has no feelings. It doesn't exaggerate, and it has no reticence."

"You show us some more pictures?" asked Justly.

Sylvester took out a sheaf of pictures he had not already shown, and put them in front of Justly. There were more scenes from the trail: Daniel smoking on his barrel; Henrietta stirring in a mixing bowl; Clement standing with a hand on Tickler's back; Thou-Wert reading his Bible as he sat on his wagon tongue; Dora with her children; a group of the company gathered by a campfire at evening; and suchlike records.

"The rest are earlier things," said Sylvester. "Back in Massachusetts."

He took out three more pictures. The first showed a group of young men bathing in a pool, some standing naked on a rock, others in the water. Another showed one of the bathers standing alone, close, making ready to dive.

"Like the young men in the book," said Lorelei. "Is that the one the lady chose?"

Sylvester laughed.

"He could be, couldn't he?"

"He's a handsome boy," said Lorelei. "Ain't he, Justly?"

I wondered if she was thinking of how she had made me change my britches, and I wanted Sylvester to put down the next picture. I had already glimpsed that it showed a lady standing before a long oval mirror. Now she covered the bather. She was naked and had her arms raised as if pinning up her hair, and the mirror showed her intent look, her head turned a little to one side.

"Is that her?" asked Justly.

"Who?"

"The lady at the window."

Sylvester laughed again.

"No. I call this picture *A Balcony in Boston*."

Beyond the mirror, an open door showed a balcony with curved pillars, against wispy trees.

"The lady's husband paid me to make the picture. To make a record they could keep."

"Of how she was," said Lorelei. "That's surely a nice thought."

"He didn't mind you seein' her?" asked Justly.

"I say it's my camera that does the seeing," said Sylvester. "I've learnt to look with the eye of my camera." He smiled. "I have a glass eye."

"Read to us again, please, Sylvester," said Lorelei. "Just a page or two before bed."

"I believe a leaf of grass is no less than the journeywork of the stars. . . ."

Sylvester read, and after a couple of minutes Justly folded her arms on the table, put her head down on them, and slept. Lorelei kept her arm across my waist and held her hand on my hip. My mind tried to hold lines that I would go back to the book for in daylight, but the wine was now tugging me down toward Justly. Suddenly Lorelei was thanking Sylvester.

"That was lovely, Sylvester," said Justly, springing awake. "I loved that, an' your lady in the mirror."

"You had dreams, my sweet one," said Sylvester, smiling.

" 'A leaf of grass is no less than the journeywork of the stars,' " said Lorelei. "I'll never forget that. I'm not sure what it means, but I'll never forget that."

"I don't think I'm really sure either," said Sylvester. I knew he was being kindly. "And I'll never forget these moments, Lorelei."

As Sylvester was going I said my thanks and went to follow him.

"Scrag, stay a moment." Lorelei took my hand. "Stay a moment."

"Scrag's near asleep," said Justly.

"Scrag, I just want to say how much we appreciate you thinkin' Justly an' me bright enough for Sylvester readin' to." She put her arms about my waist and kissed my cheek. "Sweet Scrag."

No words offered themselves, so I said nothing. The float and odor of hair, I thought.

Lorelei released me and Justly took her place, her arms around my waist. Perhaps she had not noticed that her mother had kissed my cheek, but suddenly her lips were on mine, and the surprise of their warm pressure stayed as I blundered into the dark.

13

JOURNAL, 1859

Sunday, July 3

We rested today on account of several horses being poorly. Thou-Wert prayed that we should find a regular trail again. Clancy said we can't depend on Axel anymore, it seems. We waste much time winding about.

Thursday, July 7

Horses still poorly. Axel says we rest three days so horses can graze in good pasture near a small stream.

Friday, July 8

Thou-Wert called the company together at sundown to make apology to Traven's boy Dick. Clement found Martha's rabbit pieces wrapped in muslin cloth and crawling with maggots in the jockey box, where Martha had put them for cool shade and forgotten. Martha apologized to Dick, too, and when Axel asked why she had accused the boy, she said the Lord had shown him to her in her mind's eye, and the dog had been sniffing around the wagon, "seeming like he was looking for more." Clement said he had accused the boy because Martha was sure. He said he thought the stink was from the horses being poorly. Thou-Wert said he couldn't take back the punishment, but doubtless the Lord would spare him chastisement on account of some future wickedness. Traven said he was sorry he larruped Dick and his brother, but they should know not to run away. Jeanie mobbed at Traven again, and the boys blubbered, and the dog barked half the night.

14

The dog's barking, starting up at intervals, sometimes near, sometimes far, made me sleep fitfully. I dreamed of the dead Indian, but the scene was that of Sylvester's picture rather than of memory, and the onlookers were as they might have been if seen by the camera, including Sylvester himself bending behind the tripod, his head under the cloth. The blood that oozed from the Indian's wounds was a dark brown, spreading as if on a picture surface. "Bury the blood," said Axel. Then the picture was of the place as we left it, brown grass strewn to cover brown soil, and we were fleeing over the crest of a hill, and careering down the steep incline on the other side, pursued by Indian cries, and plunging, plunging.

I woke, my heart thudding. At first it seemed that the wagon had just come to rest at the bottom of the drop. Then came the relief of feeling the firm board at my side and my mattress level on the floor. I lay in silence, thinking of the dream. The dog barked again, a single yap, distant, seemingly high on a hillside. As if the anxiety of my dream had persisted, I began to worry that the creature had run off and was somehow unable to return. As I drifted into sleep again, further single yaps came at intervals, and my worry increased. Then it was as if I pulled myself back from sleep and realized that the sound was not from the dog.

It was from some animal of the region. I thought of those I knew might be out there, and wondered if there were others, unfamiliar, perhaps not even known by name. As I tried to give shape in my imagination to a dark object stirring in darkness, I thought of an Indian in brief silhouette against the night sky on the rim of the nearest hill.

My heart thumped again as I went to the flap and looked out. It was so dark that my imagination of a figure against the sky was quite false, but as I peered in the direction of the hill the sound came again, and this time was answered by a more distant call somewhere away to the right. After a similar interval another came from farther off, then another, more distant still. What kind of signal was it? Were we being watched and, in some code, the subject of communication from hill to hill? Were others in the company awake? Axel would be, his turn for lookout. I thought of him sitting vigilant for hours, with his rifle cocked.

I dropped to the ground on the inner side of the circle to relieve myself against the wheel, and as I stood there I heard Daniel about the same business at his own wheel.

"Scrag," he whispered.

"Daniel."

He came close.

"You heard them Indians?"

"Yeah."

"Bannocks, I think. They won't bother us. Don't lose no sleep."

"What's it about?"

"Young ones. They send them out t' train theirself. Courage, eyes for the dark, know the world of the night. First I thought it was that Dick's mongrel." He slapped my shoulder. "Git t' sleep."

But sleep would not come. I kept drifting off into disconnected pictures of dreams and snatches of conversation, then jerking awake because something in those impressions disturbed me. After a while I thought that if I had to lose sleep, I would at least lose it pleasantly, and I began to take myself back over that evening, a week and a half ago, with Sylvester, Lorelei, and Justly. I knew again, as I had felt many times since in fancy, the shape of Justly's mouth on mine, then came the feeling of Lorelei's arms about my waist, "Sweet Scrag" on her voice, the "float and odor of hair," the "press of a bashful hand" on my hip, Sylvester saying *A Balcony in Boston,* and the slender lady's back, and the curve of her hip echoing the outline of the mirror frame and the pillar stones of the balcony, the waver and taper of candle flames, and Justly's little breasts, shadowy under the light-touched dress, surprising, first-seen things. I wanted to fall asleep with this thought, but when it merged into the fancy of Justly's breasts as two new creatures venturing forth, the word "creature" pulled me back again to the figures on the dark hillside and their strange calling.

Where were we traveling? It was as if I could sense us moving in darkness, the wagon floor gently rocking as the wheels turned in soft pasture. Slopes rose steeply on both sides, the valley opening as we approached and closing behind us. Somewhere behind was light and great distance, a distance that was vague, that dissolved its features. Ahead, and distant, too, was a featureless light landscape, separated from us by an immense night of rearing slopes and deep places. We were traveling in some deep place. "And we said, 'Here we stay,'" said Daniel, "and we called the place Halo." A moon stood high above a ravine from which I looked up, a clear halo far from it. On the rock edge, against the sky, a dog barked. ". . . know the world of the night," said Daniel.

I woke to the sound of voices, the clink of pots and pans, and the whinny of a horse. Intense light filtered through the hole I had still not bothered to repair. It must have been Clancy's head that passed, in upside-down image on my shirt draped on the chair.

"That dog barkin' half the night, man," he said. "And I got five bloody horses t' shoe t'day."

15

At mid-afternoon the only sounds in the encampment were of Clancy's hammer ringing on the anvil or its thud against a shoe on the hoof—this accompanied occasionally by a shout at an uncooperative horse. Most of the company were in the wagons, taking an opportunity to sleep after the interrupted night. Sylvester had invited me to bring Justly to watch him work, as he made pictures of Clancy and the horses.

The inside of his wagon was a workshop, the wooden sides higher than those on the other wagons, and lined with shelves and racks which held his equipment. There were strings across from one side to the other, on which a few of his new pictures were pegged.

"Watch," he said. "You can learn the mysteries of the collodion process."

We watched, but the mysteries remained somewhat in spite of Sylvester's careful explanations. A glass plate was tilted this way and that while a liquid, the collodion, spread. It was dipped into silver nitrate in a glass-lined box, which would sensitize it to the image thrown on it by the camera's lens, then put into a wooden frame with a hinged cover.

"Now we must get Clancy in the lens before the plate dries."

We followed Sylvester out, the light dazzling after the near-darkness of the wagon. The camera was already set up where Clancy was working. With an instruction to Clancy to hold himself still in one of his usual stances, Sylvester crouched under the hood.

Clancy was holding a hind hoof between his knees, strad-dling the horse's leg, his long leather apron parted up the center. The shoe was already in place, Clancy holding a nail in position ready for driving, his hammer raised a few inches above.

We hurried back to the wagon with the plate. Sylvester secured the flap and hung an extra canvas to shut out light. We were barely able to see what he did at the table.

"Now the plate comes out of the frame, and I pour ferrous sulfate over it to develop the image. Then it waits in the dark until I print the picture from it — next time we stop for rest, maybe."

"How can you wait?" said Justly.

"Oh, there's a kind of excitement in the waiting. Like knowing you might have buried treasure. What's it going to be, gold or rubies?"

"Don't know about what buried treasure feels like."

Sylvester was pouring liquid over his next plate.

"Don't you, Justly? Don't you?" He tilted the plate one way, then another. "What do you say to that, Scrag? Shouldn't Justly know about buried treasure?"

I felt as I did when Sylvester used unfamiliar words, un-comfortable but challenged, knowing that he was leading me into understanding. But now I sensed that he was leading Justly, too, and I was uncertain where.

"I don't know," I said. It felt a weak answer.

"H'm." He put the plate into the box on the glass dipper. "A quick bath in silver nitrate." As he lifted it out and held it dripping, he said, "Pirates' gold doesn't know it's pirates' gold."

The plate went into the frame, the lid closed. We went out to Clancy again. He was standing at his small fire with hand bellows, agitating the flames around a horseshoe. Sylvester quickly moved his camera and put in the plate. By the time he was ready, Clancy had taken the glowing shoe from the fire on tongs and turned to the anvil. The picture Sylvester made was of the moment the shoe touched the anvil, Clancy with the tongs in one hand, his hammer in the other.

We were with Sylvester through the afternoon. He made five pictures, all of various stages of Clancy's work, while Clancy wheezed, joked, and occasionally cursed, with an almost shy apology to Justly. When Sylvester had finished, he boiled a kettle on the fire and made us tea. He asked what work I wanted to do in Oregon. I said it would be whatever I could find at first, maybe help in a store again. A momentary memory, like one of Sylvester's photographs, came back: Lorelei and Justly come into Rodd's place, standing by the counter to be served, against the little window, people passing outside, myself in the shadowy interior sorting hardware, caught by surprise at my nervousness of coming forward.

"Think hard about what you'd really like," Sylvester said. "There's nothing closed to you."

"Bar shoein' horses," Clancy said. "Half a lifetime their wrong end. No wonder I got a chest."

Only one or two people were stirring around the wagons. Martha came to complain that smoke from Clancy's fire had gone over her clothesline, stretched between trees by the stream. Clancy said she was the only woman careless enough to leave washing out while he was working, and Martha went away in a huff.

"If Martha don't want smuts on her drawers, then Martha better not leave them out in my smoke, I say," said Clancy with a long wheeze afterward.

I ran back to my wagon to fetch two extra mugs. As I climbed up, there were voices from Lorelei's wagon and the sound as of a chair falling over, then the bulge of a figure against the canvas.

"Get out. Get out of this wagon." Lorelei's voice was raised, urgent, yet in check, sounding as if she wanted to avoid being heard by others.

Before I could decide what I should do, as I wondered if she needed help, Axel almost fell from the step, saying, "Hell, I go!"

As he came to the space between Lorelei's wagon and mine, he looked up, scowling, red-faced. Almost past, he turned.

"You still friggin' monkey, boy."

16

Daniel's wagon was wobbling over the path of small rocks in front of me. In front of Daniel, Will's was pitching downward and at the same time turning left to avoid a boulder. Will was on foot, at the left-hand horse's head, Emmy walking behind with the children, two little white caps and brown dresses beside the wide skirts of their mother. George's wagon was already far down the incline, pitching from one side to the other, Dora and the children out in front, following Sylvester. Thou-Wert and Axel had reached the bottom; now Axel was walking back up to give help with the Abbotts' timber wagon, which had been left behind.

The sky was an intense blue at midday, the sunlight making the covers gleam almost white. The valley into which we were going seemed like a basin, the hills to our left and right obscuring a view on either side, so we could see only that the way ahead rose again to a level as high as the valley we were leaving, the crests much higher.

Before beginning the descent, we had roped as much of the furniture of the wagons as possible. Daniel now called to me to get to Ebony's head, and I called to Lorelei to get to

Prancer. Daniel kept turning to see that I was managing, and
I, just as frequently, turned to Lorelei.

"Damn madness, this," he called.

Axel was almost abreast of Daniel in his climb.

"You vant go north, you damn go north. Git damn Canada,
likely."

"Canada, my ass," shouted Daniel.

Axel scowled at me, saying nothing. Lorelei let him take
Prancer's head, and he told Justly to get down from the wagon. They walked in front of Axel, following my pitching path
downward. Mixed with belief in Daniel's judgment of the
foolishness of Axel's decision to come this way, I felt admiration of the Swede's physical ability, and resentment at his
presence, once again, with Lorelei. Was it only to help her he
had come back up?

The descent took almost three hours, the timber wagon
having to be partly unloaded, the planks carried down by
hand, all the men toiling up and down the slope until the
brothers had restacked their store. Thou-Wert's wagon had
shed a wheel rim, and a spoke was broken. There was no
choice but to delay the climb from the basin until Clancy and
George had done their craftsmen's work of repair.

Sylvester set up his camera and photographed them. Justly
went to watch and help. I read Whitman, thinking at the same
time how close and strangely joined in our fortunes we had
all become. I thought of my own connections, like invisible
strings, going out — to Lorelei and Justly, to Daniel, to Sylvester; looser strings to Axel, Thou-Wert, and the others. I
thought of how, coming down the slope, seeing wagons below
me, and looking up at those threatening to topple from behind,
I had recalled words Thou-Wert had read out before we

started that morning. " 'Are not two sparrows sold for a far-thing? and one of them shall not fall on the ground without your Father. But the very hairs of your head are all numbered. Fear ye not therefore, ye are of more value than many sparrows.' " I thought of the vastness we traveled, the vastness behind and the vastness ahead, and of all the small birds falling in those vastnesses, and in the vastnesses beyond, across the world, and of all the birds that had fallen in ages past and would fall in ages to come. Could all those deaths be known? Did Thou-Wert truly believe they could? Did he say the words out of habit or because they were comforting? And how strange it was that he had read those words this very day, before knowing of the perilous descent that lay ahead. Was that by chance? From all the words he could have read, did some invisible hand guide Thou-Wert's hand to these? How strange, too, that my own thoughts could be followed so quickly by some similar thought or word-picture from the book in my own hand.

See ever so far . . . there is limitless space outside of that,
Count ever so much . . . there is limitless time around that.

Sit awhile wayfarer. . . .

The wagons were in a disorderly huddle, the flat space in the bottom of the basin too small to allow dispersal. My thoughts were distracted by the hurrying back and forth of women and the moaning of Emmy, who was in childbirth. At about four o'clock, the sun still blazing into the hollow, the only shade that cast by the wagons, a startlingly raw small cry came from under a canvas cover and seemed to say, "I am here. Do you see me, too?"

At sundown, which was early behind the hillcrests, the hollow suddenly cool, Thou-Wert called the company to prayers and thanksgiving for the new member. He said that Will and Emmy had agreed to set the name he had suggested before the name they had thought to give. Providence had chosen this precipitous path for us so that the child might be born on a Sunday in this natural cradle between the bosoms of protecting hills. "Chosen," the child should be called. With water from a hand basin he touched the baby's forehead.

"I name thee Chosen Arthur."

In the night, I was wakened by a weak, jabbering cry from Chosen Arthur, which was immediately cut short. I saw, in the dark, the dazzling light on the wagon tops ahead and below on the slope, and Emmy's wide skirts, and the two children at her side. As I went to sleep again, I glimpsed the baby nuzzling at the great globe of Emmy's breast, then Lorelei smiling at me across her table, as if she knew, again, what I had seen.

17

JOURNAL, 1859

Monday, July 11

The way out of the hollow to the west was too steep for the timber wagon, and Emmy is not able to take her turn at the reins, so Will and George told Axel we must take the shallower slope out north.

Saturday, July 16

It was a good choice to come this way. The going is good. Late Tuesday morning we found ourselves going a bit more to the west in a valley with good pasture, a little stream, and trees and shrubs. We have traveled every day for a week, and rest the animals tomorrow.

18

"It ain't the same as bein' naked for just anyone," said Justly.

"It ain't naked," said Lorelei. "Showin' a bare back ain't naked."

Lorelei took one of the photographs from the table and looked at it again, smiling.

"I just love that, bless you, Sylvester. Ain't that a pretty picture, Scrag?"

The picture showed the flaps of the wagon cover partly folded back, from outside. In the darkness of the interior, Lorelei was sitting on a box, facing away, her dress open and fallen about her hips, her back bare and slightly turning, picked out from the shadows by soft light.

I thought of something Sylvester always seemed to say.

"How it was," I said.

"How it *is*, boy," said Lorelei. She smiled, then turned serious. "That's the nice thing, Sylvester. This ain't in some book or on some wall, and it ain't some rich man's lady in Boston. It's me, and here, and now." She reached over the table and kissed Sylvester's cheek. "And you can make a damn pretty picture, Sylvester."

"Give it a name," said Justly.

"Sundown," said Sylvester.

"Put my name in," said Lorelei. "I'd be right pleased to have my name in."

"Lorelei, Sundown," said Sylvester.

As Sylvester wrote the title below the picture in pencil, at the left-hand corner, and signed his name at the right, I thought, Someone will read that and wonder, "Who was Lorelei?" But the thought of some far day was dismissed as quickly as it came. Sylvester's "how it was" meant so much less than Lorelei's "how it is." I wondered how Sylvester and Lorelei had managed to steal the moment for the photograph without anyone knowing. Again, a feeling of bafflement at the ways of achieving assurance and competence assailed me.

"It's still kind of naked," said Justly.

"I've got a glass eye," said Sylvester.

19

"The Devil waiteth for the unwary." Thou-Wert wagged his forefinger. "You're a foolish woman. I have a mind to ride after them myself."

"You do no such thing," said Lorelei angrily.

"I shall not. But it's upon my conscience that I should."

"Then damn your conscience!"

Thou-Wert stomped off, his ruddy face a deeper color than usual. Halfway to his wagon, he turned back, raised his hand as if he would say something more, then slapped it sharply to his thigh in a gesture of exasperation.

Sylvester and Justly had gone riding up the valley, their horses laden with his photographic equipment, Sylvester with a rifle across his thighs, as the camp subsided into Sunday-afternoon sleep. Thou-Wert's concern, which had brought me to look out, was not for their safety in the unknown way ahead, for the valley seemed a pleasant and untrammeled place, but for Justly's companionship with a man.

"Why did Scrag not go, too?" Thou-Wert asked. It was the point in the conversation at which I had looked out. "Why did you not go, too, Scrag?"

I pretended incomprehension.

"Because I said the child should have her own moments," said Lorelei.

"Her own moments, indeed! Ha! Her own moments! I'd have thought you recollected enough about own moments, Lorelei."

When Thou-Wert went, Lorelei relit her pipe and leaned against the wagon, upturning her face to the sun, her eyes shut. I came down to her.

"Scrag?" She kept her eyes closed. "You heard that?"

"Yeah."

Still keeping her eyes closed, she held out the pipe.

"Have a draw."

I took the pipe and took some draws, leaning against the wagon beside her. I turned my face up to the sun like her, and closed my eyes. There seemed no sound but the slight gurgle of the pipe.

"I've had enough of Thou-Wert." She said it quietly, half amused, it seemed.

I held on to the pipe, trying to master the skill of it, not taking too much smoke yet keeping it going.

"You enjoyin' that?" she asked.

My left hand was hanging at my side. Her fingers touched it, then she took it in hers.

"Come inside awhile."

She took me into the wagon, still holding my hand. I went with her feeling much as a child feels in capable hands.

"Light the candle, Scrag."

I lit the candle, watching her lace the flap.

"Light them both."

I did as she said. There was a strange pleasure in that,

and it seemed as if she knew about it. The second candle reminded me of Justly lighting it. Its light fell on Sylvester's picture of Lorelei, propped on the end of the table, against the canvas.

Lorelei came close.

"That picture makes me feel good." She took my hand. "It make you feel good, Scrag?"

"It's a pretty picture," I said.

She turned away, still holding my hand.

"You like see 'how it is'?"

The way to reply hesitated in my throat. Lorelei dropped my hand.

"Undo me."

I pushed a little round button at her waist through its loop.

"You start at the top, Scrag."

I put aside her hair. The button came undone easily. I felt nervous and inept, but the buttons slipped quickly through the loops and the dress was open. Lorelei sat on the bench beside the table and made the cotton stuff fall forward so her back was bare. She turned slightly, as in the picture.

"That how it was?"

"Just like the picture," I said.

"Touch me," she said.

I put my fingertips on her spine and traced the bones a little way down.

"Hell, Scrag, you're somethin' gentle."

"I'm hellish nervous," I said.

"Don't be. I ain't judgin'." There was a pause. "Put your hands on my shoulders."

I did as she said, and after a moment closed them in on the slope to her neck, then touched toward her shoulders again. Her flesh was very smooth, and the sensation was the sweeter because it came of my own venturing. Then Lorelei held her hands over mine and stilled them.

"Be with me, boy."

There was silence, then she pulled my hands down upon the slopes of her bosom and held them over their surprising points.

"Be with me, boy," she whispered.

In amazement at my own daring, I felt my hands going around and underneath, lifting gently.

"Boy." Then she chuckled. "You snuff candles without burnin' your fingers?"

Obediently, I snuffed the candles as Lorelei, holding her dress with one hand, spread her mattress with the other. I knelt down with her in the dark as she lay back. There was enough light coming in around the canvas to show that she was uncovered to her hips, where the dress was gathered. I was grateful for its dim play over her as I followed her indication — "Yes, Scrag, yes" — and slid the cottony things away to her feet, and paused to take in an image that would never be sharper and never dimmer all my days.

20

The light around the rim of the cover was a dim line, sharper at the lower edge against the board, blurring into darkness above. Suddenly, with voices outside, and a horse's whinny, I was fully awake, even before Lorelei shook my shoulder.

"Up, Scrag." She was bending over me. "Quick."

Then she was unlacing the flap and opening it. Evening light came in, and I was on my feet, alert, remembering, joyful at the sight of Lorelei, standing in her dress against the opening. She leaned to look out, then came in to me.

"Finish my buttons, Scrag."

She turned her back. I put the last four buttons in their loops.

"Remember — Justly must never know unless I tell."

"I'll never tell anyone."

She smiled.

"A good intention, Scrag." She kissed my mouth. "But I won't hold you to that." She pushed me to the opening. "Go and welcome Sylvester. Tell him come eat with us."

Axel had shot a small deer at dawn and shared the meat among the women. Lorelei had said she would cook at sundown.

Sylvester and Justly were tethering their horses within the circle. I went over to them and gave Lorelei's message. Sylvester said he would gladly come to eat with us as soon as he had washed and tidied himself. I went back with Justly. She was flushed from riding in the sun, and excited.

"We had just one good afternoon, Scrag."

I wanted to tell her, "So did I."

"You ride far?" I asked.

"Wait till Sylvester comes," she said. "We'll tell you it all together."

That was what she said to Lorelei, too. Lorelei went to cook on the fire that someone was starting at the middle of the circle. Justly said, "Out, Scrag," because she wanted to change her clothes before Sylvester came, so I went to my wagon to read awhile.

But I could not read, my thoughts in too much turmoil. I turned the pages to see if some line would leap up and speak what was in my mind, give shape to what I felt. Nothing offered itself, nothing could be personal enough to me. Then it occurred to me that I should write words that would be my own poem, and immediately the words were there on my lips, pressing to be written. No, not written — said, over and over. "You lay in the dark and were almost a part of it." The words matched, in some strange way, the image in my memory.

As we took our seats at Lorelei's table, I looked hard at the candle flames and thought, You snuff candles without burnin' your fingers? Then I looked at the liveliness on Justly's face and wondered if my own excitement was on mine.

"Now, the afternoon's great secrets?" Lorelei said as we ate.

"Ain't no need for secrets," said Justly.

" 'Confession' should be the word, I suppose," said Sylvester.

Justly laughed.

"It ain't confession. Mama, Sylvester made some pictures of me, that's all."

"That don't need no big confession," said Lorelei. She smiled. "You got a nice back, too, child. A bit skinny yet, maybe . . ."

My mind was still in the afternoon as I listened and ate well. When Lorelei said "skinny yet," the image I saw briefly was of Justly's narrow shoulders under the blackish blouse with tiny flowers as she stood wading weeks ago, looking away across the pool and up the slope beyond. Then I was back in the wagon again, Lorelei's dress fallen from the smooth shoulders she had asked me to touch.

"Anyway, Sylvester already told me when I was comin' from the fire. And Thou-Wert already told Sylvester he shouldn't have been ridin' alone with a young girl. And he came here hollerin' hellfire near enough at me for lettin' you go, and he told Scrag he should have gone with you."

We all laughed about Thou-Wert. Sylvester poured small rye whiskies from a bottle he had brought. Justly tried hers and gave it to Lorelei.

"I couldn't have made pictures with Scrag around," she said.

I felt only the vaguest curiosity about the photographs Sylvester had made of Justly, and it seemed that Lorelei's thoughts were elsewhere, too. Sometimes she glanced at me, and we seemed to be signaling some shared thought of the afternoon. When the meal was finished, the table cleared, and Sylvester read to us from *Leaves of Grass*, she put the tips of her fingers under my belt and occasionally made a gentle pressure against my spine. Much of the time, instead of hearing Whitman, I heard only the good, strong sound of Sylvester's voice and thought, over and over, "You lay in the dark and were almost a part of it."

21

The going being so good in the valley, Lorelei left Justly at the reins and came to ride beside me.

"There's things I should say, Scrag — yesterday an' all . . . I didn't mean to hurry you into nothin'. There's no need for you to feel obligated."

"You didn't hurry me." It seemed as if I was lying.

"Sure?"

"Just about sure."

"I don't want you to feel different about me."

"How?"

"You don't disrespect me?"

"Reckon you know how I feel."

"I guessed how you *did* feel."

"Did you?"

"It was a long time, Scrag, wasn't it — you feelin' good about me?"

"You know that."

"You tell me about that sometime?"

I shrugged.

"That's somethin' I'd like real well to hear, Scrag. Will you try sometime?"

"Yeah, I'll try."

"And you feel good about yesterday?"

"You know I did."

"But you still feel good about it today?"

"You know I do."

"Jesus, boy, it ain't a silly question! Don't you know that?"

I wanted her to stop asking me things, to put her hand in the back of my belt again.

"I feel damn good about it," I said.

22

"Watch some poor creature strangle theirself," said Daniel, "then think about the ways of humankind."

We were out in the scrub of the valley just before last light, finding tracks of rabbits and setting wire-loop snares. In the morning I would come back with him to pick up the stiff, dew-sodden rabbits with bulging eyes and bloodied mouths, to distribute to the women in the wagons. With quick knives and strong hands they would peel off skins, to make them look, briefly, almost like human babies, like Chosen Arthur looked now, before they sliced them apart for the stew. At night, around tables, we would shut from our minds any thought of the vile devices we were now laying.

"Console y'self you don't want t' git thin," Daniel added.

He knew that I was with him only because I liked his company.

"There's things you might rather be at," he said. He waited for me to answer, but I let myself think of Justly or Lorelei lighting a candle and closing the flap, and said nothing. "You bin gittin' some right nice feminine company, Scrag."

"Reckon so?"

"Don't make it sound like a question, boy. Ain't no question there. Distinctive fem*inine* company — there's a good dictionary word — tha's what you got there. And that ain't easy to come by."

What could I tell Daniel? In spite of my assertion to Lorelei, I almost wanted Daniel to ask some question that might give me the chance to share my secret with him, as he had disclosed to me a story he had told to nobody else, not even Henrietta. But I knew I would say nothing.

"There's some rich little honeypot under that lid," Daniel said. "But give it a bit of time, boy. No hurry. Leave it be awhile. Yours when the time come, if you want it."

Daniel's misjudgment half amused, half disappointed me. There was nothing I could tell.

"Must be hard," he said as he straightened from the last snare, "young fella like you, Scrag, t' think of an old 'un like me with the selfsame feelin' an' the selfsame thoughts, near enough, on that subject."

Somehow, it was, but I wanted no lie between us, so I did not reply.

"I thought to have buried all them notions under a stone in Halo sixteen years back," Daniel said. "But they don't go, boy, they don't go."

We walked back in the quickly closing dark.

"I was too old when I wed that first time." Daniel stopped to light his pipe, the matchlight flickering over his face. "But I'd alwus moved on, never settled. Alwus restless." We were walking again. "Never quite knew what I was lookin' for. Thought I'd recognize it when I found it, I suppose. When I did, it was a woman. And then I lost it, boy. Jest one more move, find a place for her, a bit of land out West. She was a spirited girl, y'see. Like I said, distinctive. And I left her under a stone in Halo."

I wanted to turn him from that thought.

"What places did you work?"

"Maine," he said, "on farms. Then up the Great Lakes for furs. Massachusetts, some land of my own, till I lost it in 'thirty-seven. Then I got a little money t'gether again, and over t' Missouri. That's where I found her."

We were back at the wagons. It appeared that most of the company were gathered at the fire in the center of the circle. We went to join them.

"And I don't even know if Halo exists. Perhaps they didn't make out, moved on. Maybe Halo's jest that stone out there, an' her under it."

I left Daniel. Lorelei was cooking trout again. They were so plentiful in the stream that Clancy had taken a dozen. You could pick them out by hand, he had told Justly — "with your eyes shut." I was asked to supper.

"When we've eaten, Justly's got somethin' to show you," said Lorelei.

Justly protested that she had not. Lorelei teased her and said she had pestered Sylvester to print her pictures straight-away, not to wait for the next long stop.

"First time I've ever had a picture," said Justly.

"You can show Scrag," said Lorelei.

When we had eaten, Justly said we should drink coffee, and when we had drained our cups, she insisted on refilling them. When the cups were empty again, she fetched some pictures from her tin trunk. They were in a cover of thick white paper, on which, in Sylvester's hand, was written, *"Justly at the Pool, 1859."*

"There's one Scrag can see, anyway," she said.

It was as if six weeks had not passed. Justly was standing near the pool, as in that other place, wearing the same blouse and skirt, and looked as if she might suddenly turn away again to drop into the water.

"You remember that day back there?"

"I remember."

"Me wadin' an' then, when I came out, puttin' a worm on the hook. 'Push it on. Like a concertina'!"

"She scritched," I told Lorelei.

Lorelei laughed.

"She told me."

"We caught nothin', anyway," said Justly.

I was thinking of her wading back there, of her un-awareness of the water's reflection that caused me turmoil.

"We've come some long ways since then," said Lorelei. The three of us caught each other's glances in a moment of seriousness. "You go an' make more coffee while I show Scrag your pictures."

When Justly had gone, making no more than token pro-tests, Lorelei passed me two photographs in turn. They were surprising in their simplicity, and beautiful. In one, a naked girl was standing in a pool, seen from a distance, from behind, streaks of the shadows of branches and leaves falling across her as they fell across the still surface of the water. In the other, the girl had turned partly toward the camera and was wading.

Lorelei was standing behind me. She put her hand on my shoulder. Without saying anything, I stood and held her close while she kissed my face and neck many times until we heard

Justly coming back from the fire. Lorelei broke away and put the photographs in their folder.

Justly looked at us inquiringly.

"They're damn good pictures," I said.

"I know," said Justly.

"Scrag means you're one small beauty," said Lorelei.

"I know," said Justly, smiling.

Lying in my bed, listening to the night sounds, I thought of the country we traveled in and the vast landscapes beyond, trying to imagine Daniel as a young man hoeing a field in Maine or clanking a bucket and casting grain to chickens; then he was in trapper's gear, following tracks in snow, great waters nearby; then scything grass in Massachusetts; then greeting a slim girl, with a beautiful face I could not see clearly, in Missouri; then standing, much older now, his hat in his hand, over a roundish white stone in a place with a great yellow moon with a halo around it. "Skin a rabbit!" a woman's voice said. It seemed to be my grandmother, or perhaps it was someone else, perhaps my mother. Could it be? Could it be? "Skin a rabbit!" it said, and my tight little undershirt was pulled up, pressing hard against my face, and slipped away over my head, and I was naked. Then somewhere a baby was crying, then somewhere it was quiet. Far away there was another cry, very small, of some hurt creature. Then silence.

23

"How old were you?"

"Bit older than Justly is now. Bit younger than you. It was young, but it was common. Not enough women to go around, so they tried the girls."

I was under Lorelei's wagon, greasing axles, at the noontime rest. Lorelei was sitting on the grass, smoking. Justly was cooking cakes on a little fire I had set.

"But Justly's father was no older than you. It was just a boy-and-girl thing—curiosity, fun. Only half a dozen times."

She was looking away from me, as if the memory could be seen halfway up the mountainside. She paused, and I waited.

"Seems a long time away. I don't even recall his face clear now. Ain't that strange? But it was only half a dozen times. I was keen for half of that, then I got scared an' didn't want it no more. Then Justly was comin'. Oh, Jesus."

She turned, and we were close, on either side of the spokes.

"Can you imagine it, Scrag? No, you just can't. If it had been a man, I guess I would have been married off, shame covered over. And with child again four or five times before twenty. I wouldn't look like I do now." She put her face close to the space between spokes. "Tell me I look good."

"Yeah."

"Tell me, boy."

"You look good."

"You are hellish shy and hellish sweet, you know that?"

"No." I wanted to know more of the story before Justly returned. "What happened then?"

"Oh, the old story. Little Miss gettin' big belly."

"What happened to him?"

"Ass whipped. Sent back East to school."

"Then?"

"Just finishin' growin' up an' helpin' kid grow up same time."

"Then?"

"Met Frank. Couldn't marry because of a wife in St. Louis. Gave me a ring for appearances. He was happy enough to use my name. Good man. Weak, restless, but he made me feel good. Then his trips down South got longer, an' he was makin' some open legs down there feel good. Like, I suppose, the wife in St. Louis thought of me." She held the pipe stem through the wheel for me to take a draw. "What sort of story does that make?"

I let the question turn in my mind as I finished the job and went to grease my own wagon. Lorelei went to help Justly, and we were soon sprawling on the grass to eat. Scrimshaw seemed so distant that I found it difficult to hold aside those miles of hill and prairie and see into any part of it. Momentarily, my mind touched on a vague sense of yearning to be noticed by the pretty lady who was Justly's mother, that had been with me for as long as I could remember her. Then the

present moment was intense with its own yearning, only relieved when Axel gave a shout to get moving again.

The good valley we were in was beginning to meander,
but generally turning westward. The sense of being lost, and
that Axel was less reliable a guide than we had thought, was
diminishing among the company after a run of beautiful days
and fine traveling. All the horses were happy, restored by
good grazing and the easy going. Whenever we turned, the
stream turned with us on our right-hand side, widening often
into tree-fringed pools by which we were inclined to linger.
Sylvester's pictures of Justly were always in my mind as we
passed such places, and it was easy in fancy to place her among
those real speckles of sunlight and shadow.

I was thinking of Sylvester's pictures as we traveled on
that afternoon. It was easy for such pictures as those of Lorelei
and Justly to fix themselves in memory, but almost all of
Sylvester's photographs had the same power. It was as if,
through the glass eye he joked about, he could see a person,
a place, an action in a way that others could not. His pictures
stood in memory like some of the lines from *Leaves of Grass*.
"These are my *Leaves of Grass*," he had said. What strange
power pictures and poems could have. "You lay in the dark
and were almost a part of it." Did my own words have power
in themselves, and not only through memory?

Lorelei was running alongside.

"I come up, Scrag?"

I stopped and helped her up. We trundled on in silence
for a minute or two. She stuck a thumb in my belt at the back.

"What sort of story was that, Scrag?"

I shrugged.

"They were lucky."

"Reckon so?" She paused. "What about Justly?"

"She's lucky."

"Thou-Wert said she was a punishment for sin. He was just the same then as he is now. Same ol' hogwash. Just a younger man givin' it. Said the child should be called Justly: 'Lorelei is justly punished. Let the child be named accordingly.' He was a power with Mama, and so it was. But she's a damn sweet punishment. Sweet sin, sweet punishment."

I hesitated a moment.

"Sweet sinner," I said.

"Am I? With you, I mean — am I? Was it a sin, temptin' you?"

"Wouldn't care if it was."

"Should we stop? Leave it just that one time?"

"You want to?"

"No. Do you?"

"No."

We went on without talking for a while.

"Tonight?" Lorelei asked.

"Yeah."

"I come to you?"

"Yeah."

"When Justly's asleep." She smiled. "You must be a bit lucky, too. Didn't think this gift was droppin' from Heaven, did you?"

"No."

"But it's mad, Scrag. You know that, don't you? It can't last, boy, can it?"

"Can't it?"

She looked up at the sky, then closed her eyes.

"Lord, forgive this boy. He's madder than I am."

24

"I go first light," Lorelei whispered.

The cover was open back to the bow, so we would not wake late. I fell into sleep with her arm around my shoulder. I must have slept deeply for some time, coming awake again only by stages of pleasant dream and sensation.

She was tracing a warm fingertip very slowly over my face. It touched across my cheek and down my nose several times, then gently over my eyelids, making them flutter to open, though I willed them to stay closed so the sensation might come again. Again and again it came, half as if to wake me, half as if to caress me asleep. Sometimes the mound of her hand touched soft and brief on my cheek as her finger moved above. Then, down in front of my ear, the finger touched in a long, gentle stroke and in toward my mouth, where it stopped at the corner, pressing.

The pressure parted my lips, and I realized it was her nipple. I opened my eyes and could just see her inclined over me, guiding the breast with her hand.

"That good?" she whispered.

I kissed her. She turned the other to me.

"Treat both alike."

She slid under the blanket.

"You want go back there?"

She took my hand and led me back. I went with her, but was someone else, older, surer than myself, and infinitely grateful for that transformation, though it was quickly over, and I lay murmuring on the strange landscape of her body.

The sleep that came then for both of us was deep, but must have been brief, for I was already aware of shapes becoming more distinct as I fell into it. I woke suddenly, to the sound of a sharp crack and, in the same instant, a tremendous searing across my backside.

I rolled to my side and looked up at the bulk of Thou-Wert silhouetted against the sky, his wide belt raised.

"Jesus!" Lorelei scrambled up, drawing her clothes to herself.

"Defilers!" It was as if Thou-Wert shouted but at the same time restrained the sound of his voice.

"Defilers! Defilers!" He stood aside to let Lorelei pass. "Out! Defiled, defiling woman!"

He clambered over the board behind her, turning back to me again.

"I could not sleep, so I walked abroad, and the Lord brought me here — to the place of the fornicator. Defiler of the defiled!" He hitched his trousers and fastened his belt. "Fornicator!"

As he jumped down, my fear of him suddenly went.

"Spurious," I said. "Spurious."

Clad only in my shirt, I put a leg over the board, as if to follow him, and the pain in my backside bit deep.

"Spurious," I shouted after him.

He hesitated, as if he would come back, then, to my relief, strode off.

As I hurried into my clothes, Clancy was standing by his wheel, in his shirt and underdrawers.

"You all right, Scrag?"

"Fine," I said.

25

The first to be about in the camp, while it was still not fully light, I broke sticks and started a fire at the center of the circle. There was a plentiful supply of sear wood in the valley, from trees fallen and undisturbed over ages, and I soon had, first, a good blaze and then a widespread cooking glow going, at which the women assembled. Too often, they had the task of fire lighting while the men attended the animals and wagons, or took the chance of catching fish, lifting rabbits from snares, or taking shots at early birds or creatures venturing from their night cover to the dewy pastures of the new day. This morning, as one by one the women came with their pots and pans and small sacks, I found myself so well regarded, and overwhelmed with offers of breakfasts and future meals, that I thought I would light the fire quite often.

The pain from Thou-Wert's belt was sharp, every bend renewing it. I saw my grandmother striding across the backyard with a hazel switch or putting her strap back in the kitchen-table drawer as I stood up from the end of the horsehair couch, bawling. I was no stranger to the flame of punishment on flesh, but this was pain of a different order.

Between conversations with the women, and the shouts or whines of the children, I tried to imagine confrontations with Thou-Wert in which I devastated his standing in this little company, where his word seemed always law. At the same time, I was relieved that he did not appear by the fireside, as the men gradually arrived, looking for their breakfasts.

I accepted breakfast of fried eggs and oatmeal cakes from Jane, who was the first to use my fire, feeling uneasy in the smile of her squinty little eyes behind their small gold-rimmed glasses, in case she and Clancy had discussed the commotion. But she seemed unaware, and I was grateful to wily old Clancy for his discretion. As the others assembled, exchanged small conversation, and departed, some to eat on the ground a little way out from the fire, others to their wagons, I judged that, for the time being, at least, no word of my disgrace had gone around.

Lorelei and Justly came and cooked porridge. Lorelei and I exchanged glances across the fire, but an understanding between us kept us apart, until she came to offer me a helping, going away with no more than a smile when I said I had already eaten Jane's oat cakes. As she went back to the wagon it was strange and good to think of the body under that swing-ing blue dress naked on my mattress through the small hours of this very morning.

Walking together for those few yards, mother and daugh-ter seemed much alike. Both were carrying a pot in their right hand — Lorelei, the porridge; Justly, the coffee — both moved their free arm at the same angle, both carried themselves with the same upright, easy motion. Justly seemed a smaller version of her mother. Watching them, I remembered how I had thought that once before, on the day I watched her wading. But not so pretty, I had thought then, and I thought that now, but Justly was changing.

In spite of Thou-Wert's intrusion, I felt a surge of joy in the thought that only two hours ago I had been with Lorelei in the darkness. As we traveled on, the thought became "only three hours," then "only four hours," and the joy remained. Five hours, then six hours, and then we pulled up in a wide expanse of valley for a day and a half of rest.

There had been no stop at mid-morning, as Axel wanted to press on as far as possible before the break. I now found that the slight unease in approaching Lorelei that I had felt at breakfast still lingered. It was a new feeling, different from the shyness or nervousness I had felt often enough before. It was an instinct that said, "Not now, not now."

Instead of waiting for the midday meal, I went fishing, requesting Sylvester to tell Lorelei where I had gone if she asked.

"Bring something back and eat it with me tonight," he called.

After wading through the stream, I found a spot in the pool where fish waited under a tree for grubs or flies to drop. I sat on the bank there through most of the afternoon, occasionally taking a fish, occasionally dozing.

It was interesting to watch the camp from a little distance. After the meal most activity ceased, as the company took their rest. The horses moved slowly about on their long tethers or in hobbles, steadily grazing. A stallion paced restlessly, with his yard out. Clement's two cows wandered freely, watched by Tickler on his short chain. The hens pecked close to the wagons where crumbs had fallen. Daniel came down and stood briefly against his wheel. When I woke from dozing, all was as before, but Daniel must have settled to sleep.

At about four o'clock, by the sun, the people began to stir and go about tasks. Horses and mules were taken to the nearest point of the stream to water. The cows followed, making their own way, and when they had returned, stopping partway to piss, their tails raised like pump handles, Clement led Tickler out for his turn. Tickler showed more interest in one of the cows as they passed and went reluctantly, Clement urging him along by a pole attached to the ring in his nose. In the stream the bull suddenly lurched on the stony bed, and Clement was knocked sideways by the great flank, sitting with a shout of anger into the water. Then the cow began to respond to the interest shown in her and returned to the stream, prodded off by Clement with the flat of his boot, but shortly following Tickler back to his chain. Clement whacked the cow across her bony hindquarters and sent her careering away, to the amusement of the children. She bellowed from a distance in protest while the children gathered in curiosity a few yards beyond Tickler's range. Dora went over and took the Abbott children away; Martha sent her boy to gather wood for the fire and took the girls in, so only Dick and his brother were left. Their dog went in close to the bull, making him put his head down, and then followed the tracks down to the stream and lapped water. I thought that someone would offer me tea or coffee if I returned now, so I pushed a stick through the gills of my eight trout and waded back through the stream.

I called on Sylvester, had my coffee, and left four fish for our evening meal. He said he was printing new pictures and invited me to stay to watch, but I said I would take fish to Lorelei.

"I'll cook for sundown," he said.

Lorelei and Justly were about to go to the stream with two buckets to fetch water for hair washing. I said I would go for them while they prepared their fire. Lorelei said she would light the fire and Justly could come with me and take extra pans.

"What were you hollerin' about this mornin', Scrag?" Justly asked.

"Not much."

"Hell, it woke me up. Woke Mama, too. She looked out to see."

"Sorry about that. Nothin' special."

She saw I wouldn't tell.

"You bin fishin' all day?"

"Caught eight."

I pointed out the spot I had fished from. We filled the pans with water and turned back.

"Ol' Tickler wanted a cow," she said.

"I could see from there," I said. "It was the cow wanted Tickler."

"Same thing, ain't it?"

"In the end," I said.

Justly giggled.

"Some joke, Scrag. I tell Mama? *In the end*—that ain't bad."

"I didn't mean it," I said.

"You don't have to be embarrassed," Justly said. "I ain't. Guess I'm learnin' not t' be. Like Mama."

"Ain't she?" I said.

The dishonesty slipped out. I felt false, pretending to know

Lorelei so little, but the chance to ward off suspicion had come and had been taken. Justly quickly showed me that she would not be deceived.

"You know Mama better than that, Scrag."

When we were back at the center of the circle, where Lorelei had a small fire going, with two boiling pans ready, Justly related our conversation, including her final comment. Lorelei laughed, but at that point caught my eye with a look I had seen across the fire at breakfast. To leave them to their task, I made the excuse that I would read and went to sit by my wagon. Soon, mother and daughter came to theirs, and, between lines of Whitman, I watched them wash their hair.

There was something strangely pleasurable in watching the careful, homely actions. They had rolled sleeves high and turned collars low. Justly bent over a bowl set on a bench, soaping her hair with both hands, cupping water a few times and letting it run back, then squeezing the hair all over, the soap frothing between her fingers, suds falling. After a little of this, Lorelei took a jug and poured water, the straight hair falling with it in steady cascades till the jug had been emptied two or three times, and Justly was moving about squeezing the strands. Finally, Lorelei stood behind her, gathering the girl's hair in a towel and rubbing, as Justly turned up her face to the sun. Then it was Lorelei's turn, Justly going through the same motions as her mother, both of them chattering and exclaiming as before, Lorelei's shorter, bulkier locks becoming a frothy cap that her daughter sloshed the water over with delight.

It was good to be sitting there in the sun, the open book on my knee, seeing these ordinary actions, hearing these voices, enjoying the look of bared arms and necks, the shapes and movements of two bodies that had become more exciting to me than any others.

And I could come every afternoon of my life to look at the farmer's girl boiling her iron tea-kettle and baking shortcake.

I thought of Walt Whitman's farm girl and saw her counterparts here, a few yards away from me. The simple actions I had just looked at were as compelling to me as the boiling of the kettle and baking of shortcake were to Walt. This, and other such scenes, I could, truly, come and see every day of my life.

"Scrag, it's your turn. There's water to spare."

My protest was only halfhearted. I put *Leaves of Grass* in my trunk and submitted. Lorelei said I was too gentle with the soap and took over, kneading my scalp roughly. I felt slightly foolish, wondering what the men would think if they noticed me. Then I remembered Axel calling to her, the day we moved rocks in the river, that she could change his britches, and realized that, though this had been a joke, he would probably be happy to have her wash his hair, for the same reason that I stood here.

"A little more rinse, Justly."

Justly poured the warm water gently over the back of my head. Lorelei's fingers continued to move, more gently now, touching around my ears and temples in a way that made me think that, yes, Axel would happily come for this. Then she stopped and told Justly to finish the rinsing, and when this was finished, she handed me the towel.

"Justly, fetch the scissors. Sit on the bench, Scrag."

She trimmed my hair, which had not been cut for months before we left Scrimshaw. Justly was walking around, brushing her tresses to dry them. When she was out of earshot, Lorelei asked, "You hurt where Thou-Wert hit you?"

"Hellish."

"I ain't seen that man all day."

"Anyone know about us? He tell anyone, you think?"

"Guess Axel, maybe. He looked at me funny. But Axel don't fret me much. An' he looks at me funny, anyway. You can guess what he'd like. But he ain't got a cat in hell's chance."

I thought how Axel would like to be sitting here on this bench, her bosom above his face, having his hair cut, on a long bright day after lying with her.

"It was good," I said.

"It was best you went fishin', an' best we don't be together too much, a day or two. You understand that?"

"Yeah."

She put the comb through my hair, then stood back and looked at me.

"Next time, your hair won't hang in my eyes."

I went walking to let my hair dry and to ease my backside after the hard bench. Clancy was attending to a sore fetlock on one of Traven's horses. I went on by, in case he asked me about Thou-Wert.

"Oh, smart, Scrag! You goin' a weddin'?"

"Smartenin' for Oregon."

"You don't think we'll ever get there, do you, boy?" he called behind me. "Axel leadin'?"

I sauntered about, avoiding Axel's and Thou-Wert's wagons. Axel, I could see, was cleaning a rifle. Thou-Wert was not out. I stood awhile watching George and Will working with plane and spokeshave at a wheel repair, shaping a new felloe and spokes. Dora and Emmy were sitting together by Will's wagon, Dora stitching, Emmy nursing Chosen Arthur, their children chasing around. Dick's dog came up and scampered after the children, till Dora sent him off. He went away, turning back to make sure whether Dora would insist, which she did, after which he stopped to sniff at Daniel's back wheel, then briefly spattered it. Sylvester was not out, and I did not want to be in the dark of his wagon, so I went back, took my book, and lay facedown in the grass with it. That position, and the sun's warmth, eased the pain somewhat.

Lorelei and Justly were taking turns at brushing each other's hair. I watched the gleam of hair, their moving arms and tilting heads, but made no contact. The pleasure in being there was enough, but I thought they might be getting their own pleasure from being watched. Then, no, I thought, they would be doing it just like this with nobody else in sight.

Before long, I stirred the remains of the fire and boiled a kettle to make tea. I took some to the bench for Lorelei and Justly, and went back to Whitman.

"You read us that *Leaves of Grass* sometime, Scrag," Lorelei called. "Not Sylvester. You read us that, Scrag."

"Maybe."

"Do it, boy," said Justly.

Lorelei had pinned up Justly's hair. She looked elegant, and she knew that. She wanted me to notice.

As the sun went down I watered my horses and then joined Sylvester at the fire, where he was cooking our fish. Over the meal, in his wagon, I told him I had seen the pictures of Justly and that they were beautiful.

"She seemed the spirit of that place," he said. "Seeing her

standing there, I could imagine she'd always been there and always would be. Too lovely to be quite real — but she's also as real as bread and trout. That girl's a poem, Scrag."

On an impulse, I wanted him to know about Lorelei.

"I tell you something?" I asked.

"Sure."

"Lorelei . . ." I began. Then the words were not right, and I refused them. Sylvester stopped a forkful of fish halfway to his mouth and gave me a sidelong look, smiling.

"For you, she's the poem."

I nodded.

"Why not? Why not?" Pouring me a whiskey, he said, "Well, you've found your direction, Scrag. And Lorelei's a good compass. Life being what it is, you'll move on, but she'll have shown you the way."

As if it were possible to know some future emotion, to be momentarily a future self, I felt, as he said these last words, an untellable sense of loss. He seemed to understand. He reached across the table and held my arm.

"But today's today. Be a hedonist and enjoy what you have while it's there." He paused, gripped my arm firmly. "But record things, Scrag. Find some way of showing how it was, if you're given that grace."

We sipped at our drinks and were silent.

"You never had a wife, Sylvester?" I asked after a while.

"Never did. Wrong direction. No compass, you might say." Then he grinned. "Are you going to start telling me what I'm missing?"

I drank too much whiskey. I went unsteadily back toward my wagon, carrying a copy of Lorelei's photograph that Sylvester had mounted for me. Under his signature he had written, "For my good friend Scrag—picture of a poem— July, 1859."

Daniel was sitting on his barrel, smoking, the tiny spot of pipe glow a friendly beacon. I stopped, leaned on the wheel.

"What do 'spurious' mean?" Daniel asked.

"Another dictionary word," I said.

In the wagon, I looked up "hedonist."

Waiting for sleep, with the mattress seeming to tilt on a moving floor as if we were traveling, without the rumble of wheels, through the night, I thought of Sylvester saying, "But record things, Scrag. Find some way of showing how it was, if you're given that grace." Might I be given that grace? "You lay in the dark and were almost a part of it." Was there a grace in that? Was the grace in the experience, too? Lorelei's breast in her hand, touching my eyelids and the corner of my mouth—could there be sweeter grace than that? And how could I ever have the grace to tell how it was?

26

" 'Moon of the Red Cherries,' " said Daniel. "That's July in the Sioux tongue."

Justly had gathered cherries from a little tree overhanging from the slope above us, and was handing them around at nooning. They were unripe, but she was taking pleasure in the giving, and we ate them.

"They need to darken," Henrietta said in her odd, muffled voice. With white cotton bonnet, apron, and full skirts, wide-bosomed, and holding up the cherry by its stalk, she looked like an illustration from a book of children's stories.

"August they call 'Moon of the Cherries Turning Black,' " said Daniel. He spoke loudly, slowly, as if, for once, Henrietta might hear.

"Yes," she said, but it was what she always replied.

Lorelei said, as we were ready to move on, "Hell with Thou-Wert," and came up behind me to the seat. We had mostly kept apart for several days, and we came together now uneasily and rode on for a while saying little. It was a splendid day, with hazy blue distances when we came to the higher places, but intensely hot on the south-facing slopes. We sat well back for the cover's shade.

"Daniel's a good old man," she said. "Sad, his age, to come west and leave everything behind."

I wanted to tell her about Halo, but said nothing.

"I saw my backyard in Scrimshaw when Justly picked them cherries."

In my memory, the old picture of her came, pretty lady, pretty lady. I wavered between boyhood and this moment, with the good scent of her beside me. We were silent, with our thoughts. I glanced at her after a while and saw that her eyes were wet.

Lorelei and Justly took to riding with me in turns, and sometimes Justly went with Sylvester. We saw few cherries, but their color was darkening. The days were bright; nights, star filled and chilly. We were surprised that we were still seeing no sign of other wagon trains. At each new meeting of valley with valley, we looked for wheel ruts or fire embers, but there was nothing. Only occasionally was there sighting of an Indian, and always at a distance. It seemed that we were in a land almost without people.

Axel said that a regular route could not be far away. "Two days avay," he would say, but after two days we were still lost. Thou-Wert preached about promised lands and milk and honey, but the horses were suffering on the rocky slopes and from lack of pasture and water, and the company were filled with apprehension that we might encounter some obstacle — gorge or river or mountain — that would stay us in our tracks.

We knew that Axel had made wrong decisions, but there had been voices enough to support him at the time, and the doubters, like Daniel and Clancy, had been silenced. When

Henrietta fell ill, and lay delirious on the floor of the wagon, the women said that at the first valley with pasture they would go no farther without a rest of several days.

On Sunday Thou-Wert prayed for pasture, and on Monday evening it was there, a narrow valley, with a fast stream in which the wagons could stand in turn to swell the shrinking, dried-out wood of the wheels, while the company and animals took rest. There was no width to form the circle, so we stood in line, spaced by shrubs and rocks, but reassured by the knowledge that Axel's rifle was at one end and Clement's at the other. At the fire, Martha made Clement call for a thanksgiving prayer for Thou-Wert's guidance while Axel walked about tapping his boot with a fire poker, muttering that we were "led by vimen."

"Now you need pray for sense to listen to vot I say," he said. "You had damn easy journeyink so far. Vot fool made you expect no hardship? Don't you know there's dead bodies for every mile of this goink vest? Ve stay three days here, then go."

Thou-Wert took the power of his prayer to Henrietta's bedside while Daniel sat on his barrel. Henrietta had said that George should make her a box, but in two days she was mending.

Coming to water his horses while I was watering mine, Thou-Wert confronted me.

"It has troubled me, Scrag, that I gave no opportunity for withdrawal of that word."

When I pretended puzzlement, he slapped his thigh in irritation.

" 'Spurious,' boy, a vile word."

"You used vile words," I said.

"Aye, that I did. 'Defiler' I withdraw."

I said that I would withdraw "spurious."

"Defile, thou did not. Boy, thou wert defiled."

"I was not," I said angrily.

"At the very least thou wert led astray. A temptress led thee, boy. Led thee to be a fornicator. Nothing can undo that, Scrag." Thou-Wert shook his head sadly. "A fornicator once, a fornicator thereafter. On thy knees on the bare wagon boards and ask forgiveness, boy. This night, this very night. Ask forgiveness for the woman, too, boy, who has the burden of her comeliness. Pray for her, too. She offered herself as easily as her sweet child offered cherries by the trailside, Scrag. Ah, the fruit of evil can be very tempting, boy. Refuse it. Refuse it. Say to me now, you will refuse it."

I shrugged in embarrassment.

"Ah, stubbornness I understand, Scrag. But I see thou hast heard and understood."

That night, in Lorelei's wagon, I took turns with Sylvester in reading from *Leaves of Grass*, speaking the lines that had taken my liking from the first days I had turned these pages. I read about the bathers, and the lady "aft the blinds of the window," the trapper and the red girl, and coming to watch the farmer's girl. I finished with a passage about the animals:

> *"I think I could turn and live awhile with the animals . . .*
> *they are so placid and self-contained,*
> *I stand and look at them sometimes half a day long."*

As we were leaving, Sylvester unwrapped a new picture of Justly, which he had tantalizingly kept as a surprise for the end of the evening. It was a portrait in profile, showing her hair pinned up in the new way, and cherries held to her lips.

"Strange," he said. "I showed it to Daniel as I came by. *'Moon of the Red Cherries,'* I said. And, do you know, that old man cried."

27

"Listen, Scrag," Lorelei said, "just listen, and don't say anything till I've finished or I won't be able to tell you right. When I was still a kid, though Justly was already a year nearly, and Mama was tendin' her and had taken her for the day to Grandmama on Vine Hill, this man came by the house and asked after Mama and the child. I said they were on Vine Hill for the day, and asked him in to take tea, for he was a frequent visitor. While he was sippin', I went up to my bedroom to fetch a letter from an aunt of Justly's father, sayin' that the boy was close to her and that now she had learned about Justly at last—for the boy had been forbidden by his family to let on—she would like to contribute money for Justly's welfare. I was findin' the letter when I heard steps on the stair. I called that I was just on my way, but he said, 'Stay, child, I'll come to you.' I can see the picture in my mind still, how, because he was tall, he filled the little doorway, standin' there lookin' around my pretty room, smilin'. 'This is a pretty room,' he said, 'and you're a pretty girl. Do you know that?' I said I didn't know. He said I must know that because that was why I got Justly. Then he said, 'I'll show you how pretty you are,' and came in and took my wrists and said, 'Kiss me, child.' I was scared to death, but he was smilin' and pleasant still, and when he put down his face, I gave him a kiss. 'A proper kiss, on the mouth,' he said, so I kissed his mouth. 'That was nice of you, child, now I'll kiss you,' he said. He was still holdin' my wrists, and he turned me, still gentle enough, though, so I was back against the bed, which was high, and pushed on my wrists and tipped me. He let go my wrists and just bent over me, propped up with a hand on either side, still smilin'. 'Show me how pretty you are,' he said. I asked him to stop now, let us go and drink our tea. He said, 'When I've seen how pretty you are.' I said he was frightenin' me. Mama might come. He said, no, she wouldn't come home for hours and I shouldn't tell lies. He said he had only asked a simple thing from a girl who had been with a boy and got herself a child. 'Open your bodice.' Then he went serious. 'Open your bodice!' So I opened it, and he said, 'See how pretty you are — just as I told you,' and that sort of thing. No, don't say anything, Scrag. Let me just tell you. I want to tell — this is the first time ever. So he touched me a bit, gentle at first, then hurtin', and I told him, 'Leave me now, please, leave me.' 'But you know it's not finished,' he said. 'I'm not that boy, with his lust. I only want beauty. Let me see you, girl, then we'll drink our tea.' He stood up from me and went and stood in the doorway again and told me to undress — and he would not enter the room. I did as he said, thinkin' that would be the quickest way to end it, because he seemed to mean what he said. And he did, because he stayed at the door, havin' me turn about a bit before he said I should put my dress on and come down to him. I said the tea would be cold. He said he would pour a fresh cup. When I followed him down, he said, 'You see, I told you, child, that you were pretty—and I had to show you.' Scrag, I was so scared I actually said, 'Thank you.' 'No, child, thank the Lord who made you,' he said. That man was Thou-Wert.

"No, don't say anythin', Scrag. The story ain't finished, and I'll have a hard time tellin'.

"I never breathed a word of what happened. I'd had shame enough over Justly comin'—an' didn't want more, all the shame of explainin'. Who'd have believed me? They'd have said I was lyin', because he had shamed me through his namin' of Justly. Though, God, Scrag, I soon enough loved both the child and her name, forgot, pretty well, how the name was come by. The child *was* her name, I couldn't separate. And, Jesus, I loved her, hard and fierce, like I do now, boy. Let no harm come near her! The truth of the story is that he would come to the house as if nothin' had happened. Sit takin' tea with my Mama—Papa out workin'—with me in and out, Justly a-growin'. 'A pretty child and a pretty mother,' he'd say to Mama. He just knew I'd not tell, not then, maybe never. And time passed, and it seemed a bit like it had never happened. So I didn't much care that it had—it was past and done with. I could even smile at my sayin' 'Thank you.' Sometimes, undressin', I thought of him stood there, fillin' the doorway, but that was early on. As I learnt men's ways I guess it seemed fairly normal, till I remembered the fear sometimes—not often—an' knew fear wasn't a part of how it should be, fear or forcin'. And today I had both. Just after you went with Sylvester and Justly, Thou-Wert came, tapped on the wagon, said could he talk with me, said you had spoken. I said, 'Sure, come in,' and that there was still some coffee. Scrag, all them years had passed! I had a mind to rightin' the wrong of his words to us — defiler, fornicator, an' that — so I sat with him an' heard all his stuff about seducin' a boy — no, don't say nothin', Scrag, let me tell you — thinkin' when he's finished I'll give him my mind. 'Seducing a boy,' he says, 'like a long time ago.' I said it wasn't seducin' — I mean, with you, Scrag, an' you know it — no, don't say a thing — an' he said, 'What was it?' An' I couldn't tell him because I didn't know no right word. I couldn't say 'love' because that didn't seem right, our difference in age an' all, and we hadn't spoken of what it was, so I had no business to say, though 'love' can't be far from it. Some folk might understand if I said 'a damn sweet sport' or 'joy' or 'sweet pleasure,' but not that one. 'You tempted and took him,' he said. 'Like a long time ago. A mere child then, even then a temptress.' He looked half mad: that smile that ain't smilin'. 'And there's unfinished business. What would they say if I told them, those people out there? How I found you with Scrag, not a stitch on you. That boy long ago. Why Justly is Justly. And the visitor calling and a young girl shameless. What would they say? So there's unfinished business.' The dark of the wagon was like that light bedroom, him blockin' the way. He took my wrists the same grip. 'Won't the temptress tempt me? Tempt, you bitch, tempt me. Do as that girl did.' I thought how the seein', that time, had appeased him, how endin' it quickly had been the best way. So I undid my dress, though my hands were so shakin' I could hardly unbutton, an' let it fall off. Then he did the rest . . . did the rest. I knelt. I knelt on bare boards. On bare boards, and he took me. That bastard took me. Like some old mule, Scrag. Then he drank his coffee. Justly came in a little time after, as I was dressin'. No, don't speak, Scrag. You can say those things later."

28

Emmy was sitting on the top of the little stepladder Will had made for the children, her feet on the bottom step, Chosen Arthur at her bosom. She had her head down, watching the baby, and did not see us till we were near. At the last moment I wanted to walk on by, but Justly pushed my arm.

"Excuse us, Emmy."

I was nervous enough because of the baby feeding, without the concern over helping out Justly with what we had decided she should ask. Emmy looked up, welcoming. She was always friendly, a smile on her round, pale face.

"Hello, you two."

I found it difficult to meet her eyes because of Chosen Arthur guzzling at that globe, and looked at the straight line of the parting down the middle of her tight-drawn dark hair.

"Justly wanted to ask you things."

"Excuse me askin' when you're nursin', Emmy, but we wanted to see you alone."

"How can I help you?"

"This ain't easy," said Justly. "And don't mind me askin' in front of Scrag, because I wouldn't have the courage, maybe,

without him. Emmy, when a man forces a woman, shamin'
her an' all, is that what you'd call rapin'?"

"Heavens, Justly! What's this?"

"Is that rapin'?" Justly insisted. "When she hain't said
yes."

Emmy looked at me, but I kept my eyes on her hair.

"That's what it sounds like child, unless . . ." Emmy
shrugged slightly.

"Unless what?" said Justly.

Emmy shrugged again, looking down at the baby.

"Unless he was just that keen — maybe a boy — and he was
just not mindful." She glanced at me again. "About takin' his
time, and suchlike."

"Not a boy," Justly said. "Not just unmindful."

"Who has done this to you, Justly?"

"Not Justly," I said quickly. I looked at Emmy's face, now
full of concern.

"Not me, Emmy," Justly exclaimed. "Mama. Yesterday."

Emmy straightened on her seat and Chosen Arthur slipped
from her breast. A jet of milk arced in the space between us
like a fine thread. For a moment, fascination overcame embarrassment as the wet nipple stood on the white globe.

"And the man was Thou-Wert," said Justly.

Emmy put Chosen Arthur, who had called his brief protest,
back to his sucking. She waited, as if uncertain of what to
say.

"It was Thou-Wert," Justly said again.

A sudden wailing sound broke from her. Her face distorted
into anguish, as it had when she had come to tell me about
finding Lorelei weeping in the wagon. She caught her breath
in deep sobs.

Emmy jumped up, her breast slipping into her dress, and held out Chosen Arthur to me.

"Take him, Scrag."

She put both arms tightly around Justly and held her, swaying gently.

"Quietly, Justly, quietly."

Justly's breath went on drawing deeply, with a strange sound I only remembered from childhood. Emmy patted her back as a mother would a child's. Chosen Arthur looked at me with one eye, sleepily, the other hidden in his bonnet, which had gone awry. There was milk running from the corner of his mouth and over his chin. I pushed his clothes on it and wiped it away, grateful that he was not crying.

"Ssssh," Emmy soothed. "Ssssh, child."

Before long, Justly's breathing was near normal again, and she was simply crying, quietly, her head under Emmy's chin, Emmy's hand stroking her neck under the pinned-up hair.

"How lovely your hair is, Justly. Lovely, lovely." She looked at me. "And now look at Scrag holding Chosen Arthur."

I moved so Justly might be able to see. She opened her eyes. I took the baby close. She looked for a while, managed a smile for a moment, then closed her eyes and cried again, gently, till she needed to cry no more.

"Let's go in the wagon," Emmy said.

She took Chosen Arthur, her dress darkened in a patch from Justly's tears, and led us up. I touched Justly's shoulder to comfort her as she put a foot on the step, and she turned and kissed me.

"I'm sorry, Scrag."

Emmy gave us biscuits and covered the baby in his cot. Her children were with Dora's children, but might be back soon.

"Now tell me."

Justly told what she knew. I judged, as I had earlier, when she had told me, that Lorelei had told her the story in less detail than she had given me. Mainly, Justly spoke of finding her mother, and of Lorelei's concern that nothing should be said.

"Then why are you telling me, Justly? Do you know what you're saying?"

"Was what I've told you rapin'?"

"If it was just like you say."

"It was just like I say. Just worse, maybe."

"Then that's what it would be called. But do you know what you're saying?"

"Thou-Wert raped Mama, that's what I'm sayin'."

"Think carefully, child. Do you know what would happen if everyone knew — if they believed you?"

"Everyone should know."

"But would they believe you?"

"They'd believe Mama."

"But if Lorelei didn't want you to tell?"

"Jesus, she'd have to want me to tell."

"But she didn't."

"Jesus, Emmy, should that ol' man be able to do that an' nobody know? And, maybe, do it again, and again. Jesus, Emmy!"

"Don't blaspheme, child."

"What's that? What's 'blaspheme'?"

"Taking the Lord's name in vain. Saying 'Jesus' as if you were swearing."

"I don't know about the right or wrong of that, Emmy, but I know about the wrong of rapin'. If you'd been Mama still half kneelin' there when I came in, you'd have known all there was to know about rapin'."

Emmy put out her arms across the table and took one of Justly's hands and one of mine in hers. Her face was shadowy, her back to the light outside, the sky against the open bow, but I could see her serious expression.

"If it was rape, Justly . . . Scrag, do you know what could happen to Thou-Wert? No? Where we came from or where we're going, they would hang him."

"Jesus, no, they wouldn't do that, Emmy! Put him in jail, maybe. They wouldn't hang him!"

"Oh, wouldn't they?" said Emmy. "There's not much forgiveness in this land, child."

"Even Mama would forgive if he admitted an' was shamed," said Justly.

I was thinking how when the sun is shining it is hard to believe terrible things. The sky was an intense blue, a single white cloud sailing across it, small and high. There was a glow of some golden shrub on the mountainside. Somewhere near, a bird cheeped. It was impossible to think of Thou-Wert being hanged.

"We aren't where we came from, and we aren't where we're goin'." Before I had finished saying it, I knew it sounded foolish, but Emmy understood.

"We would have to make our own law, perhaps," she said. "And our own punishment."

"What can I do, Emmy?" Tears were welling again.

"Go and be with Lorelei. Leave me to talk with Will."

We went down. I held my hand to Justly and remembered holding it to Lorelei that day after she had watched me change my britches.

29

"Ve have a court," said Axel.

Emmy had told Justly's story to Will, Will had told George, George had told Dora, Dora had told Martha, Martha had told Clement, and Clement had gone to Axel. We had traveled for two days since the long rest, and it was the morning of the third. Now, though it was Sunday, we were to press on. Axel was angry at being delayed, stomping about impatiently as the company gathered in the space behind his wagon. Some people sat on the ground; some stood. Thou-Wert looked sick, restlessly walking around his wagon with his Bible in his hand.

Axel said he would hear the evidence with Clement, who would be judge, and that Dora would represent the women.

"This ain't no real court," said Clement, "but it is the best we have." He sat perched on Will's stepladder. He asked Lorelei to step forward.

"What have you to say, Lorelei?"

"Nothin'."

"Lorelei, word has been rife in this company that you was raped three days ago. Is that so?"

"I don't wish to say nothin'."

Everyone was silent. Clement sat considering.

"A very serious thing has been said, woman, and it could only have started with you. Are you sayin' you lied?"

"I've lied to nobody."

"In that case, I order you to tell this court what happened."

"I'll say nothin'."

Clement turned to Dora and talked quietly, Dora nodding. Then he turned to Axel. The company were murmuring among themselves. I thought Axel might be saying "stubborn voman."

"You stand before this company as a woman who has been — so it is said — dishonored, yet you are willin' to say nothin'. I demand that you tell me why it is that, after startin' this story, you refuse to say more."

Lorelei stood silent.

"I am losin' patience, Lorelei. Speak."

"It is a serious matter," said Lorelei. "I won't speak."

"It is a serious matter, and you must speak."

Lorelei was silent. Dora said something to Clement.

"Do I understand that you are protectin' the man?" asked Clement.

"I don't wish him punishment."

"The court decides about punishment."

"This ain't a court," said Lorelei.

"It's the best we have," said Clement.

Thou-Wert was pounding his fist on his Bible in agitation. "May I speak?"

"Speak."

"My good name is besmirched," said Thou-Wert. "This woman has said she makes no charge. The matter seems ended. But cannot the court condemn the wickedness of the lie?"

"Would you accuse the woman who has refused to accuse you?" asked Clement.

"If she has not accused me, why are we here?"

Justly broke away from beside me and pushed forward.

"I accused you," she shouted. "You raped her, an' you know that for sure."

Everybody was talking at once.

"Quiet," called Clement.

Lorelei crossed over and put an arm around Justly.

"Am I accused on the word of a child?" said Thou-Wert. "Does this vileness come from the mouth of a child? How can a child even know such things?"

"Let Justly speak," said Clement.

"Justly will say no more," said Lorelei.

"I will, Mama," Justly protested.

Clement looked uneasily around the faces before him.

"I am loath to ask a child to disobey her mother," he said, "but in these serious circumstances I must. Do you know what rape is, child?"

"Yes, I do."

Dora said something quietly to Clement. He nodded and looked at Justly.

"I accept that you do," he said. He sat looking at the ground for a few moments, then looked at Justly. "You must say nothin' more."

"She will not," said Lorelei.

"This matter is ended," said Clement. "Let no man, woman, or child in this company say more of it."

"But it is not ended," protested Thou-Wert. "With respect to the court, my good name is besmirched. How can I hold up my head?"

"You may hold it up in this company, as ever," said Clement. "The company respects the man of God."

Thou-Wert held up his Bible.

"I would speak," he said. "Sin lies about us and within us. It is in the man of God as in any other. It is in me as it is in you. It is in the woman as it is in the man. Verily, it is in the woman often, in the temptation she offers the flesh, to which the man, any man, may succumb. To which, yes, even the man of God may succumb. To which this man of God, I must confess before you, succumbed three days ago. For which sin I have, three days and nights, asked the Lord's forgiveness on my knees. My dear friends, I am not a man of force but of gentleness, as the Lamb of God bade us be. But I am a man of sin, as we all are, for which we seek forgiveness in the blood of our dear Lord Jesus Christ. I came unto the woman as a man sinning, but sinning in yielding to temptation, as another in this company yielded not a great time before. Eve was a temptress ever, and this woman is comely, as Eve was comely, and men and boys will yield themselves to her. I would go to my wagon now and pray, having bared my sin to you, as I had already bared it to my Judge above. May I ask the court to be lenient with those who have accused me of a sin too vile to name?"

"Stay," said Clement. "We are not ended."

There was a general commotion as Clement talked with Axel and Dora. Lorelei held her arm around Justly, but turned to see where I was standing. I saw others glance at me in their talking. Sylvester came behind me, put a hand on each shoulder, and spoke quietly in my ear.

"I know no word for that performance. But don't worry about the anonymous mention. It's a step on a journey, boy."

I was glad at Sylvester's guessing. Suddenly I felt that I loved this man.

"All silent," shouted Clement. "We have been delayed too long, and this matter must be ended. No, this is not a real court, but as we travel through the wilderness we must have justice. If it is rough justice, it is justice seen by all and, I trust, accepted by all as our honest keepin' to the right and decent. The court decides that an accusation was falsely made by misunderstandin'. Lorelei, by allowin' the misunderstandin' to go forward in the first place, you are responsible for this trouble, though we recognize that you did your best to draw back things before the court. For that, you will be shamed by walkin' behind the rear wagon for two hours in the mornin' and two in the afternoon. Justly, as a child you will be punished as a child, and whipped by your mother."

"She will not," shouted Lorelei. "I'll not touch her, Clement."

"Then someone else will," said Clement. "Martha will whip her."

"Don't let that bitch come near her," shouted Lorelei.

"Leave her alone," shouted Dick, "you gabbin' old — " He was cut short by Traven's hand across his ear.

"Silence!" Clement pointed at Dick. "Traven, take that brat behind yon wagon and larrup him."

Traven seized Dick by the ear and led him past Axel's wagon. Jeanie yelled in protest, following.

"Hell, larrup her, too," Clement called, at which the tension broke and everyone laughed, including Justly and Lorelei. Then I saw that Lorelei was near to crying.

Clement held up his hand for quiet. There was the sound

of Dick being leathered, and Jeanie's yelling, from behind the wagon.

"Mama will do it," Justly said.

"Dora and Martha will see that it's done," said Clement.

"Not Martha," said Lorelei.

"Dora and Emmy," said Clement.

He got up as people began to move away.

"Oh, go behind the bushes and get it done with, Lorelei. It's better than hangin' the minister."

"How could you believe him?" said Justly.

"I didn't," said Clement.

30

At nooning Lorelei would not join the company to eat. Justly and I went to her, where she sat in the trailside scrub, but she sent us away.

"Just bring me water."

Justly said I could take it. She grinned.

"Tell her I got a sore ass."

I gave Lorelei the message.

"You know somethin'?" she said. "I meant to hurt her as little as may be, an' I knew Emmy an' Dora would go along with that, but then, sudden, I felt that mean with her, all unaccountable, for her blabbin' about things, I guess, an' bringin' all this fuss. Go tell her I love her, Scrag. I'm havin' a sleep in the sun. Don't let anyone come talkin'."

At mid-afternoon we were going down a long slope into a wide valley. I had the cover open at both ends and could see Justly driving behind me. She laughed and waved, and stood up at the reins, pretending that she found it hard to sit down. When we stopped for a short rest, she went back to her mother with a mug of water and a biscuit.

When she came back, she stretched on the ground beside me.

"She didn't want t' gab, but she's happy enough." Justly suddenly rolled over with laughter. "Jeez, Scrag, Mama said Thou-Wert's got an ol' mule's dick an' next time she'll shoot the end off it." She rolled close and clutched me, and we lay laughing madly together till we were in tears. "And jeez, Scrag, I've got the sorest ass in Christendom." "In Christendom" was one of Thou-Wert's preaching phrases. It was funny, coming from Justly. I rolled about laughing. She took my hand. "Feel." As I turned she put my hand on the waistband of her skirt. "Feel," she said. We both stopped laughing, but the laughter was still there, pulsing just below my chest, ready to burst free again. I pushed my hand under the waistband and felt the cotton of her drawers. "Underneath," she said. She was smooth and cool. "Further," she said. Further, she was smooth and warmer, with fine smooth lines crossing. "That don't bother me a damn thing," she said. "I'll tell you somethin', Scrag. When Mama gave me that first cut, I was still a kid. When she gave me the last, I wasn't. That was the damn fastest growin' up! And, boy, I kinda feel good. You know that, Scrag?"

"You feel good," I said.

"Reckon I've done enough growin' for one day," she said, chuckling again.

I pulled my hand away and looked around. There was nobody watching us.

"Water the horses," I said.

There was a narrow trickle of water running among rocks at the side of the trail. We took buckets and tipped them sideways to catch the flow. Sylvester came, about the same business.

"You all right, Justly?"

"I'm fine, Sylvester."

"And Lorelei?"

"She's fine, too."

"You don't look too sorry for yourself."

"Oh, I ain't." As Sylvester went, she said, "You missed a good picture behind them bushes this mornin', Sylvester. How it was, an' all."

"Never another chance," he called back.

"Never no more," she called. She turned to me, laughing. "That even sounds kinda sad, don't it?"

The view of the valley below was deceptive, the distance down to it much greater than it seemed. Though the surface over which we rolled was fairly even, the evenness was narrow and stony, so we ground along slowly, taking the increasing steepness with care, in case horses skidded or were strained by the weight of wagons bearing down on them. In a part where the incline was particularly steep, I looked back, seeing over the tops of the four wagons to the trail behind, and saw Lorelei walking at some distance beyond Clement's wagon, a figure in pale blue against the sandy rocks, out in the clear air behind the cloud of our dust. Though it was too far to tell, I thought she looked jaunty and proud, and that she was enjoying the aloneness, and maybe telling herself that nobody in this world would ever take away her pride or make her kneel for them again. Did she know that her two hours for walking behind us there had passed? Did she disdain to come hurrying back to us, wanting to show this "punishment" for

the petty matter it was to a woman who was proud and beautiful? Was she, possibly, thinking that this Scrag boy — yes,
that couldn't be far from it, as she had said — loved her? And
would she be thinking that — as she had said here on my
wagon, that day — mad? I thought of her words: "Lord, forgive
this boy, he's madder than I am." I felt a rush of mad joy and
began to laugh. The laughter that had pulsed down under my
chest an hour ago with Justly broke free again, and I laughed
and laughed. I stood up and leaned out the side of the wagon
as far as I dared and waved to Lorelei, hardly thinking that
she would notice through the dust and distance, but she did,
and waved back.

Then an amazing thing happened. Jeanie dropped
down from her wagon and walked back to Lorelei, and
they embraced, standing for a moment, being left behind, then walked on together, hand in hand. Then Clancy
pulled up to help Jane down, and Jane walked back, and
the three women put arms around each other's waists and
walked together. Then, in front of me, Daniel stopped to
help Henrietta down, and Will stopped for Emmy, and
the old woman and the younger one with her baby on her arm
stood waiting while the wagons passed, until they were with
Lorelei, Jane, and Jeanie. So we came down to the wide
valley.

When the circle had formed, and the women were standing
in it, Sylvester began to clap, Daniel and Clancy following,
and in a moment almost all the company had joined them,
only Thou-Wert and Martha not showing themselves. I attended to Lorelei's horses, then my own, and waited for Lorelei
and Justly to come.

"You come in an' stop us from blubberin' now, Scrag?" Lorelei asked.

I went in, but did not stop them. We sat, and they held each other for a long time, then held me together till they were still.

"You know what I'll see in my dreams tonight?" Lorelei asked. "That old bull Tickler's got the amazin'est balls."

31

" 'The beautiful uncut hair of graves,' " Lorelei quoted. We were lying with Sylvester on the grass beside Lorelei's wagon, after eating. There was a sunset glow along the valley. "How does it go next, Sylvester?"

"Tenderly will I use you curling grass,
It may be you transpire from the breasts of young men,
It may be if I had known them I would have loved them.

"Is that what you were thinking of?"
"And 'This grass is very dark . . .' " She hesitated. Sylvester took up the quotation:

". . . to be from the white heads of old mothers,
Darker than the colourless beards of old men,
Dark to come from under the faint red roofs of mouths."

Sylvester pulled a blade of grass and twiddled it between finger and thumb.

" 'The smallest sprout shows there is really no death . . .' " he added.

"I'm gettin' uncomfortable settin' on this grass," said Justly.

"I'm just gone serious a bit," said Lorelei.

"A serious day," said Sylvester.

"Not all," said Lorelei. "But when I was up on that hill, lookin' down on you all, I was thinkin' there's three I damn well love down there. You'll excuse me sayin' that, Sylvester, I know."

Sylvester crooked a finger and brushed an eye with the knuckle.

"Hell, Lorelei, you say the most surprising things. What have I ever done to deserve love?"

"It don't have to be deserved," said Lorelei. "Though this is, over and over. An' if you want to know why, it's for talkin' to me like I mattered more than just for maybe looks or cookin' or woman things. And talkin' to Justly like she mattered for herself an' not just because she can make you a pretty picture, though I know what you made of her is more than just that."

The spirit of that place, I thought.

"This is the moment to say how you all mean much to me," said Sylvester. "Though Scrag will remember that a couple of times I've told him the thing I love women for is apple pie."

"I understand that, Sylvester, if Scrag don't."

"I'm grateful, Lorelei." He smiled. "One thing I'm sure of is that Scrag will look back on this journey as his halcyon days."

"You're a discernin' man," said Lorelei. "You're one dear, discernin' man."

"What's 'halcyon'?" Justly asked.

"I must go and work," said Sylvester. "I'll leave you to find out — hey, Scrag?"

"When we get to apples, I'll bake you apple pie," Lorelei called after him.

When the grass was dampening with dew, we went into their wagon.

"Spread the mattress, Justly," said Lorelei. "I don't have a feelin' for benches right now."

"Justly don't, either," I said.

"What about Scrag?" asked Justly.

"You kick them dusty boots off, boy, an' you can lie with women."

I kicked them off.

"You like the middle?" Lorelei said.

"Anywhere," I said.

"You're a sweet liar. Get in the middle."

We lay on our backs, looking at the glow of reddish light spreading up the canvas through chinks around the side. Lorelei took my left arm and pulled it under her neck. After a moment, Justly took my right arm, turning her face toward me on it.

"For a boy who didn't know his mother or have a sister, you ain't doin' bad," said Lorelei.

"No," I said. I felt nervous but at the same time like a child held close and secure.

"I don't feel like Scrag's sister," said Justly.

"What am I supposed to say?" said Lorelei.

"Go on, say it," said Justly.

"Say what?"

"Say you don't feel like his mother."

"I don't," said Lorelei.

"I knew that," said Justly.

"You mind?"

"I don't mind."

"This is an embarrassin' conversation for Scrag. You know that?" said Lorelei.

"I ain't embarrassed," I said.

"Scrag ain't embarrassed," said Justly.

There was a pause.

"Scrag ain't embarrassed, but I seen him embarrassed," Justly said.

"If you don't shut up about Scrag bein' embarrassed, I'll tell him put his boots on an' go," said Lorelei.

"I'll put my boots on," I joked.

"There, you see," said Lorelei.

"Talk about Sylvester," I said. "You said you loved him."

"Did he mind me sayin' that?"

"He should like that, shouldn't he?" I said.

"He's a shy man with women."

"He ain't too shy with me," said Justly.

"You ain't a woman," said Lorelei.

"Tell that woman what I told you this afternoon rest time," said Justly.

"Justly said she grew up today."

"While you was whippin' my ass this mornin', I was growin' up that fast I can't believe it. You know that, Mama?"

"I'd forgotten somethin'."

"What's that?"

"I grew up the same way, so damn fast."

"Tell me."

"When a child to be called Justly was startin'. Oh, this is

a borin' subject, girl. Scrag don't want t' be hearin' talk about sore asses."

"I told Scrag feel mine," said Justly.

"And I told a boy feel mine," said Lorelei. "Ain't there somethin' new we can talk about?"

"Sylvester," I said.

She was thoughtful a moment.

"It ain't easy to put. Maybe Sylvester's deepest feelin' would be for men, not women. Like in *Leaves of Grass* an' that woman watchin' the young men bathin'. The woman is watchin', but it's really a man sayin' they're beautiful, naked there. It's the writer sayin' that. And I guess Sylvester feels like that."

"You feel like that, Scrag?" said Justly.

"I don't know how I feel."

"Shall I try guessin'?" asked Lorelei.

"Try."

"I guess you'd be thinkin' about the woman bein' excited."

"I reckon so."

"And the other things you like special are the red girl with the trapper, an' the farmer's girl in the kitchen."

"Whitman liked them, too," I said.

"Lovin' ain't simple," Lorelei said.

We talked on, now serious, now teasing, now turning to trivialities, our thoughts and feelings spoken from the floor of the wagon in our loose embrace. Again, as the light faded from the edges of the cover, I had the odd feeling that the wagon was traveling on and I was being carried toward unknown places that lay in darkness.

"Scrag, I've no mind to kick you out tonight," Lorelei said.

"If you'd like to pull them boots on an' go make us coffee while we get ready for sleepin', you'd be welcome to lie there. Justly won't grumble."

I made coffee at the dwindling fire. There were a few people coming and going still. Thou-Wert was sitting alone on a boulder, elbow on knee, hand under chin, firelight just catching his face. Daniel was having his last pee against the wheel.

"Good night, Scrag. Bin a bad day."

"Not all bad," I said.

"Did I see you tryin' the lid, mid-afternoon?"

"No, you didn't."

"There's all the time in the world for you, boy."

"Good night, Daniel."

I took the coffee to Lorelei, then stood at my own wagon wheel, thinking of Daniel, wondering what it was like not to have all the time in the world. I could hear the voices of Lorelei and Justly on one side, Henrietta unusually loud on the other, Chosen Arthur briefly letting out farther on, and Axel playing quietly on his harmonica, a sad tune I could not recognize, that seemed to do with loneliness.

I tapped on Lorelei's cover.

"Come up, Scrag."

A candle was lit. They were both under blankets. There was one in the middle for me. Lorelei's dress and Justly's skirt and blouse were draped across the table. I sat on the bench and poured the coffee.

They sat up to take the mugs, their shimmy tops surprising and pretty in the candlelight, the light on their arms and on one side of their faces, large shadows thrown on the canvas.

"Thou-Wert was sat by the fire," I said. "He looked miserable."

"There's one good thing come of that foolishness," said Lorelei. "I don't ever have to pay respect to that man again. An' I'll surely never have that ol' mule bangin' up behind me or any other way in this sweet world. Look in that table drawer, Scrag."

I opened the drawer. At the front of it was a little derringer pistol.

"I told Scrag what you said." Justly chuckled.

"You can grin, Scrag, but I meant every word," Lorelei said. "Close that drawer and come to bed. I take it you'll put your boots off, an' you'd be more gracious without them britches. Justly'll blow the candle."

Justly blew a long breath at the candle. The flame fluttered and bent but stayed there. I kicked off my boots. On the second blow the light went out. I folded my britches on the bench.

The blanket had a good fresh smell. Lorelei first, and Justly quickly after, moved half out of theirs, and put an arm across me, as if laying claim to some new possession. We lay in the dark without speaking.

"Justly, you asleep?" Lorelei asked after a while.

"Jesus, this is nice," said Justly.

"Justly, you asleep?" Lorelei asked after a further wait.

Justly stirred slightly, but there was no reply.

"You want to sleep yet, Scrag?"

"No."

"I can't sleep yet," Lorelei said. "It don't matter about talkin'. Justly don't wake. I'm so full of feelin's, I can't sleep yet. You mind if I talk a bit?"

"I like you talkin'."

"Turn to me."

I turned.

"Will these be your halcyon days?"

"I guess so."

"You know what 'halcyon' means, Scrag?"

"No."

"I don't know, either, but it sounds like somethin' good an' special, don't it?"

"I'll look in my dictionary."

"You do that, an' tell me. There's so much I'm learnin' an' wantin' to know, an' so much I'm feelin', I feel like I'm made new, some moments." She paused. I waited. "Hal-cy-on. That's a nice word. Halcyon days. Maybe you can say halcyon nights. Would there be halcyon nights? I guess there would. You want to touch me, Scrag? Don't wait for askin'. Loosen that. Jesu. Just touchin', boy. No more, no more. Just touchin', talkin'. Hal-cy-on. 'I contain multitudes'—you remember that from the book? That's how I feel. I know what he meant by that . . ."

"Tell me."

"I'll tell you my multitudes. First, I contain the tiny child I was, in earliest memories. Then the little girl, an' all the little girls she was, inside, the happy one, the sad one, puzzled one, the frightened sometime, and the others she imagined that she sometime was, or heard about in stories. I contain all them. An' I contain the older child that grew from her, an' somethin' of the people around, those that she thought enough about to know their ways of talkin', thinkin', young an' old. An' then the boy she started Justly with, an' what it was to be so stirred, and standin' into her. Yes, I contain him, for his lovin'. An', most from then, there is the girl who knew what she contained, the movin' child. An' then the girl who suckled, held that tiny helpless thing. An' I contain that child, them blue, first-openin' eyes, an' what they saw as time passed. Is this borin', Scrag?"

"Go on."

"And then the girl I told you of, him fillin' up that little bedroom door, her fear. Yes, that one I contain. And others from that time, an' after. She who worked at tasks. Who knew a man or two, and has each one inside her still. Especially Frank. Oh, I contain that Frank, wherever he is, whoever he's lyin' by tonight, some half whore, Mississippi way. Yes, I contain her, too, the way that he'll be usin' her, an' all that stuff of love. Oh, Jesu, boy, that's nice. You like that smooth? This gathered part? An' you'll contain all that, Scrag, won't you? Always. Always. Come what may. Oh, Jesu, boy. Some part of what Sylvester said. Your halcyon days. An' I contain you, Scrag. That kid who used to saunter by my gate, an' crossed my path as if he'd have me notice him. Don't mind me sayin' that, it's long ago, or seems so. Now you know I knew. An' that was good, so I contain that kid. An' all that's passed between us on this trail. We both contain that sure enough. Maybe I'm nearer sleepin' now. You, too? Jesu. This gentle madness, boy. Jesu."

We were silent, and Lorelei soon slipped into sleep. I lay for a while thinking of the events of the day, of Lorelei's "multitudes," and of some of my own. How strange it was that a day that had begun so badly could end in such happiness. "What have I done to deserve love?" Sylvester said again, and Lorelei answered again, "It don't have to be deserved." Apart from that one night in my wagon, I had never before, since my earliest years, slept in a bed with someone else. Had I really slept in my grandmother's bed or only imagined it? Was it true memory, the high-buttoned nightdress with the broad button band down the middle, my face close to it, or only from wishing? It seemed to be true, for I caught again the stifling scent of its cotton or of the deep pillow. But I would think of that some other time. Now I wanted to think of lying on the floor of this wagon moving gently into the night.

"Scrag."

I was awakened by Lorelei's whisper.

"You don't mind me wakin' you? I think it ain't far off from dawn. I woke from dreamin'. Can't get back to sleep. I dreamed I was whippin' Justly over again. Oh, the relief to find it wasn't true. Is there someplace called Halo, do you know?"

"You say Halo?"

"Is there someplace called Halo?"

"I think so. Maybe. I don't know." What should I say, with Daniel's secret in my keeping? "Why Halo?"

"Up on that hill there, yesterday. Where I slept at noon-time, it was chipped in rock — Halo — half hidden in the grass."

"No pointer?"

"Nothin', but the rock was flaked. There could have been."

"You should have called."

"I was thinkin' other things."

"Maybe we're near someplace."

"Should I tell Axel? I was laughin' back up there, to think he'd passed, not noticin'."

I wondered what Daniel would say. I wanted to tell Lorelei about Halo, but held back from it.

"Yes, tell Axel."

We talked quietly till morning. Lorelei said she was a

schoolroom where I could come to learn what I might need for the world. One day I would leave and just think back sometime. Then, lying facedown, she said her back was America and my fingertips were wagons on the trail we'd come. They wandered in the valley of her spine and over the ridges and around the mountains of her shoulder blades. She said I was as lost as Axel was. I said I was not sure I wanted the trail to end, that being lost was the best thing I had known. We were quiet for a while, and when light began to come in around the rim, she sat up to show me how the tips of her breasts would gather in the cold. I felt she was teaching me but being in my mind as I learned, as if she were learning with me. When she covered herself again, and we lay in a quiet embrace, I thought of Sylvester wiping a tear from his eye and saying, "Hell, Lorelei, you say the most surprising things."

Justly woke and asked Lorelei if I was still sleeping. I turned on my back. Lorelei leaned over and kissed Justly. We heard the company stirring.

"Can you see the look on Clancy's face when Scrag steps out of here?" said Justly.

32

Turning from the first crackling of my fire, I noticed that Thou-Wert was sitting on a box by his wagon. As I saw him, he raised a hand and beckoned me. Though I had no inclination to talk to him, I went a few steps in his direction before hesitating. When he had seen me coming, he had dropped his hand, but now he raised it again and beckoned slowly, insistently. There seemed nothing I wanted less at this moment than to speak with Thou-Wert, but I slouched toward his beckoning finger, which he dropped only when I reached him. He stood up, looking distraught, suddenly grasping my shoulder.

"Thank you, boy." He pressed my shoulder and turned me partly around, falling in beside me. "Let us walk together, Scrag." His black garb had an unpleasant smell that seemed of stale sweat and horses. On his sleeves there were horse hairs he had not bothered to brush off, as he would have done usually. His trousers were filthy at the knees. "Scrag, you walk with a woeful and penitent man."

I said nothing, trying to edge away from the grip of his

hand, but he did not seem to be aware of how tightly he was holding me. We walked back toward the fire, to which nobody had yet come.

"I could walk through those flames and they would not consume me like those of the remorse I walk through now. Do you understand me, Scrag?"

I said I did. Thou-Wert let go his hold on me, stooped to take a faggot, and threw it into the fire. The flames livened as the twigs crackled.

"I'd scorch in similar flames of penitence." He grasped my shoulder again and guided me past the fire. "But there is a story I must tell. Let us walk beyond. A circle of hell these wagons have become to me."

Thou-Wert guided me past Tickler and the cows, and we walked around the outside of the circle, putting the wagons out of earshot. He gestured to the valley and the mountains, turning about.

"Is this not Eden, Scrag?"

"I like it," I said.

"And who was in Eden?"

I felt foolish.

"Adam and Eve," I said.

"You and I are Adams, Scrag."

I wanted to go. I thought that Axel and Daniel would be out now, and I wanted to tell them about the Halo rock.

"And there is Eve," Thou-Wert went on. "Unfortunately there is Eve."

"Should we have breakfast?" I said.

"I've eaten," said Thou-Wert. "The penitential crust. I'll not keep you long from yours."

I thought how changed Thou-Wert's language was, how until now he would have said, "I'll not keep thee long from thine."

He paused, gripped my shoulder tightly for a moment.

"A story I must tell. The temptation to which I succumbed one recent afternoon was not the first I knew with that Eve, Scrag. I, too, was young once. And young enough I was when this mischance befell. Not young like you. A man, but quite a young one still. God's ministry had called me several years. It was my wont to visit with those souls who needed me. And thus, one afternoon, I came to little Lorelei's house to see her mother, who was not at home. The child—for so I thought her then, and so she was, although she'd borne a child herself, her Justly, as you know—invited me to take some tea, and I went in. Mother had gone with baby Justly to Vine Hill. Lorelei went upstairs to fetch some letter, so she said, that I should see, she said, concerning Justly's welfare. I was a young man, Scrag, and something made me follow up the stairs. You'll know the feeling, boy. She'd been a long time gone. The memory that's fastened in my mind—would it were not!—is of standing at the bedroom door and seeing her unclothed—a young and very pretty Eve. My calling told me, 'Turn, go down,' and so I turned away, went down, and drank my tea."

"That wasn't all," I said.

"How's that, Scrag?"

"Lorelei told me."

"What did she tell?"

"That there was more to it."

"She was a young girl, Scrag. They're fanciful."

"I know." I twisted away from the hand on my shoulder. "And she still remembers everything you did."

"She said 'Thank you.' I tell you, boy, she said 'Thank you.' "

"I know that, too."

"She was a pretty child — no, not a child, although I called her so. Somewhere between. There was a vagueness, boy, in what she was. And in my mind, too, there has been. Did I do this or that? Say this or that? Lean over her? I see myself leaned over her. Did she say that, Scrag? Maybe my fancy added things, I've told myself, but known it otherwise."

"Yes, she said that."

"There was no hurt, though, Scrag. There was no hurt in it. I did not touch. Oh, it was long ago."

" 'Unfinished business,' so you said."

Thou-Wert suddenly dropped to his knees, beating the ground with his hands.

"Walk away, Scrag." He clasped his hands together. "Leave me to do penance for that once again."

I walked away. When I looked back, Martha was running out to Thou-Wert. As I reached the wagons, she was trying to pull him to his feet.

33

"I've had that feelin'," Daniel said. "I know this place. I lay awake last night. That long incline—I felt I'd bin down there before. But I'd never thought it this far north. Still, sixteen years . . ."

"How far would Halo be?"

"A week. Or less, could be. Maybe I'll let on now, tell Axel I was here before." Daniel grinned. "Come see his face, Scrag."

We went to Axel. He was under the wagon, with hammer and wrench. I told him about the rock Lorelei had seen. He crawled out, wiping grease from his hands.

"I never heard no place called Halo."

"I wish I hadn't," Daniel said.

"Vot's that you mean?"

"I come this way in 'forty-three. Not all the ways we bin, but two days back or so, we met the way I come before."

"You keep a friggin' secret, man."

"I do, I friggin' do. There's reasons, though. There's only you an' Scrag that know."

"Vy you not say?"

"Can't hev two leaders," Daniel said.

"You tell me that?" said Axel scornfully. "You tell them folk!" He gestured toward the other wagons with his thumb. "Ah, vell!" He changed tone. "Daniel, I tink that jus' damn nice of you." Axel's face became a wide beam. "Tell them ve rest today. I got axle trouble. How that for joke, Scrag, hey?" His beam slackened. "And how's that pretty ass you got back there? Two pretty asses. If you ain't sometink friggin' lucky, boy! How far, this Halo, Daniel?"

"Five, six days, maybe."

"Some pretty ass there?"

"Used to be," said Daniel. "Used to be." He looked at me, knowing I would understand.

We went around the wagons, giving Axel's instruction, anticipating reactions to the joke and hearing people repeating it as we went on.

"Life's a simple thing," Daniel said. "A few laughs, a few sorrers, an', like Axel says, a pretty ass or two if you're lucky."

I'm friggin' lucky, I thought. I sat in my wagon for a time, thinking that.

34

Lorelei stood with her back to the sun, under the bow of the cover, holding the little sheet of paper in both hands, reading to herself. The light through the paper made my writing stand out in reverse, unfamiliar, better formed than I had thought it.

"If this ain't one of the most beautiful things in the wide world, Scrag," she said quietly. "If this ain't just that . . ."

"Not that good," I said, but felt a surge of joy.

"Read it out," said Justly.

"You read it out, Scrag," said Lorelei.

"You," I said.

She looked at the paper again for a while, then read, her voice careful and correct, its softness making my words sound better than I had thought they could possibly be.

"The wagon is moving into night, with no horse pulling.
Lorelei and Justly lie on the floor
And enfold me between them. It is heaven here.
One holds her smooth breasts to me and says 'Jesu'

As I gently touch them. The other sleeps,
The warmth of her close, and does not stir."

"Jesus," said Justly. "Jesus, Scrag. Hey, did you do that, Mama?"

"It says so."

"Jesu," Justly giggled. "She say that, Scrag? What I missed, sleepin'!"

"Now you do somethin' for me, Scrag?" Lorelei asked. "You say that for me, for us both — Justly an' me. I'd love to hear that on your voice."

I read the poem. I was nervous, but I thought it sounded good. It pleased me that it was about my own life, and was true, and had both Lorelei and Justly in it.

When I had finished, Lorelei said, "It's good to be in there, ain't it, Justly?"

"I wish I wasn't just asleep in it," Justly said.

"There's worse ways of bein' asleep," said Lorelei.

"When's Scrag stayin' again?" said Justly.

"That's for him," said Lorelei.

"Five, six days to Halo now," I said.

Suddenly I had a feeling of not, perhaps, wholly wanting to arrive anywhere in five or six days. Halcyon days, I thought, and realized that in the notion of such days there was also a notion of their ending.

35

Martha was weaving a withy basket from osiers freshly cut from where the trickle of water down the incline fed the small pool by which we had camped.

"Scrag, Justly," she called as we passed her. We were setting out across the valley with my rod to where there appeared to be a wider stream. We turned and went over to Martha, who had her withies strewn about her feet as she sat on a box by a front wheel. Clement was on the other side of the wagon, trying out a longbow he had made for his boy.

"I won't delay you, Scrag and Justly, if it's fishin' you're goin', but I would ask a favor of you both. It's our poor minister. Oh, you know, Scrag — you've talked with him. He's a man distraught, an anguished man."

"He should be," Justly said.

"I have no doubt he should be, Justly girl. He leaves no doubt of that. The thing I'd ask of you — on his behalf — is that you put to Lorelei that he should make a true, contrite apology for what occurred, and seek forgiveness of her . . . what he called . . . her generous heart. You think that possible?"

I looked to Justly, leaving her to answer. Martha's hands were trembling with nervousness, the white, stripped withy in them twitching.

"He should be shamed," said Justly.

"Oh, is he not shamed, Justly? Is he not? He will not preach, say prayers . . . He is a broken, broken man."

"So he should be," I said.

"I'm so embarrassed, Scrag—you see I am, look how I tremble, Scrag—to talk of this thing that we all know occurred. A woman would avoid such talking if she could, and to a young man, Scrag. So you can see how earnest is my wish in this, to have some end to that man's agony."

We said we would tell Lorelei what Martha had asked when we returned from fishing. Martha kissed Justly and shook my hand, then went into the wagon and fetched us shortcakes in a tin to take with us.

The cakes were heavy and overmoist, and we laughed about them and about Martha's nervousness and earnestness. When we had eaten enough, we rolled pellets of shortcake and threw them to attract fish. A shoal of small fish I could not identify came and took them, darting about, disputing, chasing each other, the pellets too large to swallow. Then they suddenly departed, as a great chub came below them and slowly rose to take what they had left. He moved among the pellets without hurry, his mouth sometimes breaking the surface, gliding, turning, until the food had gone. Then he dipped his head and hung a few inches down, merging with the darkness underneath but for an occasional slight dip or uptilt or turn.

We had become still and silent, watching him.

"What you thinkin'?" I asked.

"He looks like somethin' else," Justly said.

I guessed what she meant, but left her to say it.

"Like Thou-Wert's dick." She spluttered with laughter, and the chub disappeared. "What you thinkin', Scrag?"

"Somethin' same as you."

I lay back into the grass and closed my eyes against the sun. After a moment Justly lay back, too. I could feel her arm alongside mine.

"You know I didn't want to blow that candle out last night?" she said.

"I guessed."

"What would you have done?"

"What you think?"

"Maybe I just don't know."

I tried to imagine what she was thinking as she lay silent.

"She seen it, Scrag?"

"Seen what?"

"Oh, hell! Has Mama seen it?"

"Why don't you ask her?"

"I'm askin' you."

"Ask her."

"You let me see sometime?"

"Sometime."

"Like when?"

"Like when you want to."

She paused.

"Like now?"

"You don't mean that."

"Maybe I do."

I waited. She sat up.

"Maybe I do."

I wondered what she would say if I did not reply. Her fingers tapped my leg lightly. There was the splash of a fish leaping in the stream.

"I do," she said. "You help me, Scrag?"

I undid my belt. She waited again, then undid the buttons, taking her time. Her touch was surprisingly cool, so light I could barely feel its pressure. It seemed an age she waited, silent. I wanted her to speak. She did up the buttons as slowly as she had undone them, and buckled the belt. She lay back, then turned and kissed my cheek.

"Thanks, Scrag."

"You satisfied?"

"What sort of word is that?"

"You like that, girl?"

She put her head close to mine, her brow against my ear.

"You could say that. Say, Scrag—I come back there sometime?"

"Sometime."

"When's sometime?"

"When you want."

"Like now?"

"Like now."

"We'd better fish. There was some big fish on your line, you know that, boy? Don't you care?"

"There's plenty fish," I said.

"Did Lorelei do that?"

It was the first time I had ever known her to use her mother's name.

"There's things ain't right to tell," I said.

"Will she ask you?"

"What's that?"

"What I might do. Will she ask you what I might do?"

"How do I know?"

"Scrag, would you tell?"

"Hell, no."

"There's things ain't right to tell."

"Or ask," I said.

We were silent for a while. I thought of the fish pulling on the line, wondering what kind it was.

"You love her, Scrag?"

"Guess so."

"Love me?"

"Guess so."

"I tell her you said that?"

"Hell, no."

"Love ain't for talkin' of?"

"Guess not," I said.

"That was some poem. Her titties an' all . . . *Jesu*. You like them some! I guess I'd whisper that 'Jesu.' You put me in some poem, Scrag?"

"You're in that one."

"Asleep!"

"I guess you'll be in one." I thought of her in Sylvester's pictures, and how the girl of that pool, "the spirit of that place," was different from the girl lying beside me in the afternoon sun, who was different again from the girl I had always known in Scrimshaw.

"What are you thinking of?" Justly said.

"Sylvester's pictures," I said.

"You like them, Scrag?"

"You know."

"I guess I do. I like them, too. You look at them you say 'Jesu'?"

"Somethin' like that."

I put my hand to the buttons of her blouse.

"You mind not now?" she asked. "You let me take you by surprise sometime, like Lorelei?"

"Let's fish," I said.

There was a trout on the hook. I made her take it off. It slid from her hands and lay jerking in the grass. I showed her how to kill with a neat blow. We took four more, at long intervals. She put the stick through their gills, and we walked back toward the wagons. I put a trout in Martha's tin and left it in the finished withy basket, which stood on the tailboard, glad that Martha was not there for conversation.

36

Lorelei and Martha were on opposite sides of the fire at sundown. Martha had thanked me for the trout and was cooking it on a stick. She kept glancing across, as if wanting to ask Lorelei her decision.

"Scrag, Justly, come. I'll end her Christian misery."

We followed Lorelei through the group of people at the fire and came to Martha.

"Martha," said Lorelei, "I thank you for your message. I want no grovelin'. He's shamed enough. Forgiveness ain't the word I'd use. Say it is ended. Also, I trust he'll tell how Justly was unfairly whipped, for what she said was honest truth. You tell him that, an' let it be ended."

She was turning away, but Martha seized her tearfully and kissed her, the blackened trout jerking as wildly on the end of the stick as it had on the line.

"I'm so relieved, dear Lorelei. I'm glad I spoke. It was an agony to talk such things to that young man. God bless you, dear."

"Scrag ain't no stranger to such talk, nor should he be," said Lorelei. "Don't make no bones."

Going back to our place by the fire, where our trout were sizzling, I felt some pleasure in knowing that several members of the company had heard those parting words and observed that Lorelei and Justly both linked arms with me. Sylvester was just arriving with his coffeepot. Justly mentioned that we had four trout between the three of us, so Sylvester was invited to make coffee and follow us to the wagon.

During the meal Sylvester seemed ill at ease, and I guessed that he had not realized how well Lorelei and Justly had put aside their shaming. After we had finished the coffee, and he had begun to understand, he went back to his wagon to fetch rye whiskey. Lorelei spread a blanket and we retired to the floor. Justly now ventured to try whiskey, and then to take some more, and Sylvester said her taste was improving. Sylvester himself seemed a little drunk, and he said I seemed so to him. We all leaned against each other and embraced somewhat, and Lorelei said she wondered what we might sound like to someone passing. Sylvester said he would go outside to listen, but he went to his wagon and came back with a poem he said he had finished just before coming to the fireside. He said it might not be very good, but he would feel privileged if we would hear it. We asked him to read, and he sat up on the bench to be near the candle, reading with the light casting his shadow on the canvas, one hand moving there in shadowy gesture to the rhythm of his words, his features touched by light and dark.

"Not the handsome young man, nor the beautiful young woman
Can turn me from the lure of falling light
Upon the objects of this world—sunlight, moonlight,
Gracelight of candles, flickering of fires,

Each with its cast shadows shapes all forms
To the passing loveliness my camera holds.

This old man sits by his wagon, his clay pipe clenched
In a weathered hand, so peacefully smoking.
This farrier straddles on an upturned hock,
The high June sun on his white-shirted shoulders.
The pipe's fine stem casts its shadow from westward,
The hammer shadow strikes its blow on the ground.

This young man sits by his wagon reading,
Stayed by a poem at noon rest time.
This slim nude girl stands in a dappled pool,
Here, half turned toward me, here, facing away.
The book's gleaming page throws its angles on grasses,
The Mount of Venus has its own small shade.

Ah, this poem began with easy abstractions.
Now the real young fellow puts his book aside,
The girl puts on clothes. They are walking over
The sunlit valley, their shadows beside them.
I could wish mine there, merging, a rod in my hand,
My heart in his heart, her hand in my hand."

There was a silence in which each of us seemed reluctant
to break the poem's spell.

"You're surely in there, Justly," said Lorelei, "and ain't
that beautiful?"

"What's 'easy abstractions'?" Justly asked.

"In the beginning I was only thinking of the *idea* of a
handsome young man or a beautiful young woman," said

Sylvester, "not really of anyone in particular. Thinking in the abstract. And I suppose I was contrasting that with the way, for me, the light and shade my camera registers is always so real, the light on particular things, the shade from particular things."

"I like that 'passing loveliness,' " said Lorelei — "and your camera holding it from passing."

"You can't hold the real thing from passing," said Sylvester, "but you can show how it was."

"Daniel an' Clancy," said Justly, "I could see their pictures."

"The spirit of that place," I said. I knew the whiskey had given me the confidence to say that, but at the same time I was gratified that Sylvester would be pleased to know I had remembered his words.

"Justly at the pool," he explained.

"You mean that I was the spirit?" she asked.

"Something like that."

Justly pushed her hand into Sylvester's.

"That how you wanted it?"

Lorelei was putting her hand into the pocket of my britches.

"Where's your poem, Scrag?" She drew it out. "You let me read this?"

I was glad that she would read it, excited at the thought of her speaking of holding her breasts to me, knowing the words would carry even more feeling that way. I longed for Sylvester's approval.

He gave it. Lorelei read slowly, carefully, with her face and the paper close against the candle. Gracelight of candles, I thought, and wondered at the look of her features caught in that soft light and their turning into shadow, her color heightened by yesterday's long walk in the sun and, perhaps, by the sweet embarrassment of the poem.

"Scrag, I'd be proud to have Lorelei take that out of my britches pocket and read it to anyone," Sylvester said. He lifted his hand that enclosed Justly's and looked at it for a moment, as if thinking of his own poem. Lorelei's fingers pushed my folded poem back into my britches, lingering. "All the time in the world," I thought, and wanted her to take it.

37

I woke at first light and saw Lorelei standing under the open bow in her long drawers, sponging herself at a hand washbasin set on a bench. I did not know if she had seen me stirring, and let my eyes half close again, reticent to surprise her and pleased to watch, half guiltily, with Justly curled close beside me, still soundly asleep. When she had finished, she put on her dress and went down. There was the sound of the water being poured against a wheel, then silence. I guessed that she had gone to gather wood for the fire, and had a mind to join her, then thought that if she had wanted company, she would have roused me. I turned toward Justly, put my arm across her gently, and fell asleep again.

I dreamed something like a jumble of moments from the stream bank when we had fished together, and woke to her telling me to find what sort of fish was on the line. Looking up, I found Lorelei standing over us with dishes of porridge in her hands and a pot of coffee on the table. She said we should eat quickly and get dressed before someone in the company came and saw us in bed together.

"Though that ain't of overmuch importance, maybe," she

added. "But them that want to dress in private should wake early."

We finished the porridge, then while we dressed, Lorelei went outside, pulling down the canvas. We were modest and awkward, turning away.

"I ain't that much bothered, are you?" Justly said.

"Not that much."

Lorelei was untethering the horses. I went for mine, and we harnessed up. I went in the bushes to pee, and watched mother and daughter walk down to greet Daniel and Sylvester, who were busy around their creatures, Sylvester trying to coax a hen back into its coop under the wagon. There seemed to be an eagerness to be off early, with the prospect of the place called Halo somewhere over the horizon, only Tickler making protest.

The going was easy, but every jolt made me aware of how tender my head was after Sylvester's whiskey. At the mid-morning stop, I sat with my coffee in the shade by the wagon and closed my eyes. I was almost dozing when Lorelei came up.

"Scrag, you lend me a pencil?"

I fetched her one of my three pencils.

"Scrag, you hain't got a piece of paper, too? Just a piece like your poem was on?"

"I got some."

"I'll show you somethin' in a bit," she said as she went away. "Somethin'll surprise you, boy."

Toward noon we met two wagons, after watching them slowly draw nearer from a great distance out of the haze. Voices hailed us, and we gladly drew up to greet the first strangers in weeks. A rough-looking group of eight men dropped down, and some of us did likewise. A burly man with a ginger beard, open shirt, and a mat of ginger hair on his chest asked us if we had a farrier in the company.

"You got nails for a loose shoe?" he asked Clancy.

"I got some."

"You put 'em in for me?"

"I'll put 'em in."

"Come an' look," said Ginger.

While Clancy went about his job we prepared for the midday stop, the strangers walking around our wagons and surveying us. Axel was scowling.

"Who say ve stop?" he asked me. "I never say ve stop here. You go tie your cover down, boy. Lotta friggin' thieves, likely. You go round tellin' others be careful."

I did as Axel said, sensing that some of the strangers were noticing what I was doing. Someone had started the fire, and people were cooking. A couple of the strangers brought over a big frying pan. There was the smell of rabbit Daniel had taken from his snares this morning.

A small bony man with broken teeth was eyeing Justly, nudging a companion, as she tethered the horses. Daniel was watching them, and followed them as they followed her back to the wagon. Seeing him, they sidled away, then the little man changed his mind and came over to Daniel, who was muttering a warning to me to keep an eye on them. He asked if we knew where Pike's Peak country was.

"Up my ass," said Daniel.

The little man grinned.

"You keep the female stock, Crusoe?"

He went off toward the fire, turning back to call to Daniel, "You watch them around Jack Pewter's town, Crusoe."

Daniel scowled.

"I traveled with Jack Pewter," he muttered. "He still there? Jack Pewter's town. I don't like that."

I noticed that Lorelei was coming over, so I went to her. She had the piece of paper in her hand, folded. She folded it again and slipped it into my pocket. I thought she would be thinking of putting my poem there last night, putting her head on my shoulder just before Sylvester poured another whiskey and Justly unpinned her hair to be like the red girl in the book.

"You read that when you're alone," she said. "It ain't much, Scrag, but I done it on my own, for you an' for Sylvester — you don't show him, though. You keep it close down there. That ain't a bad place for a poem, boy."

"Hell, I love you," I said.

I sensed that some of the roughs were watching us.

"You best go in."

"Who are they, Scrag?"

"Axel said they're gold men. One asked where Pike's Peak country is."

"Where's that?"

I thought, Up Daniel's ass. I said, "God knows."

Lorelei went. I walked back to Daniel. Soon the roughs were eating, and soon after that they were making ready to go. Sylvester had his camera out and asked them to pose for a picture in front of their wagons. As he went under the hood, and the eight roughs stood there grinning or scowling, I could imagine the finished picture in its tones of brown, something for people to look at years and years hence, and wonder who these men were, and what became of them. In that moment I understood something more of Sylvester's passion for recording what his life encountered, not only the things that would be pleasant in memory, or that might, as with the picture of the dead Indian, rouse people's pity or indignation, but also almost anything at all, simply because it existed or was happening. I knew that even a picture of this group of men, as unpleasant as any I had ever met, would give him that excitement of "treasure" he had spoken of one day to Justly and me in his wagon.

As soon as the roughs had gone from the fire, Lorelei cooked for us, and now, as we ate on the grass, I thought of that other day again, when Sylvester had photographed Clancy shoeing the horses. He had compared the excitement of waiting for a new picture to be printed to knowing you might find buried treasure. "What's it going to be, gold or rubies?" his voice came back. "Don't know what buried treasure feels like," I heard Justly say again. "Don't you, Justly? Don't you?" I recalled my sense of unease when Justly had not seemed to sense that Sylvester was, in that teasing way, gently leading her into knowledge of herself, and, recalling, I realized that I, too, had not understood his intention as well as I did now. I wondered if Justly would be more aware if the conversation could be taking place today, and thought that likely. "Treasure": I thought of the notion of darkness and deepness the word somehow carried, and of the intimation in Sylvester's gentle teasing, and saw the shadowy reflection in the pool at Justly Wading, while the real girl sat here in sunshine, her skirt carelessly rucked, chattering in total unawareness of how I was thinking of her. Then I caught a smile from Lorelei and knew that *she* was not unaware.

"You ain't read what I gave you," she said. "You go read that while I make coffee, Scrag."

"You don't want me wait till dark?" I joked. Sylvester had said that one way of testing whether a poem was good was to read it in broad daylight. Sometimes words that were not very special could be quite impressive in the dark: "Dark lowers your critical faculties."

I walked away from the wagons and took out the paper, wanting the words to be good, thinking of Sylvester's notion of waiting for treasure — "gold or rubies?" As I opened the folds, I was touched by the thought that Lorelei owned neither paper nor pencil. Let it be good, let it be good.

> *This man is rawhide*
> *But his heart is kid glove.*
> *This boy is new leather*
> *I soap with my love.*

I read the words over again and still did not know whether they were good, because they were surprising. At first, there seemed something odd, even funny, in making Sylvester and myself into kinds of leather, and I smiled at the idea. Then the oddness seemed pleasing, but I was not sure why. What should I say to Lorelei?

I waited for her to come to me, so that we would be alone. Sharply, I remembered the strangely satisfying scent of new leather, and then the pleasure of soaping it, feeling its suppleness growing under my fingers, and I said aloud to myself, "Jesus, Lorelei, I love you," then looked around in embarrassment to see if anyone had heard. When I folded the paper again and put it back in my pocket, I found I could say the words over from memory, so I walked about murmuring them. "I soap with my love" gave the true, soft sound of her voice in darkness, and in the middle of this bright day I had the sensation of her there.

"You like it, Scrag?" She came over.

"I like it."

Not caring who might see, I held her with my arms hard around her and kissed her, and, not caring who might see, she kissed me back and pressed close.

"My poem made you feel that good? There must be somethin' to it, boy, if it done that. But, hell, we mustn't stand here close like this in broad daylight." We broke apart. "I'll promise you some sweetness soon."

We walked toward Justly, who was drinking coffee.

"You honest, truly like them words?" Lorelei asked. "It ain't just that they 'mind you of sweet times?"

"They do, but that ain't all."

"I want it good, Scrag. Could it be?"

We drank coffee. Justly asked if she could read Lorelei's poem, and Lorelei, smiling, told her she'd find it in Scrag's pocket. I took it out myself, and Justly read it.

"Aw, Mama, this ain't good, is it? Did Scrag say this was good? Did you say that, Scrag?"

"Good," I said.

"I don't mean bad, but, Mama, how can Sylvester be *rawhide?* He ain't rawhide. He just ain't rough enough."

"He's tough," said Lorelei, "like rawhide, an' he's gentle like kid glove. It seemed to me that's how he is, them both."

"But he's an educated man! He's studied, been to Europe. He ain't like us an' Scrag. He's smarter than rawhide."

"He's sharp an' keen, ain't he?" said Lorelei. "You think of rawhide whips. That's how he is."

"He's plain like rawhide," I put in.

"He shows his nature like rawhide," said Lorelei. "He don't disguise. You think how that first night in the wagon, readin' *Leaves of Grass*, he showed them photographs. That *Balcony in Boston*, with her there unclothed, or that naked boy stood on the rock. It took a plain an' honest man to let us see his nature like he did. There's somethin' rawhide there, I reckon, Justly girl."

"I see how you mean that," said Justly. "Yes, maybe." A different thought struck her. "Funny to think that if he hadn't shown them pictures, he would never have made ours."

"That's sure," said Lorelei. She smiled. "What did he say to you that day you waded for him there?"

"How *say?*"

"How did he ask you put your clothes off, girl?"

"That ain't for tellin'," Justly said. "I'll harness up."

Axel was coming around, calling for us to be ready to move.

"You like my writin' now?" Lorelei asked.

"I'm thinkin'," Justly called over her shoulder. "Maybe I do."

The valley we continued to travel through all afternoon was a flattish plain with blue ranges running parallel to our route for a great distance, higher on the right, peaks standing above the haze. I said Lorelei's poem over and over, sometimes in thought, sometimes aloud. A line from *Leaves of Grass* stood in my mind: "Thinking of me the driver does not mind the jolt of his wagon." How true it was, all afternoon, of what Lorelei had written, too.

Once, she came running alongside and climbed up to ride with me a way.

"You don't think 'soap' a funny word, Scrag, do you? I don't think it is."

"It's true," I said. "First I was surprised, then it seemed true."

"I thought," she said, "I ease Scrag into lovin'. So it seemed like soapin' leather. Leather new, you young, an' all. Jesus, I thought that beautiful — I cried, boy, cried. But Justly don't appreciate the feel of that — how could she?"

As she spoke of easing into loving, I had a memory of something Sylvester said in his wagon on the night I had told him of my feelings for Lorelei. "Lorelei's a good compass . . . you'll move on, but she'll have shown you the way." As on that occasion, an untellable sense of loss, as if from some future self, assailed me, only momentarily now, for it was merely memory, and the sun was shining, but it tore at my throat.

"Hell, I love you."

"I know that, boy, and I ain't sayin' 'madness' anymore. We'll just go with it for a while. Here, put my poem back there. Carry it."

She pushed the paper into my pocket again and after a while jumped down.

Once, Justly came. She told me how she had hurt Lorelei's feelings by saying "soap" seemed a funny word.

"I don't feel jealous, Scrag," she said after riding quietly for a while, "and I don't think it wrong, her lovin' you." She was quiet again, looking about at the landscape. "You want me sleepin' with you two?"

"Yeah."

"Leave you an' her alone sometimes?"

"Sometimes," I said.

"She said you had your arm across me when you woke."

"I guess I did."

"Cherishin'," she said. "That true, Scrag — cherishin'?"

"I guess I do."

"I like that, Scrag."

At night, under a great moon, we lay together again on the floor of the wagon. After talking, we were lying quietly on our backs, looking at the sky, with its luminous clouds.

"You like to know what Sylvester said that day?" asked Justly.

"Justly, you don't have to tell. You keep your moments, girl."

"It was so simple. He just said, 'I'd make a timeless picture of you, Justly. Do you see, in your mind's eye, how it should be?' I teasin' said, 'Like Eve.' He said, 'That's what I see.' He busied with his plates. He said, 'You call to me.' I can hear my voice now in the trees, like echoin': 'Syl-ves-ter.' He said, 'Hold still, like that.' It was the first one, turned away. He said, 'Now turn.' He made it just simplicity. He like that with you, Mama?"

"It was simplicity."

We lay silent. I was thinking of Justly's pictures and imagining the scene by the pool, seeing Sylvester putting his head under the little black tent he carried for preparing and developing his plates. Then I thought of Lorelei posed behind the half-open canvas and, after that, of the afternoon when she had told me to unbutton her dress.

"Maybe your poem's good, Mama," Justly said. She was sounding sleepy. "Except, maybe, *rawhide*." After a moment she said, "You mind I go your mattress, Scrag?"

"If you'd like that."

She stood up and gathered clothes from the table. She climbed over the board, silhouetted against the moonlight.

Holding Lorelei, I found myself saying something I did not want to think about.

"Three days to Halo, them roughs said."

She lay on my left arm, turned toward me, so that I felt the whole length of her body against my side.

"How long to Oregon?"

I let her question go.

"You ever wish somethin' wasn't true?" she said.

How could I begin to answer? She traced a finger slowly about my chest.

"All the years between you an' me," she said. "I wish like hell that wasn't true."

"They don't matter."

"In here they don't. But out there they do."

"We're here."

She let me follow the next thought silently. I tried to imagine some scene at the end of the journey, but no street or building would shape itself in my mind. She must have been reaching out toward the same blankness.

"You come buy buns from me?"

She had talked sometimes of how in Oregon she would make her living by baking bread and buns and patties. Hungry, wifeless men would buy from her at "The Little Bunshop." Her pile of baking tins sometimes clattered out from their store place when the wagon pitched, till I fixed some twine to hold them.

"Yeah, I'll do that."

"I'll give you twice your money's worth," she said.

I said I knew that.

38

Justly was standing at the inner end of my wagon, facing the shadowy canvas and only dimly discernible, her body red-gold, unmoving, her arms straight by her sides, her hair down but taken forward over the right shoulder. I woke from the dream, hearing Lorelei say she would go and wake Justly before the company stirred.

I thought I would light the fire, so I pulled my clothes on quickly and met Lorelei and Justly outside. There was nobody about, the grass drenched with dew, the eastern sky red clouded. As we went along the bank of the creek to gather twigs and sear wood, I remembered my grandmother saying, "A red sky in the morning is the shepherd's warning." Occasionally a fish broke surface with a gentle plip, and once we disturbed a pair of waterfowl that startled us as they took off. The circle of wagons looked as if it might have been deserted by the company, the animals motionless, mostly lying down, merging into the grass. The canvas covers, which usually gleamed white in the brightness of day, were darkened with dew, touched with reddish tints in the dawn glow.

We made our excuses to each other and took the opportunity of going into the bushes before carrying the wood back. Thou-Wert was the first of the company to appear, jumping down, turning briefly to his wheel. Becoming aware of us, he came striding over, calling, "Allow me, Justly, allow me," taking her pile of wood and walking ahead of us. Dropping the pile at the center, he brushed his clothes with his hands, avoiding our eyes until just before he turned and strode away, saying, "I'm grateful, I'm grateful."

While Lorelei attended to making the fire I went to catch fish for breakfast. Justly came with me, not saying much. I sensed that she was feeling that a space was coming between us, as I moved closer to Lorelei, and that she was beside me now only to know if this were so.

"I slept good, Scrag. Your mattress was that comfortable. You sleep good, too?"

"It don't change nothin'—me an' Lorelei," I said. "You know we're close. You didn't have to go."

"I wanted to. It was her time."

She did the fishing, and caught five trout in twenty minutes. We returned, bright and laughing, Justly taking my hand on one side, carrying her catch on the other.

Sylvester was out with the camera, setting it up near Axel's wagon. Justly told him she had caught him a trout for breakfast. She went with the fish to the fire while I stayed with Sylvester. He said he wanted to make a set of pictures of wagon wheels, using at least one from each wagon, taking photographs at different times of day so the shadows would be varied. Each wheel would tell a story of the journey, the gouges from sharp rocks, the shallower indentations from the rounded ones, the cracks from drying-out on the plains, the grasses caught up in cracks and around spokes. Though each would tell the same story, each would tell it differently. He could never tell, he said, which interested him most, the human story behind a picture or the patterns on its surface. With a smile, he said that this was the wagon wheel of a lone man, pointing out how the undershirt Axel had washed late in the day, hung out to dry on a string between cover hooks and forgotten overnight, would be in the left-hand corner of the picture, partly behind the spokes. I looked under the hood at the screen of ground glass. The features he had mentioned stood there distinctly, upside down and reversed. As he went off to fetch his glass plate he said he would take one photograph, then join me at the fire. I went, wondering at the skill behind every picture Sylvester made, and at the feeling he brought to that polished box standing there on its tripod.

As I turned to go, Thou-Wert called behind me and hurried to catch up.

"Please, Scrag, tell Lorelei, I thank my God for the charity of her soul. She understands the wrack that's brought by what the Holy One endowed us with. And that must be some kind of grace, Scrag — grace. Tell her I'll not hurt her again, in any way, in any way. God grant that I may one day make amends."

I said I would tell Lorelei. He thanked me and touched my shoulder — this time, briefly.

"It is a dog that howls there, Scrag, between our legs."

I hurried on in front so that he should not see the splutter of mirth I could not hold back.

"Scrag looks pleased with hisself," said Justly.

Lorelei smiled.

"That ain't so remarkable."

We took out benches and table for breakfast, as the grass was still wet. The red glow was fading from the sky, the red girl still standing in my dream.

39

"Hey, Scrag, tell me this Crusoe thing," said Daniel. " 'Crusoe,' he said, that ruffian yisterday, that little leerin' runt with them black teeth."

"I guess because he had long hair."

"Who had?"

"Crusoe."

"Who was this Crusoe, then?"

"He was in a book by Daniel Defoe. A shipwrecked sailor on an island all alone. His hair grew long."

"You read that book?"

"I read the most of it."

"I'll git mine cut for Halo," Daniel said.

40

"You'd be the one she chose, Scrag, watchin' there."

Lorelei was again reading *Leaves of Grass*, sitting on my tailboard. She had told me how she was excited by suddenly finding that she could read much more easily than ever before, and that words stood in her mind.

I knew that she was meaning the lady aft the blinds of the window, watching the young men bathing.

"I ain't there," I called from under the wagon, where I was greasing.

"Boy, you sure are."

She was silent again. I carried on greasing, seeing her bare feet swinging below the board.

"You're that homeliest one," she said. "You don't think I know that lady's mind, boy? I know her."

I was smiling to myself, pleased at her teasing, which I knew was also serious, and amused not to reply but to see what she might say next. Her feet swung, and she hummed to herself for a time.

"You nearly finished, Scrag?"

Her legs were bare and long as she slid off the tailboard, her skirt riding up. She bobbed down, looking under.

"You do one thing really special for me, Scrag?"

"What's that?"

She dropped to her knees, walking her hands toward me through the grass, her breasts shadowy where the blouse was hanging away.

"The rock in the pool by that pretty cascade — you stand on that for me? I get Sylvester take you like that young man in the photograph he showed? For my own an' no one else's eyes?"

"Hell," I said.

"That 'hell' mean 'maybe,' boy? I ask Sylvester now? You go back there first light? It's hid from here. It wouldn't take five minutes, Scrag. I'd treasure that."

41

I was ready for the photograph some minutes before Sylvester finished preparing the plate. After putting off my clothes and wading out, there had been a difficult climb onto the rock, which was almost sheer on three sides but sloping at the back. I sat in the sun and watched Sylvester standing with the top half of his body enclosed in his black tentlike contraption.

It was early. Nobody had stirred as we left the circle. As Lorelei had said, the rock could not be seen from the wagons, hidden by a group of trees and bushes. I felt strangely unconcerned at being naked, then the realization came that I was pleased that Sylvester should see me.

I looked east, into the hazy brightness, and thought of Scrimshaw. The self I could remember there seemed as if it must be from some time further back than the weeks immediately before departure. I felt larger, solider, much more assured. I looked at my thighs, spread somewhat by the pressure of the rock, and had a momentary memory of sitting on the edge of my bed regarding them, then of looking at myself in my grandmother's sloping mirror. Was it possible that I had filled out so much in four months? I tried to encircle my wrist with my thumb and forefinger, and found that the tips could no longer meet.

I stood up, knowing that Sylvester must be almost ready. Waiting, I turned slowly in the sun, then realized that he was watching.

"Still, Scrag. Just like that."

The sun was warm on my left side. Sylvester went under the hood. I thought of my image upside down and in reverse, and felt a knock of excitement in my chest. When Sylvester emerged and slid out the plate, he looked at me and grinned.

"She'll hold this to that bosom, Scrag." Just as he was going under the tent, he turned. "You swim. I'll join you when I've fixed this plate."

I was going to tell him that I was no swimmer, but his head had already disappeared. I climbed down to the water and tried a few strokes, desperately trying to swim, remembering my lie to Justly at that other pool. When Sylvester was ready, he stood by his folded clothes for a moment, regarding the pool, his hand shading his eyes from the sun's glare, which was now intense. He was taking in an impression of light and shade, I thought, relieved that he did not seem to be amused at my incompetence. He was very slim, his skin much darker than mine, as if used to light. I remembered how he had talked one night of "lying like a lizard" among Italian olive groves. Suddenly he put out his arms, arched forward, and dived. I saw him gliding, then swimming underwater, turning toward me before he surfaced.

"Some slight tuition, Scrag?"

"Scrimshaw was no place to learn," I said.

I felt the excuse was weak. I wanted to let myself relax

into the water as he indicated, relying on his firm hand under me, the other on my back. I moved my arms as he instructed, then my legs, then all limbs together, as he walked forward with me.

"It's pattern, Scrag, as most things are."

I sensed the patterning, and was beginning to achieve it, but when he said he was withdrawing his hand from under me, I struggled and sank. We worked at it for a while, then Sylvester left me to practice while he swam around. He emerged near the cascade and called to me to come under it with him. We stood in the space between the falling water and the rock behind it, enclosed, the silvery screen seeming to separate us, briefly, from more than just the landscape beyond.

"This seems the kind of spot for wishing in," Sylvester said. A little way apart, we looked at each other, unashamed. "I'll make a wish, Scrag, mine for you. You mind?"

"Make that."

"I'll wish you to be some kind of artist, Scrag. An artist of some kind. Maybe in words. You've made a start."

I shrugged.

"Small start."

"But felt, and true, and competent."

"I've had no schoolin', though."

"Scrag, that's the least of it. There's nothing it will take you haven't got or soon will come by."

I looked at the falling water, then back at Sylvester. His body was shadowy, with flickering light from the cascade playing over it. The look on his face seemed to ask for trust in his words.

"Yes, I'd like that," I said.

"Our resolution, then, to be good artists. Let's get ourselves baptized."

He came and put his arm across my shoulder, and we stepped under the cascade. It was icy, and we shouted in surprise and exhilaration, staying under it only a moment.

"Breakfast with Lorelei," Sylvester said as we dressed. "Now, isn't that perfection after this? And with that blossoming girl."

Walking back toward the camp and the smell of cooking, he said, "And don't forget that art must also eat. Its food is experience."

42

"This was my lifeblood at the time, ten years ago. It seems a bit thin now." Sylvester handed me a small tan-colored book. "But you have that."

His name was on the cover beneath the title, *An Eastern Window*. I turned the pages. The poems were mostly set in neat verses, with shortish lines, and looked quite unlike the Whitman he now so much admired. He smiled.

"You're thinking how trim and spare. It was my ideal then — that elegance."

"The title —" I started.

"In one, a youth stands at a window facing east. From Boston, that meant Europe. It's about his dream of Europe, art and literature and love. Authentic then, but we move on. We need a different truth, our own. The funny thing is that this book seemed just that, then. I have affection for it still, but I've moved on."

He took the book and signed it on the title page, writing underneath, "For my dear friend Scrag, approaching Halo, August 1859."

"One day you'll sign your own book, Scrag. You see that one finds me."

I said that such a day seemed some distance off, but that if it ever came, I would find him.

"We're distance men," he said.

We went down from the wagon and I walked with him as he watered his horses.

"So much that good art needs," he said. "Maybe the thing I value most now is surprise. Not novelty — that fades. Surprise of recognition of the true, seen differently."

"You mean like this?" On an impulse, I took out the small piece of folded paper from my britches.

He looked at me quizzically, as if I might be making the claim for something of my own. I unfolded the paper and handed it to him, feeling slightly guilty at disobeying Lorelei's instruction not to show it. He read it several times, glancing at me occasionally, while the horses slurped water.

"You think this good?" he asked.

I thought with dismay that he was about to tell me the poem was bad, and I felt a moment's foolishness, as if my judgment had been swayed by love.

"Yes," I said. The word seemed barely to pass my lips.

"I talk of what art needs." He was still looking at the paper. "She gives it without knowing it."

"It's good," I said.

"There'll never be a time when I won't know these lines," he said. " 'I soap with my love.' As she might say, 'Ain't that

a line for tears?' " He tried an imitation of Lorelei's voice. I
smiled at it. I heard again her words from yesterday: "Jesus,
I thought that beautiful — I cried, boy, cried." Remembering,
I felt again the pulse of loving as she pressed against me in
that embrace. It stayed as I hurried off to my horses.

Part Two

Halo

43

We entered Halo in the late afternoon. Rounding a hill, we suddenly found it before us, timber buildings, some white painted and surprisingly stylish, on either side of a straight, very wide thoroughfare. A short way down on the right, the buildings gave way to a square of trees, with crossing paths, on which a few people were walking or had stopped to converse. Blinds in store windows were drawn, whether for a rest period or a holiday it was not possible to tell. A few curious children approached when we stopped a few yards short of the square, and stood regarding us, two of the older girls giggling when Axel stepped down to ask for guidance.

"Ve need place to pull up vagons," I heard him say.

"Compound," one of the girls said. "Behind the Palace." She gestured over to the left, opposite the square. Gleaming white in the sun, with shuttered windows on two stories, the largest building in the street had a long board across it, with decorative lettering proclaiming Pewter's Palace Hotel.

"Vere else?" asked Axel.

"There ain't nowhere else." One of the girls put her hand to her mouth, eyed her companion, and spluttered with giggles.

"Novere," the other girl said. They giggled and turned away.

An old man touched his hat to Thou-Wert, who had stepped down.

"Reverend, there's rules. There's nowheres 'cept Jack Pewter's yard, what's called the compound, back of the big hotel. Go down the lane by Pewter's Palace there."

"I thank thee, friend," said Thou-Wert, and we trundled down the lane until the first wagon came to a wide opening in the compound fence. Axel stood reading a large notice, tilting his hat to the back of his head, then walked back along the train, shouting its contents.

"Vagon space free for residents an' wisiters . . . oddervise dollar a day . . . hosses an' animals extra. Vot you say?"

There seemed to be agreement that we should stay a night or two. Axel came back saying that we should follow him into the yard and draw up closely alongside each other. He would go to the back door to make inquiries. While I sat waiting to move forward, I saw that the two girls from the main street had followed us down the lane and now stood looking at me. They were of about twelve years, thin, with dark straight hair. They were looking with what I took to be, in a phrase of my grandmother's that instantly came into my mind, familiar eyes. The one who had been first to respond to Axel in the street now spoke, while the other looked down, smirking.

"That your own wagon?"

"It's mine."

She smiled slightly, then glanced toward the hotel.

"That's Jack Pewter's whorehouse."

"Belle!" The other's exclamation was accompanied by a

slap on the bottom, and they walked away laughing, looking back a few times, waving.

By the time we had all drawn up, Axel had found the price of accommodation and that the animals could be put in an orchard beyond the yard. While we unharnessed and took the horses away, the women talked together and decided that they would all sleep under a roof and take a bath, with the exception of Henrietta, who preferred her own bed. All the men decided to stay with the wagons but to have some meals in the hotel. As we sat on the rough benches around the compound and chatted, four boys were already dashing with buckets to an outhouse with a smoking chimney, and staggering away with hot water.

"Cleanliness is next to godliness," said Clancy. "Especially among women, ain't that so, Scrag?" He grinned. "Most of us only got one to go by. Scrag, he got two."

I saw that Daniel smiled faintly, as if only half listening.

"Distinctive," he said.

"True," said Clancy. "I don't deny that." He looked uneasy, as if he thought Daniel had disapproved of his joke, and went off, saying he had left his matches in the wagon.

I sat beside Daniel.

"You come a Sunday walk in the mornin', Scrag? Keep me company?"

I knew where he meant to go.

"You want me come?"

"I'd like that, Scrag boy, if you would."

"I'll come, then, if you want me to."

"I do."

He was silent for a while.

"I used t' think I'd go an' stand there all alone an hour. But I don't want that, now the time has come." As if he guessed my thought, he added, "No, Scrag, I don't know why the change. I thought the other night, maybe she'd hardly know me now if she could see me there." He paused. "Though I'd know her."

Daniel lit his pipe. He sat smoking, the good smell drifting across me occasionally, the pipe's gurgle gradually increasing. I knew he was deep in his thoughts and did not disturb him. Sylvester came out with his camera and set it up at the entrance to the orchard, to make a picture of the animals dappled beneath the trees. In the yard, a plump girl had joined the four boys in the task of carrying water. Sylvester had her pose for a moment with her empty buckets, as if striding toward the outhouse, while a boy went in the other direction, his shoulders pulled down by his brimming load. Daniel tapped his pipe on the end of the bench, refilled it, and lit up again.

"You know what I'd do, Scrag, if I was your age now?"

"No."

"Not that I ever did sich things, but lookin' back . . ."

"Tell me."

"I'd go in that hotel, an' find that room where them distinctive women are."

"They'll be at bathin' now."

"Quite so," said Daniel. "Boy, that's why I'd go."

I hesitated a long while, until he said I might soon be too late. He assumed the reason was the same shyness that would have held him back at my age. I told him that it was more that I had never yet seen inside any hotel.

"Faint heart never won fair lady," he said.

The plump girl said that I could follow her and she would

show me the room. I offered to carry her buckets, but she said she would not be allowed to let me do that. I mounted the narrow back stairs behind her, wondering at the width of her haunches and whether Daniel might really follow his own advice if given the chance of living his life again. As we reached the carpeted landing, with its dark red calico wallcovering, my nervousness increased, and I thought that he would not. Under the carpet, the boards creaked slightly. Perhaps, from some point ahead in life we would know it foolish to waste time in nervousness, I thought, and was grateful for the notion as the girl set down her pails and tapped lightly on the door.

Lorelei called to her to come in. The girl opened the door and told her that she had a visitor.

"Is it Scrag?" I heard Lorelei say.

The girl looked back at me. I nodded.

"It's Scrag," she said.

As she stood aside to let me pass, she smiled, and her wide brown eyes gave me a glance. The door closed gently. The room was light, with pale green walls and a pineboard floor from which the sun reflected, a shutter standing partly open. Lorelei was lying on a large brass-railed bed in her chemise. Justly, in nothing but her drawers, was sitting at a dressing table by the far wall, brushing her hair. A little way back from the window was a flower-painted screen, behind which I could see the end of a bathtub.

"You had a notion you might see some bathin', Scrag?" Lorelei was smiling.

"Daniel had."

"Oh, did he, now? That's some cute horny notion for a man his age. A shame you waited on it, though. Still, boy, ain't this enough?" She put hands under her head, elbows on the pillow, and smiled again. "You'll pardon that language, Scrag."

The word she had used excited and embarrassed me. I looked away. Justly was looking at me in the mirror. She had brought her hair forward in front of both shoulders and was brushing it there. As I watched, there was a tap on the door, and the plump girl came in to ask if she could empty the bathtub. She moved the screen and bent over the tub to fill her pails. Departing, she said she would have to return several times. When she had gone, Justly stood up and brushed her hair for a few moments more, parting the ends of it on either side of each breast, knowing that I was watching and would remember how she had said, "I'll take you by surprise." When the plump girl had come and gone once more, Justly dressed and suggested we should go out into the street to explore Halo. Lorelei said Justly and I should go together while she enjoyed the luxury of a real bed for a little longer. The plump girl came, and poured a half bucket of water from the window onto the head of one of the bucket boys in the yard before departing again. Lorelei set up Justly's hair beautifully, and when we stood aside on the stairs for the girl to pass us with her buckets, she turned to look down on us and said, "Don't your hair look just beautiful!" We decided to go out by the back door because we were too nervous to venture through the unfamiliar building. We were aware of the bucket boys watching Justly as we crossed the yard. Her cheeks colored and she smiled at me, half pleased, half shy.

At the far end of the lane, the two young girls were standing. They looked at us as we came toward them, looked down, saying something to each other, and looked back again, smiling to us when we came near.

"She your girl?" one asked from behind us.

"Maybe," I said.

"Maybe," one said. They giggled.

"You go see Joe," one said. "Down in the square."

We passed the front of the hotel. The plump girl was opening shutters upstairs. She waved to us and we waved back. We went on down the same side of the street and saw that some of the buildings were now showing signs of life, shutters and doors opening, people passing in or out. There was the usual array of stores and offices of a little town, the usual sights, sounds, smells. Outside a saloon at the bottom end, several horses were tethered at a rail, a simple-looking hunchback youth in a grubby white apron gathering up dung with besom and shovel, watched by a few children, who seemed to be teasing him. A horse broke wind and they all laughed, mimicking the sound loudly, running around sticking out their backsides. The youth stopped his work, grinning. One of them kicked through his pile of dung, scattering it, and the youth swung his besom at him.

"A place like anywhere," Justly said as we crossed the street.

The buildings on the other side were wider apart, with space between them for access to dwellings behind. Outside a small church a minister stood with his arm around an old lady who was weeping. When we came to the gap where the square opened, we found that the girls had come over, as if to await us.

"You go see Joe," one said. "He's down the far side."

Two old men were getting up from a seat, so we took it and sat in the lowering sun. The girls still hung around, moving off a bit, coming back, circling.

"You got nice hair," the bolder one said to Justly.

"You like her hair?" the other said to me.

"I like it," I said.

"She your girl?"

"Maybe," said Justly.

"What's your names?" I said.

"She's Ruth, I'm Belle," said the bolder one.

"What's yours?" asked the other.

"I'm George, she's Jessica," I said.

"I go by Jess," said Justly.

"You got nice hair, Jess," said Belle.

"Have I?"

Belle went around behind the seat.

"You have that, Jess. How's that done up?"

"Some ways, my mother's secret," Justly said.

"She can sure dress hair," said Belle. "Your mom a whore?"

"She ain't!" said Justly.

"Belle's mama is a whore," said Ruth.

"She's pretty, too," said Belle. "She ain't an everyday whore. Just when the crowds come an' Jack Pewter sends for her."

"What crowds is that?" I asked.

"The gold prispecters, most."

"There gold around here?"

"There used to be. I don't remember that. There ain't much now. They just go through to elsewheres."

"Where's elsewheres?"

"All ways. Anywheres. Just searchin', mostly."

"Pike's Peak," said Ruth. "That's where they're goin' now. They struck gold there."

"You heard of that?" Belle asked.

"I heard."

"Where's Pike's Peak, then?"

"It's up my ass."

Belle and Ruth staggered about laughing, repeating what I had said, declaring that I was rude, attracting the attention of people passing by, until I regretted using Daniel's insult. I told Justly that we should go on a bit and the girls that we would see them some other time.

"You go down there see Joe," said Belle.

"Who's Joe?"

"He's just down there."

The trees of the square were bright, with spangles of sunlight on leaves and earth, dark shadows of trunks lying away from us, as did our own images. People looked at us as we passed, as small-town people always look at newcomers, some nodding and smiling because we were boy and girl together, perhaps. As we were coming to the edge of the square, we could see that all there was beyond was a scattering of poor-looking shacks and workshops to either side of a wide sweep of uneven track leading to another group of trees before the steep hillside. Suddenly Justly screamed. In the same instant, I looked up and saw a man hanging from a branch of the square's last tree.

44

In the moment we stood there, the hanging man high above us, so that we looked at the broad soles of his boots and into the stained crotch of his britches, and then to the foreshortened body in its dirty yellow shirt and to his misshapen features and the rope and branch, and some smaller, dead branches above, against a high gray cloud, I felt a sense of revulsion unlike anything I had ever known. Yet, at the same time, there was a sense of the ordinariness of the terrible — a man, a tree, a piece of rope, sky, walls of houses, voices, all ordinary yet terrible. We swung away, my arm around Justly's shoulders, into the square, laughter behind us, weaving our way between trees, through patches of sunlight and shadow, till we reached the seat we had left. Belle and Ruth emerged from somewhere and stood looking at us.

"Jess upset?" Belle asked. "You upset, Jess? You seen Joe?"

Justly wrenched away from my arm, went against the nearest tree, and puked.

"Ruth spewed when she seen Nell," Belle said.

"Who's Nell?"

"She's down in the wood. Just out of town."

"Who's Nell?"

"Joe's girl. They hung her, too. They done it in the wood."

Ruth was touching Justly's back, tender.

"You all right, Jess? You better now? You come sit down." She put an arm around Justly's waist and drew her to the seat. "Jess better not go see Nell. I spewed when I seen her first."

"I nearly did," said Belle.

"We go back the hotel?" Justly said.

We crossed the street, followed by the two girls.

"Don't you go in the front way?" asked Belle.

"We like the back."

Lorelei had slipped into bed and was awakened by our tap at the door. I told her Justly was feeling sick, and left them. She said we should meet in an hour for supper in the hotel, and that she would be pleased if I would ask Sylvester to join us. If I wanted to smoke, she said, I could take her pipe and tobacco from the wagon. It was good to be in her wagon alone, with the sense of feminine things around. I stayed sitting on her bench to light the pipe, and decided to delay seeing Sylvester until I came back from the wood.

The yard was deserted, so I guessed everybody was taking the opportunity of resting or, perhaps, of looking at Halo. As I came to the end of the lane, Belle and Ruth were there again, as if they had known I might come.

"Jess feelin' better?" Ruth asked.

"A bit."

"She a nervous girl?" Belle asked.

"A bit."

"I ain't." She fell in beside me, then Ruth came the other side. "You nervous, George? I bet you ain't."

"Ain't nothin' wrong with nervous," Ruth said.

"I ain't," I said. "Not normal things." I put the pipe back in my mouth and tried to revive it. "Hangin' ain't a normal thing."

"That's some pipe," Ruth said.

"It's normal here," Belle said. "You come see Nell?"

"We best don't take George there," said Ruth.

I stopped to relight the pipe.

"What was she hung for?"

The girls were not sure. I wondered if what Joe and Nell had done was something kept from children's ears. But there seemed little kept from the ears of Belle and Ruth, and their childhood seemed devoid of innocence. They appeared, too, hardly curious about the crime of Joe and Nell, who seemed to be remarkable only in their fate, not in what had led them to it.

"Don't you know what they did?"

"They was lovers," said Ruth.

"What was they hung for?"

We had come to the place where Joe was.

"Don't know," said Belle.

A short way past, we stood and looked back. I wondered at the way the girls seemed so unappalled. Their feelings seemed to stop short at interest, as any event in a small town might arouse interest, with a tinge of awe because death was involved.

"He's pissed hisself," said Ruth.

"They'll leave him there all Sunday. On Monday, bury him," Belle said. "An' Nell. You come see Nell."

We walked past the shacks. Outside the last one, an old woman wearing a man's broad-brimmed hat stared at us from behind a rickety gate and grumbled.

"You shouldn't go down there. Ain't fittin'."

"George wanna see," said Belle.

"Ain't fittin', wanna see her, that poor gal," the old woman called behind us, and she continued grumbling to herself as we went down the track.

I knew that I did want to see. I felt sickened, appalled, but I wanted to see.

"What did they bring her right out here for?"

"They always do. The kids call it the Woman Tree. I guess you'll see the reason why it's bin called that."

There seemed to be some amusement in what Belle had said. There was a suggestion of giggles, and the girls' long shadows on the dusty track before us collided and parted, collided and parted as we went.

As we neared the wood, I could see Nell, caught by the sunset light against the shadows. The tree's lowest branch was high, but she was lower than Joe. At first, when we reached her, I wanted not to look closely. An old man, with his hat on the ground in front of him, was sitting on a tree stump, his face and fringe of rough white hair in his hands, his elbows on his knees, crying and talking to himself, turned half away. The trunk of the tree was thick and smooth. I did not know what kind of tree it was, but the reason for the name the children gave it was plain. Where it forked there was a deep oval scar in the bark, as if made by a split during early growth.

The roots were wide where they entered the earth, like arms reaching underground. I let my eyes go from them to the bottom of Nell's skirts, her feet hanging limp below in little black shoes with brass buckles. She must be very young, I thought, her shoes so dainty. I wondered that they had not come off, then I saw that the flesh was bulging in her white stockings, holding the shoes in place, and that her ankles were swollen under the lacy petticoat.

"George don't wanna look at her," Ruth murmured behind me.

It was true, but I wanted to know this thing that was there to be known. I let my eyes follow up a fold of the dark blue silky shirt, shining purplish here and there in the sun glow, to the gathering at her hips and to the tight waist, then to the bulge of her bosom in a frilly white bodice, and at last, in a glance that immediately withdrew in horror, to the rope and its mark on her neck, and the once-pretty face with its bulging eyes and lolling tongue.

"Jesus Christ!"

I backed away and tripped in a cart rut, sitting into the grass. I was shivering. Belle and Ruth stood looking at me. The old man took a hand from his face and turned his head vaguely, his features a sight of pure agony. I continued to shiver. The girls still stood there, not speaking. The old man screwed up his eyes against the sun and stared at me.

"I'm sorry, sir," I said.

The old man still stared, and his head started to nod slowly.

"My Nell, my Nell," he murmured. "I'll stay here till they take her down." He nodded for a while, still looking at me. "No one will touch her till they come." At last he turned away, his head down again. "Jack Pewter's good as fuckin' dead."

I got up, grabbed Lorelei's pipe from the grass, relieved that it had not broken, and lurched away blindly. After a short way I tried to run, but my legs would not take me, and the girls caught up.

"I felt like that, George, too," said Ruth.

"I did an' all," said Belle. "You mind we took you there?"

"I come," I said. "Who's that ol' man?"

"Nell's Granper Judd," Ruth said.

The sun was suddenly dropping below dark hills, the sky crimson. There were lights in windows of darkening buildings, the lines of roofs sharp in silhouette against the sky.

"We live down there," said Belle, indicating past the church, and they ran into the dark as I crossed the street. When I looked back at the entrance to the lane, they had gone.

45

"She's a work of art," said Daniel.

She was seated alone at a round table a few yards away from us, a startlingly large lady who had entered the hotel saloon a few minutes earlier. I thought that she might once have been beautiful. She had taken her place at the table reserved for her with the manner of someone accustomed to being looked at, seated where her presence could not be missed by anyone passing down the room or turning from the bar. Her hair was a frizzy nut brown, set with several small gold combs. From her ears, there were gold pendants. Her eyes were large, with long lashes curled and darkened. There were bright patches of rouge on her cheeks, too near the eyes, the puffy flesh below them too wide an expanse of powdery pale pinkness, except for a mole spot on either side, darkly emphasized. Her crimsoned lips were shaped to a rosebud effect, but her mouth was small to be set in such an acreage, her face merging into the white neck. Her wide shoulders were bare, the upper part of her bosom an enormous sweep decorated by a gold chain from which hung an array of charms that lay across the high swell of her breasts. Occasionally she took a sip from the smallest of glasses on a delicate stem. Once she took a tiny handkerchief from a bangle on her wrist and touched a spill from between the mounds. My eyes kept going back to the knots of her nipples under the silky green stuff some way below. I wondered if she knew they were quite that prominent.

"She ought not be under the light," Lorelei said.

Pewter's Palace saloon was an L-shaped room with a bar along the inner angle, tables along the walls, a few grouped for diners at the wider end. There were oil lamps suspended, the largest one above the corner of the bar, near where the "work of art" had her table.

"Maybe she likes the dramatic effect," Sylvester said.

"Like you say, Sylvester," Justly said, "nothing that light and shade can't make beautiful."

"She needs more shade," said Lorelei.

"It brings back Paris days," Sylvester said.

"Paris full of fat ladies?" Justly asked.

"Full of colorful ones."

"There's colorful and colorful," said Lorelei.

We had finished the good meal of venison and were drinking. Our conversation was uneasy. Daniel seemed to be brooding on something. I wondered if it was on thoughts of the walk we would take in the morning, or on memories of another time here, when Halo was only a space under a yellow moon, or if it was simply on Henrietta's silence. Justly had been looking pale, but was now reviving. Daniel had told me, when I came back from the wood, that Lorelei and Sylvester had been looking for me, so my meal had begun with an apology for not giving Sylvester her message. Sylvester had already heard of Justly's experience of seeing Joe and was intending to take a photograph of him. The thought of that sickened me, but I respected his purpose. I was reluctant to tell where I had been, and when I was persuaded to say something about Nell, he said he would go to the wood, too. Perhaps a magazine editor in Boston would be interested in the justice of the West. Beyond all the conversation, the clatter, the bustle, the features and attitudes of people at tables or bar, I saw the terrible forms of Joe and Nell in stains of sepia. Lorelei was almost morose at moments. She apologized, saying that it was the effect of taking a sleep at an unusual time. I felt guilty, wondering if her mood was connected with the fact that I had gone off mysteriously, without calling on Sylvester. After a glass of wine her cheeks were flushed, and in her white lacy dress she looked smoldering and beautiful. Then something she had said came back to me, and I understood. "And, Jesus, I loved her, hard and fierce, like I do now, boy. Let no harm come near her!" I heard Justly's scream under the tree again and felt myself reeling away with her through the square.

"You got a taste for that rye whiskey, Scrag," Daniel said.

"I got a taste for that."

We were talking, drinking, watching the people at various tables or those who went up to the bar, taking in the experience of being in a room again for the first time in four months, when Henrietta became agitated, indicating in the direction of the stairs.

" 'Ores," she said. " 'Ores."

Two women were going up the stairs with men, another nearby leading a man between tables toward the banister.

"Ssssh!" Daniel protested.

" 'Ore'ouse," Henrietta said.

Lorelei giggled at Daniel's embarrassment.

"Jack Pewter's whorehouse," my whiskey said.

"She just ain't used t' wine," Daniel said.

He indicated the back door, asking Henrietta if she wanted to go. She nodded and said good night to us. Daniel said he would come back after seeing her to the wagon. At the signal of Daniel going, a few others left. Passing our table, Clement and Martha said they were going to the church in the morning and that Thou-Wert was going with them to hear the preacher. I looked along the wall a little way and saw Thou-Wert, his face deeply flushed, talking with Clancy. I wondered if Clancy might be goading him with his jokes, but Thou-Wert looked happier than he had been for some time. Fornicator, I thought, and began to laugh to myself. Then, suddenly, feeling my body shaking and seeing Justly staring at me across the table, I thought how similar that sensation was to sitting in a rut a few yards from Nell, shivering, watched by Ruth and Belle.

"You all right, Scrag?"

"I'm fine."

Justly came around the table and took Daniel's place.

"You sure you're fine?"

Daniel came back and sat on the other side of Justly. Whenever Justly turned her head toward me, he looked at her hair. It was a look that spoke of something beyond simple liking of a girl's pretty hair, beyond admiration of the skill of its putting up, as if some sweet memory had been roused.

"You sure got some nice hair, Justly," Daniel said. He looked across the table to Lorelei and Sylvester. "Justly sure got nice hair."

"Oh, if that ain't kind, Daniel." Justly turned and kissed Daniel's cheek. His eyes brimmed and he quickly picked up his drink.

"I ain't much used t' kissin', these days." Uselessly, he tilted the glass again, then set it down and wiped his sleeve across his eyes. "What a spectacle," he apologized.

"Daniel, there ain't no better tribute than a tear." Lorelei reached out and touched his hand. Daniel took her hand into his own, turning it and looking at it as if it had become something precious to him.

"You're two distinctive women, I told Scrag. And, hell, you are." Without looking up, he went on: "You ain't seen their like, Sylvester, where you bin? An' Scrag, he don't need no askin'—"

We were suddenly aware of a stranger looking down on us, a tall, badly shaven man in a black suit. I had noticed him sometime earlier, standing by tables at the other end of the room, then at the bar, seeming to regard us with some kind of interest—because of Lorelei, I had guessed. Now he held out a small, highly polished wooden box, about the size of a prayer book. He smiled, showing buck teeth, his right eye slightly wayward.

"Excuse me, gentlemen and ladies, I have a small memento here. Unusual and beautiful. Would you be interested?" He glanced toward the "work of art," still sipping from her tiny glass a few feet away. "You seen that necklace there Lil wears? Them charms? They grace her bosom, you might say. There's ten on there, and you might say there's room for all. My handsome box has just the one. The price is cheap for somethin' rare."

"What is the charm?" Lorelei asked.

The man smiled and put the box on the table.

"You open it, lady."

Lorelei undid the brass hook and opened the lid. Inside,

on a bed of creamy velvet, was a strip of leather, like a little finger, smooth and polished.

"Tanned to perfection, polished with the finest leather soap. The one of its kind. The word I should use is *unique*."

"How come, a charm?"

"A charm for luck. A lady's charm for love and travelin'. It knows a bit about them both."

"What is it?" Justly asked.

"It's changed somewhat. The curin', tannin', polishin'. A shadow of itself, but potent still—a potent charm. A part."

"A what?" said Lorelei.

"A part. An Indian part. This one is Sioux. I got Cheyenne, Arapaho. All prime an' young. What would you think of offerin'?"

Daniel flared, his face red, his hand, which had remained on the table near Lorelei's, clenching.

"My boot agin yer ass, you cockeyed frigger! Sling yer hook!"

The man grabbed his box as Daniel swept it toward the edge of the table.

"Never thought for no offense," he protested. "You seemed a likely customer."

"I ain't, you trash!"

The man was backing away, but keen enough for a sale to take a final chance.

"Mebbe your friends don't feel the same."

"Hook it," I said. I heard my rye whiskey talking.

Everyone at our end of the room was watching. The man edged away to the bar, muttering something to Lil as he passed. She started to laugh, high-pitched, her bosom shaking.

"It was my fault, encouragin'," Lorelei said to Daniel. She glanced, with a look of anger, toward the laughter.

"It worn't no nicety that made me fly," said Daniel. "No 'not in front of women'—all that stuff. I like an Indian." As he spoke Lil's laughter went on. "Hell, that woman's scritch!" he said in her direction.

Lil took a drink, and then her laughter resumed.

"Lady, lady, all in white," she screeched. "Virgin white. Don't she like no Indian parts? Hey, you, Miss Virginal, don't you like a nice Sioux part? She don't like no . . ." The words passed into laughter again, other voices joining in, through amusement at Lil's half-drunken nerve, I thought. I was near to amusement myself, as I had been in the moment of Daniel's outburst.

Lorelei was suddenly out of her seat, and all the laughter except Lil's died away. Lorelei stood opposite the "work of art," looking down on her, then reached her hands well across the table, leaning over.

"Don't you disgust yourself, you ancient whore?"

Lil stopped laughing.

"What did you say?"

"Don't you disgust yourself?"

"Finish it."

"You ancient whore."

Lil stood up, tipping the table, thrusting it away from her, the bottle and glass falling, Lorelei staggering backward, for a moment sitting on the floor. As she scrambled up, Lil caught her with a swinging, backhanded blow on the face, which sent her reeling again, the heavy woman pursuing her, with amazing agility, as she fell. Lil hurled herself onto the woman on the floor as if she would crush her, but Lorelei turned aside, and she landed on hands and knees with only the boards under her, to the amusement of the onlookers. Lorelei grabbed her hair and tugged, Lil turning helplessly onto her side to free her hands for retaliation, reaching to claw at the wrist above her head, her legs thrashing. As she thrashed, she rolled upon her back and her black-stockinged limbs came free of skirt and petticoat, and there was an increase in laughter as it was seen that she wore no drawers. One of the barmen moved to intervene, but his fellow and the cockeyed man held him. People from the other end of the room were coming forward, two women screeching to Lil to get off her back. Lil's legs continued to thrash until she managed to swing the left one far enough to the side to clench it upon Lorelei's ankle. Then she swung the other close, jabbing the heel of her shoe against the trapped foot. Lorelei yelled, tugging at Lil's hair the harder, and Lil jabbed again. Lorelei's wrist was bleeding from the scratches of Lil's nails, and as Lil dug them in again, she let the hair go. Lil made to sit up, but as she did so Lorelei clawed once more and her fingers went down the back of the green dress. It opened at the buttons, then started to rip as Lil tried to pull away. Suddenly Lil let herself fall sideways, at the same time swinging the leg that had been jabbing at Lorelei's ankle to a position on her thighs, so that she could straddle the "lacy lady," sitting on her knees, trying to pinion her arms. One arm she did succeed in holding, forcing it to the ground beside Lorelei's face, but the other was able to tug at the necklace, pulling off a handful of Indian parts that were immediately thrown away with a cry.

They fought somewhat as children fight, and the onlookers laughed, jeered, and cheered as a crowd of children will, but, unlike a children's fight, this would not be stopped by anyone stepping in or by tears, yet at any moment there might be injury. Lil had seized one of the charms and was wrestling with Lorelei's arms in an attempt to push the thing into her mouth. She was now sitting astride Lorelei's waist, the frilly long drawers behind her flailing and bucking.

Thou-Wert had come behind me.

"Cannot something be done, Scrag?"

"You like to try?"

"I will, that I will."

He pushed forward, holding up a hand.

"This must stop," he called.

Lil glanced at him.

"Git back!" She threw the thing in her hand at him, ripped another from her necklace, and pushed it at Lorelei's face.

"Stop!" Thou-Wert shouted.

"Git back, preacher."

In this second moment of distraction, Lorelei jerked her knees into Lil's back and, as the whore's body came forward, grasped at the white bodice from which the dress had already dropped away. There were howls of laughter as a great dug came out on one side and the bodice pulled low on the other. Lil gave a bellow of anger, took a fistful of Lorelei's hair and tugged, lifting her head a moment, then banging it back to the floor, repeating this several times. Lorelei's hand reached out, clawing desperately to find flesh, found a shoulder and scratched it, the arm, and scratched again, then groped over the swinging globe until it found the nipple, and fastened upon it. Lil gave a shriek, pitched forward, rolling off, letting herself go in the direction that would give most relief, as Lorelei held on.

Some of the onlookers were weeping with laughter.

"Hold on, Mama." Justly clenched the air.

"She's got her," Daniel said.

"Let go, you bitch," Lil yelled.

Their scrambling and rolling had brought them to the feet of some bystanders just beyond the end of the bar. Lorelei suddenly let go, rolled away, and got to her feet. Lil got to hers and was pulled aside by two women. Lorelei ran for the back door.

"Go see her, Scrag," Justly said.

As I pushed my way to the door, I saw that Lil had broken from the women and gone to follow Lorelei herself. By the time I was in the passage between the saloon and the door into the yard, she was standing outside in the moonlight, shouting.

"Where are you, bitch? Come outa hidin', Fancy Drawers. I'll have every stitch off yer."

Through the open doorway I could hear no other sound. After swearing to herself, Lil turned to come in, confronting me and several others who were trying to see what was happening.

"You was wid that bitch," she shouted, pushing me. I fell back against one of the whores and the reek of perfume.

"Boy, you wanna come upstairs?" the woman screeched. She pushed me aside to her companion. "You have this young one, Beth?"

Beth let me by, and I pushed back into the room. In a while the commotion was dying away, and Lil and the two whores had gone up the front stairs, Lil taking a few Indian charms that had been gathered from the floor by the cockeyed man.

I said I would go and look for Lorelei again. Sylvester said he would come, but Justly said it might be better if I went alone. I stood out in the yard and listened. The wagon covers were white under the moon, shadows cast over the bare earth. As I came near Lorelei's wagon I could hear her crying, very quietly. I listened, uncertain whether I should leave her for a while. Then I realized that the sounds she was making were between crying and laughter.

"Lorelei," I called quietly. At first she did not hear. "Lorelei."

"You come, Scrag."

She was sitting on a bench in the darkness. I stood behind her and put my arms around her. She cried again for some time, then started to shake with laughter.

"Scrag boy, she got nipples like a nanny goat, hain't she?" She pulled my hands down.

"You remember that first time you stood behind me like this?"

"I remember."

"What did I say?"

"I remember that, too."

46

Beside me, Justly was already asleep, her hair down, her head deep in the soft pillow. For a few moments we had watched together as Lorelei poured water from the pitcher into the large china bowl decorated with a rose pattern and started to "wash that old whore off me."

"Scrag, ain't this Lorelei just one awful show-off?" Justly had murmured amiably.

"You reckon that?" Propped on my elbow, I had watched her eyelids flickering.

"I reckon . . . that."

The washing finished, Lorelei stood looking in the mirror above the washstand at the red patch on her face where Lil's backhander had caught her. As she held her fingers to the place, saying that she was going to "look a sight" in the morning, the candlelight caught the momentary stillness of the long curve of her side, like the curve of its own flame, momentarily unflickering. I thought how perfect are some moments, recognized as never-to-be-forgotten even as they occur. This was one such. Another was when she turned and came with the candle toward the bed, pleased with herself, smiling, knowing the knocking under my ribs, though, as I delighted in this moment, I knew the rarer vision had been in the moment earlier. A third followed, the candle on the bedside table, Lorelei swaying her breasts above me, saying that her nipples were Sioux August cherries and I should eat them. But the moment became prolonged and ended in tumult, Lorelei kissing hotly across my face as I let her go.

"Aw, hell, I made you spend, boy. You cure me . . ."

She guided my hand and pressed down on it, soon muffling her cries into the pillow and clenching, "Jesu, Jesu," pausing briefly in silence, then chuckling and turning to me with happy murmurs.

When she was silent, I thought she was sleeping, and put my arm across her as I dropped toward sleep myself.

"How would you ever tell 'how it was' with lovin', Scrag?"

I was thinking about that, wondering what the words might be.

"Could you ever tell how *that* was, boy?"

"Maybe."

"Maybe you'll try someday?"

"Maybe."

"You show that me?"

"I reckon so."

"Oh, how I'd like that, Scrag."

I remembered the time when she said her back was America and my fingers were wagons on the trail. I started moving them about on her skin again, a slow, erratic trail, a wagon train with a mad captain, and soon slept.

We must have come awake at the same time, after, it seemed, an hour or so. Perhaps it was because she had turned under my arm, as she was now lying on her back. The candle was still alight, but had dwindled. She surprised me by saying again the last thing she had said before we slept.

"How I would like that, Scrag — you tellin' how it was. I wonder, maybe soon, or years an' years away. If it was years, I wonder where I'll be, an' where you'll be. Oh, I won't think about that."

She turned again, slid one hand under my neck while the other moved on me.

"I just remembered somethin' I forgot to tell you earlier. When we were lookin' for you, early evenin', Sylvester brought this mornin's photograph. He rushed an' printed it a little while before, a gift for me, then one for you an' one he kept. Scrag, it's so good. You standin' on that rock. Boy, it's just beautiful! I thought of what I said that day way back. That day I made you take your britches off. Do you recall?"

"You standin' there. You wouldn't durn well go."

"Oh, I know that. But what I said when we stepped down an' you held out your arm to me. Do you remember that?"

"I guess I do."

"What did I say?"

"Have you forgotten, then?"

"I ain't forgotten my own words."

"What was it, then?"

"I said, 'You're some man now.' Ain't that just what I said?"

"Somethin' like that."

"Hell, boy, not *like*, not like. Exactly that. 'You're some man now.' "

She pressed her face onto my chest and was silent, her hand still. My mind drifted.

"Can you imagine, Scrag, what sort of man could cut that Sioux boy's prick off? Scrag, can you?"

I said I thought I could imagine him. Her hand on me, and her easy use of the word I would not have spoken to her, had aroused me again.

"In that saloon, that old whore sittin' there, I thought of them dead boys, all prime an' beautiful, an' not so different from them handsome bathin' boys in *Leaves of Grass*, or like you in the photograph I'd just bin lookin' at, an' I was thinkin', Is this just what it comes to, just them shriveled, danglin' bits around a painted whore? Is it just that, Scrag?"

I was wanting her, was impatient with her for talking in a way that, somehow, I could not follow.

"Just what *what* comes to?"

"Oh, hell, I can't explain. Like, maybe, this good America. Some such . . ." She was exasperated, but shrugged the feeling off, nuzzling close. "You wanna go back there? Then, boy, you go."

Later, just before sleeping, the candle dead, moonlight streaming through the shutters she had just opened, she returned to a thought of the little polished box open on the saloon table.

"Somehow it's like it wasn't just a shriveled part laid there."

"What was it, then?" I was too tired to care.

"Oh, I don't know. But it was more."

47

Waiting for Daniel to be ready for our walk, I watched the animals in the orchard. Unhobbled or untethered for the first time since we left Scrimshaw, they were enjoying the freedom of movement in the dappled grass, nuzzling each other, one or two kicking up, one rolling, Axel's young ginger gelding uselessly trying to mount Dick's little roan, who kept moving forward as if she knew the futility he could not understand. Only Tickler was restricted, his chain looped around a tree in the near right-hand corner, where he stood surveying the scene, his head low, making an occasional irritated shake to test whether iron links might no longer hold him. Nearby, the cow with his seed in her stood looking at him — in what sort of soundless communication? I wondered — while her usual companion turned away, showing him a crusted rump.

I leaned on the gate, noticing how the curving line of one horse's neck and back flowed gracefully into the line of another's; how a small movement might alter the outlines but not the grace of them. I thought of Lorelei in last night's candlelight, and was beginning upon an imaginary conversation, to tell her how good that was, when Daniel came up behind me.

"We fit now, Scrag?"

"I'm fit."

"We're both fit, then."

I knew that Daniel was feeling nervous. When I had called at his wagon, he had been shaving and had nicked his chin, so blood was trickling. He would have to polish his boots, he had said, and have Henrietta sew a button on his shirt. I had said I would be happy enough to wait by the orchard. Now his boots were shining as I had never seen them, and he was acting so nervously that he tripped and dashed dust over them before we were out of the compound.

"Look at them," he said. He stood on one leg, alternately, rubbing a boot up the calf of his trousers to restore the shine.

The old man who had given Thou-Wert directions yesterday was standing at the entrance to the compound, looking across to our wagons.

"Good day," he said.

"Good day," said Daniel. "You tell me how the graveyard might be come upon from here? I jes' don't git my bearin's anymore."

"You mean the old one, then," the stranger said. "You'd mean the old graveyard."

"Well, yes . . ."

"The old graveyard ain't there no more."

"Where was the place, then? A bit up here, I guess." Daniel indicated up the lane, which beyond this point dwindled to a narrow path with high weeds on either side.

"Your guess is good enough. But it ain't there no more, I say."

"How ain't it there?"

"You hed someone up there?"

"Yes, friend, I got someone up there. The first. The first was ever put up there. With these two hands. I put her there."

"Oh, pitiful Christ!" The old man put out a hand to Daniel's wrist. "I've heard of her. The young one what the fever took. You speak of her?"

"I speak of her."

"Oh, pitiful Christ!"

Daniel glanced at me, as if to ask if I thought the old man might be an odd one.

"How far?" I asked.

"Oh, it ain't far," Daniel said quickly. "I pushed her on a small handcart. They walked behind." He turned, looking up the lane. "This was all just pasture then."

He stood looking away, and I had a momentary glimpse of a little company walking behind a bumping handcart under this same cloudless sky, pasture going up a little slope.

"Two hundred yard, no more," the old man said. "But there ain't nuttin' there you'd want t' see."

"I'll be the judge of that." Daniel was suddenly impatient. "Good day, an' thank you, friend."

We turned up the path. Urgent with something to say, the old man followed us.

"It was all Jack Pewter's doin', what was done."

Daniel stopped, turned around.

"What was?"

"The diggin' what they done."

"What diggin'?"

"Jack Pewter's diggin'."

"Hell, what for?"

"Fer gold."

"He got a strike?"

"Up in the little stream some twelve year back. Panned there awhile. Then traced back up the hill an' found some more. Bought up everything with that — all what he hadn't took already."

"What about the graveyard, then?"

"Sometime later he worked down — or paid the men who did, an' I was one — an' hed another strike jes' where the stream go underground. You know the spot?"

"Can't say I do. I wusn't here that long."

"It ain't much of a stream, an' dry in summer, anyway. Beyond them little trees, you'll see a rock outcrop. By there the stream went down, an' Jack struck his last gold."

"The graveyard, man?"

"Jack hed the notion there'd be more way under, so he hed us dig an' hew, an' later he brung blastin' men."

"That would be Pewter," Daniel said.

"We laid that little graveyard waste. I hev it on my conscience t' this day."

"I'd damn well think so."

"We did what Pewter said. You knew the man. Jack Pewter, he don't tell you twice. Hell, he don't hardly tell you once sometimes afore he'll hev you halfway there. You know the man. It was the last job what I ever done."

"I know the frigger," Daniel said. "C'mon, Scrag."

Daniel strode up the path. I followed, with the old man hobbling to keep up.

"Oh, pitiful Christ, he shouldn't go there." His voice came at my back. "That ain't no place f' him t' see."

I looked around at him as I walked, the path very narrow

now so that we were brushing through the branches and fronds of weeds. Back in the lane, near the compound, I noticed Belle and Ruth, and assumed they had come looking for Jess and George. They saw me and waved. I held up my hand, then regretted the action. Immediately they were following.

After a way the path opened on an area of earth piles rank with weeds.

"Take care, take care," the old man called. "There's craters in the grass. Half a dozen shafts left open all abouts. You'll hev t' mind y' step."

Daniel stood looking at the scene. I waited back for a while, then went up beside him. He put an arm around my shoulders, still silent.

"Oh, pitiful Christ." The old man's voice could hardly be heard. Sometime afterward the grass and weeds were rustling around his feet as he went away. I heard his voice and the voices of the girls, but no clear word. A quick glance over my shoulder showed Belle and Ruth standing by the path, the old man moving down the narrow space, almost shoulder high in greenery. I guessed the girls had been told to leave us alone.

"I jes' don't know the spot," said Daniel. "Is she here?"

I could not think of what answer the question might need and weakly said, "Somewhere."

"Aye, somewhere, boy." Daniel took out his pipe and tobacco. "You mind we set awhile?"

We went forward to a block of blasted rock and sat. Daniel lit his pipe.

"You hain't got a pipe, your own?"

"I hain't."

"I'll find you up a pipe when we git back. You smoke that long one, Lorelei's."

"Anytime I want. Too long t' carry, though. Afraid of breakin' it."

"That sure is elegant. I see her smokin', standin' by her wheel, I think, That sure is elegant, my dear, an' so are you. Scrag boy, you lay that curvin' stem along her anywhere, you'd find the same shape answerin'. Ain't that the truth?"

He glanced at me, his face creasing into a smile behind the smoke. I was grateful that he was breaking out of his sadness.

"I guess that's true."

"I guess you know so, Scrag, don't you?"

"I guess I do."

"I thought you'd want the young one, boy."

"I know you did." I thought I would show him the notice I had taken of his words. "There's all the time in the world," I said.

"I'm glad you left that little lid on there. She's very sweet an' innocent. Should be, awhile." He drew at his pipe, as if he had said enough. I could hear the voices of Belle and Ruth, but Daniel had not noticed them. "You know how lucky you are, Scrag?"

"I know."

"She's some uncommon woman, ain't that so?"

"I know."

"An' I don't need t' tell you make the most of it. Boy, it's such a little while." He took the pipe from his mouth and held it out, looking at it. "There's bones as white as that out there somewhere. Tha's all it come to, boy, no matter what they were." He stood up. "I'll look about a bit."

We went forward. Belle and Ruth took this as their signal to venture toward us.

"Hey, George," called Belle.

"They think I'm George," I explained to Daniel.

The girls came up.

"Ol' Pitiful Christ come with you," said Belle.

"Who?"

"Mister Kent. Ol' Pitiful."

"Pitiful Christ," said Ruth.

"He's always sayin' that," said Belle. "Didn't he say that to you?"

"We call him that," said Ruth.

"Oh, pitiful Christ," Belle mimicked.

"Maybe he got good cause," said Daniel.

He moved off. I followed. The girls came beside me, Belle nearer.

"You lookin' for a grave?"

"Yeah."

"The graves are gone."

"We know."

"This graveyard was from when they first came here."

"We know."

Daniel stood looking at the skyline behind us, with the hill running up, then turned forward again, as if trying to get his bearings.

"There was a little tree, a spruce, I think. That stump be it, you reckon, Scrag?"

"I ain't too good at trees. That ain't much of a stump."

"I put her south of it." He looked at the sun, for direction. "I'm standin' on the spot, if this is it."

"There ain't no spruces hereabouts."

"There's stumps down there," said Belle. She indicated farther down the slope.

"It stood alone." He looked across the wasted area. "I think it would be here she is."

I tried to motion Belle and Ruth away, but they looked at me without understanding.

"I ain't supposed to come down here," said Ruth.

"I ain't," said Belle.

"What you come for, then?" I knew they had no notion of their intrusion, and wished they would understand the roughness in my tone as concern for Daniel's private moment.

"Ruth said, 'We go see George,'" Belle said. "You mind us comin', George?"

"George, he don't mind," said Daniel.

"No," I said.

"I'm Belle, she's Ruth." Belle was seizing her opportunity with Daniel. "What's your name?"

"I'm Fritz. I'm General. General Fritz."

"General!"

"Well, I used t' be."

"You fight in wars?"

"Way back."

"He don't like talkin' of it much," I said.

"No, I don't talk of it too much."

"It sad?"

"Yeah, sad."

"This place is sad," said Belle.

Daniel looked at me with something in his eyes that said there was no way around the blundering innocence of children. I thought again of the strange mixture of innocence and knowledge these girls had shown yesterday.

"It's awful sad," said Ruth.

"Sometimes there's bones stuck up in grass," said Belle.

"Jack Pewter's bonefield, tha's what people say. Did Ol' Pitiful tell you that?"

"No," said Daniel. "He just said, 'That Belle, she talk too much.' Tha's all."

Ruth laughed and pushed at Belle. Belle flushed.

"You two move off a bit," Daniel said.

Belle was still more disconcerted, looking as if she wondered how she might have displeased General Fritz.

"We move off a bit," she said to Ruth.

They went some yards out, toward the center of the area, and dropped into the grass and weeds on the near side of the largest mound. Daniel stood looking at his boots, over which a light dusting of pollen now lay.

"She's down there, Scrag." He said it without the sadness I had expected. I had assumed I would have to walk away when the moment came. He walked about a bit, still looking down, almost with wonderment. "This is the spot."

"You know for sure?"

"I know for sure. That Fritz. That General Fritz, when that kid asked my name. I knew it then, this is the spot. It came out natural. The General, too. That was her mark. Boy, she was fanciful. All fun an' foolin'. She'd hev t' be down there, t' strike me that lighthearted, boy. I felt that low till she spoke then. Scrag, I ain't low now. You look at me."

I looked at him. His tanned face was red, its map of lines and creases an untroubled country. But his eyes were moist.

"Tha's good," I said.

We kicked about in the grass and weeds for half an hour, slamming our heels into the earth, trying to find Daniel's stone. Gradually we moved farther apart. It would be a rounded boulder, no more than a foot high, flat on one side, with

"Anne" chiseled there by his own hand. I turned several expectantly, but found nothing more than slugs and worms, and wondered if Daniel might be fooling himself in his notion about General Fritz. Whose grave had I been standing on when I thought up George and Jessica? Weary of the search, I saw that Daniel had gone back to the place where he supposed Anne's bones to be. He lit his pipe as I came up.

"Come rest," he said.

We sat by the tree stump. He said his Anne had been the prettiest girl who had ever come his way. He wished he could have taken Sylvester and his camera back to those days on the trail. He had no likeness of her, and sometimes her picture in his memory was blurred. What brought it clear again was when, without intending it, he saw her doing things or heard her voice. She was most fanciful and loved to play a part. "I'll be your pretty whore tonight," she'd say. He still remembered how that startled him the first time, Anne a good-bred girl of character. When Belle had asked him what his name was, it was as if his Anne had asked, expecting him to fool again. Fritz was a name he'd never spoken in his life. How was it on his lips like that, and how, inside him, sudden lightness, standing there, and certainty of where he stood?

I said I was sorry we could not find the stone. He said he might like to be alone now for a time, and maybe search again. I should go back, find Lorelei. She should have a man with her in this strange town.

I went, noticing that Belle and Ruth were already crossing toward the path. They held up hands, and I put mine up without much interest, wanting the girls to get well ahead. Daniel's smoke rose over thistles, and I thought how good it was to have been with him in Halo this morning, though this town was in no way the place his Anne had dreamed of under that moon.

Ruth waited at the entrance to the narrow path, but Belle had gone.

"What you waitin' for?" I asked.

"You wanna see Belle? Belle said I ask if you jus' like come see her, George." She was standing in the path, not moving to let me by, smiling, embarrassed.

I knew that I should push by, say I had to hurry, but I went through where she held the high weeds aside, indicating the place I should go. As I did so, I felt foolish, and younger again. Belle sat among pressed-down stalks and leaves, her skirt up, her legs a small way apart, a sketchy patch of brownish hair where I was supposed to look.

I pushed away.

"You like that, George?" Ruth tried to be saucy as I brushed past her, but looked more surprised.

"You kids go play."

Instead of going straight to find Lorelei and Justly, I went back to the orchard and leaned on the gate awhile. The animals' games had stopped, and they were grazing listlessly, shaking off flies. Tickler shook his chain. I picked up a small unripe apple and flung it at that cow's crusted rump. She started and looked around. Tickler nosed the shining green thing on the ground, then stood looking at it.

48

The congregation was coming out of church. I had stood for a few minutes with Lorelei and Justly, listening to the singing of "Rock of Ages, cleft for me," before the door opened and a group of boys and girls — the choir, perhaps — burst out, chattering, into the sunshine, hurrying down the path to the little gate, not far from where we stood, Belle and Ruth among them, now in white dresses and ribbony bonnets. I thought they were pretending not to see us until Belle turned and said, "You better now, Jess?" before being taken off by a bigger girl who linked arms with her, Ruth hanging on the other side. Briefly, faces turned back, showing that Belle and Ruth were telling of knowing us, and I wondered what else was being said. On the path, the minister was shaking hands with people emerging, giving a word to each. Some of them then came down the path, men putting on their hats, then doffing them to ladies as pairs dispersed in the street. Others stood about the little yard in groups, paying courtesies this way and that, voices rising in chatter, children weaving among them or standing impatiently waiting, one cuffed by a mother, another having his shoulder grasped by a father, a finger wagged at his face. Two of the whores from Pewter's Palace lingered with the minister. Shaking hands with one of them, he placed his free hand on the hand he held, and seemed to be saying something earnestly, the companion looking on with a smile. Nearby, waiting for him to finish, stood the old lady who had been weeping yesterday when we passed here. Behind her, talking with Clement and Martha, Thou-Wert stood ready to introduce himself.

"This could be Scrimshaw," Lorelei said.

"There ain't nobody hangin' on trees in Scrimshaw," Justly said.

The youth we had seen teased by children as he swept up dung came hurrying across the street from the direction of the bottom-end saloon, leading two saddled horses. He held one at a mounting block while a man helped a lady to mount sidesaddle, then handed over the reins of the other and the man put foot to a stirrup and swung up, reaching down to pay the boy, who immediately ran back to fetch more horses. I noticed that people were eyeing us with curiosity, as strangers, but the man on the horse, touching his hat to ladies as the pair moved off, included Lorelei in his gesture.

"Good thing he was seein' my best side," she said. Her left cheek was slightly red and swollen, but otherwise she showed no mark of her encounter with Lil. It was oddly pleasing to see her in her best bonnet again, a reminder of Scrimshaw.

We walked on and came to the opening by the square. The place looked pleasant, with people moving through patches of sunlight and shadow, a pair of lovers sitting on the bench where I had sat with Justly, some birds taking a dust bath a few yards from their feet. There was no sign to betray the horror that was waiting on the other side of the trees, nothing in the stances of the figures we could see back there that gave any indication of what their casual looking might be directed toward. I had a sudden surge of depression, and a memory of a feeling familiar in childhood, that nothing in the world mattered enough for anyone to care, even if they noticed. "The world goes on," I heard a voice say from somewhere distant. It seemed like my grandmother's, but it was a long time since I had heard her voice, and now I could not be sure of its sound, as Daniel could not be sure of his Anne's looks, and perhaps it was someone else who had said "The world goes on," anyway. Two days ago, Joe and Nell had been in the world, and now they were out of it, and this Sunday-morning world was going on as if nothing had changed, except that an old man was still sitting down there by the hanging girl in the wood.

"There's Sylvester," said Justly. Sylvester, laden with his equipment, was coming up the track from the wood.

"No matter, I ain't bein' tempted through that square," Lorelei said.

"Hell, I ain't temptin' you," said Justly.

We walked on again, coming to the top of the street, crossing and descending the other side. By Pewter's Palace, I glanced across to the square and saw that Sylvester had set up his camera on the far side of it, and was standing there looking up, a few onlookers behind him. It was not clear whether he had just taken his photograph or was about to do so, the scene discernible only through spaces between the trees. I stopped, indicating.

"Look over there." As I spoke, there was the beginning of a movement from among a group of people standing near a wall on the right-hand side of the square, and immediately two figures were running left, as if one might be chasing the other. In a moment they had reached Sylvester's onlookers, who suddenly scattered as the foremost runner leaped at Sylvester and the other took a kick at the side of the camera, sending it yards away, as Sylvester himself hit the ground, with the man on top of him.

My impulse was to dash across the street, but Lorelei seized my arm.

"No, Scrag, no, no!"

"Let him go, Mama," Justly shouted. "Let him go. Sylvester! Sylvester!"

I saw that several other men from the group had now moved forward, and I knew that Lorelei was right.

"Run tell Axel," I told her. "Anyone you can find. You too, Justly."

When they had gone, I crossed the street. Belle and Ruth were running toward me.

"Your friend, George," Belle was yelling.

"I know."

"They smashed his stuff."

"Who are they?"

"Jack Pewter's men."

We waited under the trees while the group of men took Sylvester roughly along the side of the square and out into the street. One man was carrying the broken camera; another, the tripod; another, the plate box; another, the box of bottles and the black tent. At the back, a tall, lean man carried Sylvester's hat.

Not knowing why I did it, I went out and caught up with him.

"Your pardon, sir."

He turned, still walking.

"Your pardon, sir. The hat is mine." The man stopped. "The hat is mine. He borrowed it."

"You one of his lot, boy?"

"His friend. He meant no harm."

"Mebbe."

"Where you takin' him?"

He looked at me, thrust out Sylvester's hat.

"You tek yer hat, an' tek yer ass off, fast."

He turned, followed the others.

"Where you takin' him?"

"Sheriff's office first. You tek yer ass off, son."

"Tell him Scrag, he got the hat, please, sir."

"I'll tell him that."

I stood in the middle of the street, watching them go. They turned in just before the saloon at the bottom end. Belle and Ruth came up behind me. I stood looking at Sylvester's hat, then started to brush the dust off.

"That man's John Sloan," said Belle. "I'm sorry what I done this mornin', George."

"What's that?"

"Back down the lane."

"Oh, that."

I thought how Daniel would say, "You got all the time in the world." Halo seemed no place in which that might be true.

"You're pretty, Belle."

I put on Sylvester's hat and found the black brim making a frame edge above her pretty, troubled face. I had a feeling of looking for a moment with Sylvester's eyes.

49

We stayed in the hotel bedroom, Lorelei and Justly sitting miserably, I standing by the window, while the plump maid moved around the room, making the bed, dusting things, and telling us about life in Halo under Jack Pewter. Occasionally she opened the door and looked into the corridor. Each time she did so, I wanted her to go. Her account of Pewter was making us even more anxious about Sylvester, and after a while I was wanting to be free from her wide-eyed looks at me, which somehow carried a regard for my prowess in managing to spend a night in that bed. At first I had felt some pleasure as she let her eyes hold mine slightly overlong, and with a faint smirk, but the feeling had quickly worn off. I turned my back on the room, hoping that Axel and Clement might soon return from the sheriff's office. I was wondering whether I should go out and try to fetch Thou-Wert, who had gone home with the minister, Clement said, to eat roast beef, when a commotion began in the yard.

Four of the men who had taken Sylvester from the square had come through the hotel and out of the back door and were going from wagon to wagon, asking which was Sylvester's. Finding it, two of them went inside, throwing open the cover. Two waited, one kicking dust, the other trying to coax Dick's dog, which stood off suspiciously, watching, with his nose low. Traven came to ask what was going on, followed by Will and Clancy. Some of the children gathered behind, then Dora and Emmy appeared.

Lorelei and Justly had joined me at the window. Now the maid came. She said one of the men was her uncle. He had come forward in the wagon with an armful of photographs. After pretense of throwing the pile to his companions, then a laugh as they moved as if to catch them, he started to shy them one by one over their heads. Lorelei gave a wail. I dashed for the door, ran along the corridor, and took the stairs two at a time, followed by Justly.

"Hey, what you damn well doin'?" I shouted across the yard. I ran forward and began picking up pictures, and saw Emmy and Dora stooping, too.

One of the men rushed at me and grabbed the back of my collar, twisting it tight.

"Drop!" He twisted harder. "Drop, kid."

"Leave me damn go." I could hardly croak the words.

"Drop." As I still held on to a picture of Clancy at the anvil and one of Justly at the pool, he punched me in the small of my back. "Drop."

I let the pictures go. He punched again and released me. I staggered with pain, and saw Dora take up the picture of Justly and reach for the other. As her fingers neared it, the lout set his foot on it.

"Gimme." He held out his hand to her, then noticed the girl in the picture.

Justly rushed in and grabbed the photograph from Dora. The man caught her wrist.

"Drop!" Justly winced and dropped. The picture fell face-down. The fellow picked it up and turned it over.

"Well, well. If that ain't cute."

Traven and Clancy had come over. Will was arguing with the man on the wagon, Emmy picking up photographs.

"What the hell you doin', man?" Traven demanded.

"What I'm told."

"Who told?"

"The boss."

"An' who's this damn boss?"

The man grinned and turned toward the man on the wagon.

"Hey, Jake. This fella's askin' who the damn boss is."

"Who's Jesus Christ?" Jake laughed.

"Father, Son, an' Holy Ghost," called one of the others.

"Blasphemers," said Emmy.

"You ain't a religious lot?" asked the man. "You ain't a Gospel-grindin' bunch wi' these here pitchers flyin' round."

"Your boss Jack Pewter?" Clancy asked.

"Who else?"

"Who the hell else?"

"You watch your tongue, friend. Jack Pewter, he don't like a sharpish tongue. You'll git strung up."

Lorelei had joined us. The plump girl stood watching from the back door. The four men came together, each with a pile of photographs, most unmounted, a few with white or creamy mounts now marked with dirt. The men were taking from the piles each photograph showing anyone less than fully clothed, even one of the Abbott children paddling in a creek.

They were grinning, exclaiming, showing each other, pushing others — pictures of daily life on the trail, portraits, landscapes — back into our hands.

"Don't you disgust yourself?" It was the same tone she had used last night to Lil.

The four men stopped looking at their photographs.

"Hey, I seen you last night. Sure, you're the one. You got some spunk."

"I got some anger right this minute, fella. What you want with them?"

"Now, ma'am, you know jest what we want wi' them. Such things ain't fittin'."

"Why ain't they fittin', man?"

The men laughed.

"Now, Jack, I reckon he won't mind this girlie wadin', but he ain't goin' much on others here."

"They're harmless things."

"Now, that's as may be. He'll hev t' hope Jack see it that way, ma'am."

"This Pewter kinda lackin' somethin', then?"

Across the group, Clancy caught my eye, nodding and grinning, indicating Lorelei.

"No, Jack don't lack." Jake looked around at his companions for their laughter. "No how. *You'∂* find that soon enough."

"You scared of him?"

"We do his biddin', ma'am."

"You mean you're scared."

"You could say that."

"You're scared."

"I am."

Jake made to move off.

"You bring them pictures back?"

"I cain't say that. Jack, he don't tek well t' strangers makin'
phot-e-graphs of them he's hanged. 'Go see what else you
find,' he says. No tellin' what he'll make of this. Mebbe he'll
judge this pervert stuff."

"Hell, man, it's beautiful! Can't you see that?"

"You think that, ma'am? Well, you're a one!" We were
now inside the back door, his voice suddenly sounding louder.
He looked at me. "You got some spirited women here."

They went on through the hotel toward the front door,
their boots clattering on the boards. We went back into the
yard. Clancy had gathered all the photographs together. Justly
took them to Sylvester's wagon, tidying the mess inside before
tying the cover. We were a disconsolate group. Dora said she
was surprised at some of the pictures she had seen. Lorelei
said that most of them were a younger man's work, made long
ago. Emmy said she wondered why Sylvester was interested
in making pictures of naked young men. Lorelei asked if Emmy
thought he should not be. Emmy hesitated, then said that the
pictures of Justly were beautiful. Lorelei said they were,
maybe, the most beautiful pictures she had ever seen. They
would show, for as long as anyone might be interested, what
this girl looked like on a July day in 1859. She would look
at them in her old age, and Justly would look at them in hers,
and, maybe, Justly's children and grandchildren would look
at them and say, "Jesu, she was beautiful." Wouldn't Emmy,
she asked, like to have a picture of Chosen Arthur at her
breast, to show just how it was, for him to see one day? And
wasn't there some special sweetness in a man who had a care
to make such records, unashamed? But Dora asked about the

hanging man. There was a hanging woman, too, said Lorelei. Could life always be beautiful?

I thought she might try to talk about "how it was," as Sylvester might, and of the need for truth, and begin to sound foolish in the face of their disbelief, but she suddenly was quiet, looking near to tears. When we started moving apart, Justly said they would go to their room. I said I would stay by the orchard, then buy food in the saloon.

Leaning on the gate, I heard footsteps behind. Turning, I saw Daniel, head down, kicking up dust. He came and leaned beside me.

"You find it?" I asked.

He shook his head.

"What's the word I'm lookin' for?" He sounded, and looked, ten years older than the man I had left two or three hours earlier. "I'm lookin' for a word."

"What about?"

"Life, boy. The way we fool ourself. A dictionary word."

"What would that be . . . ?" I mused aloud.

"I can't quite git the one." He turned on me irritably. "You got the friggin' dictionary, Scrag."

"Deceive?"

"That ain't the word." He thought. "Though true enough."

I wondered what he had been doing and thinking in the graveyard to bring about the change of mood, apart from failing to find his stone.

"Illusion," he said. "Illusion, tha's the word. Is it all illusion, Scrag?"

I waited.

"All what we do, an' think. How much is true?"

"Guess I don't know," I said, not knowing what else to say.

"We don't know nothin' much, do we? Three hour ago I stood there, happy as a bumpkin, Scrag. Convinced, convinced. You saw."

"I saw."

"Then I was standin' there alone, an' all that feelin' gone. Why should that be?"

"I had a feelin' she was there." I wondered if I was lying to comfort Daniel or if I had really felt as I said. It seemed that I had, but was that illusion?

We stayed side by side, leaning on the gate, vaguely watching the animals. I delayed telling Daniel about Sylvester. Occasionally something near a smile crossed his face. I thought how he was thinking of times around the year I was born.

"I wish you could've sin her, Scrag," he said. "Or I'd got some likeness I could show."

That last thought stayed in my mind and led to another — that those small pictures thrown so carelessly about the yard half an hour ago had nothing to do with illusion.

50

But was that true? I lay on the floor of the wagon, looking at the midnight stars through the open bow, and wondered. It was daylight again, and Sylvester's pictures were scattered around our feet, those yahoos laughing. Over and over, I picked up the picture of Justly wading and could not sleep. The pictures Sylvester made with such concern for truth were themselves only illusions, mere pieces of paper with brown stains shaped to the likenesses of life. How strange that was. And how strange that such a likeness could be, for the moment in which we looked at it, as if the thing itself — that face on the paper, Justly's face; that body, her body; that light-flecked stain, the water of a pool.

"The Mount of Venus has its own small shade": the line from Sylvester's poem came back to me, and I thought of how the real shade was changed to only the merest of tiny blurs on paper, yet with a strange power to disturb, even when the picture itself was no more than something in my mind. A memory of a blur on paper that was only reflection of the shade of a moment — that surely was illusion.

I had hurt Lorelei. I was lying alone tonight because I had

hurt her feelings. After we had eaten, she had said that before
going up to her room she wanted to walk a bit, for cooler air.
We had walked up and down the lane, then a little way along
the path toward the old graveyard, her dress swishing through
the weeds. At the place where Belle had hidden in the morning,
I had said that we should turn back because of the uneven
ground ahead, and Justly had suggested we walk among the
animals. The grass of the orchard was dewy. The creatures
were mostly lying, a few of the horses standing under
branches. Prancer made out Lorelei and came toward her.
She pulled his head down and stroked his nose.

"Just feel that softness on this great tough creature. Is
there anything softer in the world than that?"

I said there was.

Lorelei kicked off her shoes to feel the cool dampness of
the grass, and stood hanging on Prancer's neck, loving the
creature. Justly and I walked at the far edge of the orchard
by the bushes along the fence.

"What's softer, Scrag?"

I did not reply, and she did not ask again, so I wondered
if she knew my thoughts. She took my arm as we turned back.
Lorelei was standing with her head against Prancer's neck,
an arm over his mane.

"I guess Mama's cryin'."

"Why's that?"

"What you said about your picture."

Over the meal, I had said that I was sorry she had ever
suggested that Sylvester should take my photograph on that
rock. It was one of those taken away by Pewter's men. She
had been upset, thinking that I might be blaming her for
leading Sylvester into something that would now be laid

against him. Then she had said she blamed herself anyway.

We came up behind Lorelei and knew she was crying, though she made no sound. Justly released my arm, and I touched Lorelei's back. She rolled around slowly, leaning on the horse's shoulder, her head against his neck, her face up, cheeks wet. I brushed her face with my fingers. When she bent to put on her shoes, I touched the warm velvet of Prancer's nose.

"What's softer than that?" she said.

We went under the trees without another word. Lorelei and Justly carried on walking while I fixed the gate. By the wagon we said good night, awkwardly, as if we should not be doing so.

"We need a good sleep to face the mornin' on," she said. Axel had said that there was talk of putting Sylvester before a court in the morning.

I could not sleep. Justly's picture kept coming before me, the midday sun glaring on it, that "small shade" of Sylvester's poem disturbing, the word "illusion" saying itself over, sometimes in Daniel's voice, sometimes my own. I thought of Sylvester lying on a bunk in the jail, awake, and wondered what was in his thoughts. "If you're given that grace": his words came back in the candlelight of his wagon. "You lay in the dark and were almost a part of it": the small, beginning grace of my own words came. "Benison": a stray word from one of Thou-Wert's preachings floated back, and I liked the thought and sound.

51

People were coming out of buildings and standing at the edge of the street, children being told to stop moving. The hunchbacked youth with the besom near the saloon took off his apron, folded it across the hitching rail, and stood forward. Down the street, after a few moments, came a small procession. At the head was a light dray drawn by a horse with a black plume, led by a man in black. On the dray, which was draped with a black cloth, were two long boxes of plain white wood, surrounded by flowers. A man in black walked on either side, and behind, at a small distance, walked the old man who had sat by Nell in the wood. Behind him was a woman wearing a black veil, a younger man at either side, both red-faced, weeping. Next there was the old woman who had been weeping by the church when Justly and I passed, now with a white-haired man beside her, his head low. After another space there was the minister, his lips moving as if in prayer, behind him a straggle of silent people, the men with bare heads, who gently disturbed the dust as they moved. As the procession neared, all the watching men and boys took off their hats; women brought their hands together loosely at their laps. For an instant I was elsewhere, a small boy, wondering what it was like to be the person in the box, then an older boy, hearing someone say, as a funeral passed, "It won't always be someone else in there." Nearby, a woman spluttered into weeping, and a man said, "Ssssh." I thought, Perhaps in two or three days it will be Sylvester in there.

The events of the past hour were like the blurring and clearing pictures of a dream. Daniel tripping over a flimsy chair as we entered the courtroom, sending it skittering across the boards. "Old fella got big feet," one of Pewter's men saying to me. "I hain't got a big mouth," Daniel replying. Sitting on a bench at the back, because chairs were for people of Halo, whore Lil one of them. "Her ass needs two chairs," Lorelei whispering. Pewter, the judge, such an ordinary-looking man, with gray hair and long whiskers. Disbelief that this could be *the* Jack Pewter. Disbelief that this dingy, pine-walled room could be a court of law: a room so ordinary, where trivial things happened, like an old man tripping over a chair, a woman making a joke about the size of another's ass, a dog scratching for fleas by the door. Still grimy from being thrown to the ground yesterday, Sylvester, pale, looking with disbelief at his pictures being handled by Pewter. Pewter holding up the glass plate of Nell to the light and saying that the girl's face looked black. Laughter. Pewter listening to his men, John Sloan, Jake. Talk of lewdness. Pewter joking that he had been in photographs himself, one with the sheriff. Jake saying that was with his britches on. Laughter. Pewter holding a picture of Justly—"A perty thing. Why is this here?" Jake saying, " 'Cos she's a kid." Sylvester questioned. Saying he made pictures of life without falsifying. The men in the photographs were as men are. Pewter saying they were as men would be.

Lil screeching amid the laughter. Talk of a pervert making pictures of those brought to justice in Halo, for newspapers back East. A pause while Pewter took out his watch. The flimsy chairs creaking, the dog scratching. "Hang him." Sylvester pushed away through an inner door. Martha standing on a bench, calling, "Dear Lord, no." Lorelei wailing, Justly screaming. Panic making me want to rush out of the room, but holding me rigid. Daniel shouting, "Pewter, you callous bastard." Pewter ordering him to be brought forward. Daniel: "You know *me*, Pewter." Pewter, seeming to recognize him but immediately hiding any sign: "Two hours t' leave Halo — or you'll know me." Everyone standing. Pewter striding out, pausing to look at Lorelei and Justly, not standing, and at Martha praying. "That took her down a bit, the bitch," Lil cackling. Daniel putting his foot against the chair he had tripped on earlier, sending it hurtling.

When the funeral procession had gone, we turned away and walked up the street, without talk. I looked back and saw that other company of people turn off to the right beyond the last building.

52

The sun was well down, throwing long shadows of the cell-window bars across the floorboards. Sylvester was sitting alone on a bench against the far wall. At first neither of us knew what to say, apart from names, those three shadows between us. Then I remembered what it was that would sound ordinary and unemotional to start the conversation.

"I brought your hat."

"Dear Scrag." His voice was so low that I barely heard it.

He stood up. I thought how haggard he looked, his good clothes dirty, his shirt unbuttoned, as he never wore it. The room was stifling, heat held in the roofboards. I crossed over the pattern of shadows and held out his hat. He took it, turned it in his hands, looking at the maker's name on the inside rim, then put it on.

"It's been a good one." He tilted it.

"How Whitman wears his." I was thinking of the picture in the front of the book.

"There the resemblance ends." He smiled, took the hat off, and held it out. "You have it, Scrag."

"I can't."

He set it on my head.

"You can't refuse."

I took it off and held it, not knowing what to say.

"Sit with me."

I sat beside him, on his right. The man who had let me in came and looked through the bars in the door, and went away.

"There's not much time, Scrag." Sylvester's voice was low, as if he did not want to be overheard. "I want you to listen. It will be tomorrow morning."

"Sylvester, they just won't do that."

"Oh, they will."

"But —"

"There'll be no buts about it, Scrag. They're hanging me."

"God, they can't."

He put his arm across my shoulder.

"I won't say 'Wait and see.' Just listen now. There's something you can do for me."

I should leave Halo that night, taking his wagon, Lorelei and Justly driving mine and theirs between them. Pewter's men had seized only printed photographs. They had not been aware of all the plates packed away for safety under the floor. I should take them to John Ogilvie in Oregon City, who could be relied upon to print them well and safeguard them.

I said I would do everything he said.

"Go and make your preparations and slip away quietly. Tell everyone — I'd like them all to go."

I told him that Lorelei and Justly would come and see

him in an hour. The sheriff would allow only three visitors, then Thou-Wert. Sylvester smiled.

"Hell, Scrag, I don't want Thou-Wert."

"Spurious," I said. Suddenly the feelings I had been holding in check burst forth on that word. I wept for a minute or two, Sylvester tightening his arm across my shoulders, saying nothing. When I had finished, I was dragging at my breath with deep sounds I could not stop. When they gradually quieted, there was the face of the sheriff's man at the doorway bars again. I looked at him, and he went away.

Sylvester took his arm from my shoulder and grasped my hand instead. I set the hat down on the seat on the other side.

"I've learned from you," I said.

"It's two ways, Scrag. I've learned from you."

I tried to laugh.

"I hain't had much for you t' learn from."

"More than you know." His voice was still very quiet. He gripped my hand. I wanted to know something of what he meant.

"Tell me."

"Your ease with Lorelei."

"I'm nervous mostly, though."

"It seems like ease. I would have liked that — ease of that kind, falling into happiness, as you with her. I didn't know how good that was till I saw you with her."

"It's her. Just how she is."

"As she would say, 'An' ain't that somethin', Scrag?' " He smiled at the thought, and then his face changed. "God, Scrag, what can I say when they come here?"

I was silent, except that my breath was coming in strange

gasps again, quieter this time, but threatening to become those deep draggings of a few minutes before. Sylvester stood up, as if so agitated by his last thought that he must move around. The bars of sunlight and shadow had gone farther across the floor and were climbing the wall. Sylvester walked through them and stood at the little window. I sat and watched him standing there, thinking what a change he had made in my life. Grace, I thought; he has been given grace, but what good is that now?

"Come and look at the light, Scrag."

I stood beside him. We had to stand a little way back from the window so we could both see out together. There was a rough field, with a tree in the middle, a tree of medium size with a rounded top and a maze of tangled branches and few leaves, as if it might have been having a struggle for life, the low red sunlight through it, throwing long shadows toward us. When Sylvester spoke, his eyes remained fixed out there.

"A certain cast of light, Scrag — do you see?"

I did not know what he meant.

"Reddish?"

"Yes, that, but something more. The way it seems caught up in there."

Looking again, I saw that the mass of the top of the tree formed a perfect circle. I said the light looked strange.

"I'm not religious, Scrag. Are you? Are you a religious man?"

I liked him calling me a man. Lorelei's words came back. Then it seemed that this was the only time Sylvester would say that, and a sense of the whole future without him overcame me.

"Not enough t' worry me." My bottom lip trembled.

"I'd like my camera here — see what my glass eye makes of it." He had not looked away from the tree. "They broke it, didn't they?"

"A bit. It might not be too bad."

"So much to do." He seemed to be giving only part of his attention to the words, then suddenly it was as if their meaning rushed in on him. He turned from the window and clasped me. "So much to do. So much we could have done." He let me free and pushed a hand into his pocket, taking out a folded sheet of paper. "Scrag, you must go. You've things to do." He put the paper into my hand, still folded. "Take this and read it later. I lay awake last night, so tried to write a bit. A poem halfway made — or perhaps it's finished. Tonight I've other things to write — a few good-byes." He walked over and picked up his hat from the bench where I had set it. He looked at it once more, then handed it to me.

"As you go out through there, they'll give you some belongings, Scrag. My knife, a few spare dollars — left from what they'll need. They're yours. And anything you take safe through to Oregon, except what I'll tell those two sweet women of. And *Leaves of Grass* — keep *Leaves of Grass*. Go now." He slapped my shoulder. "Go now. No words. They're understood. All understood. It was just good, Scrag, very good."

Our hands met and gripped.

"It was so good," I said.

I tried to walk steadily to the door, where the man was looking through again. He opened it, and closed it behind me.

I looked back through the bars, my eyes met Sylvester's, then we both turned away.

The man spread out some things on his desk and made me say what they were. I signed a paper, which was a white blur on the dark wood.

"Don't blub, boy," he said. He touched my shoulder. "I'll do my best fer him t'morrer, boy."

I put my hand among the money, pushing some toward him, then took up the rest and ran out of the place.

53

The curve of the Abbotts' timber wagon swayed against
the dimness of the night sky in front of me. "Don't blub, boy,"
the voice from the sheriff's office kept saying over, and, "I'll
blub if I friggin' like," I said aloud to the darkness. I did that,
not caring who heard, occasionally hearing Justly, driving my
own wagon behind, blubbering, too. I listened for any sound
from Lorelei, but none came, and I imagined her face running
with tears of silent misery as we trundled slowly away from
Sylvester.

After a couple of hours exhaustion quieted me, and I was
almost sleeping, the horses plodding their patient way without
my attention. I had the sensation of being in that dream into
which I had fallen several times over the past weeks, of traveling onward through the night as I lay on the wagon floor,
dark hills running high on either side. Then I would jolt awake,
gripping tighter on reins that had been about to slip, missing
the familiar look of Daniel's wagon ahead, wondering if we
should soon find him. He had said he would wait at some
suitable place a few miles outside Halo. I had tried to follow
Axel's instruction to keep a lookout all around, so that we

should not pass him unawares, but now I felt guilty at dozing, hoping, as the distance increased, that we had not somehow failed to see him. He would hardly be expecting us to be traveling by night, so would not be watching out.

Briefly, Chosen Arthur cried, nearer than usual. I thought of his strange name, then of Justly's, and of Thou-Wert, who had given both. He stood over me as I turned to face him, "Defilers!" on his tongue. Then he was striding beside me toward the campfire, his heavy hand grasping my shoulder, saying, "Scrag, you walk with a woeful and penitent man." Then we were out beyond the circle, he suddenly throwing his great bulk down upon his knees in anguish, beating the ground with his hands, then clasping them for prayer, telling me to walk away and leave him to do penance once again. Then he was on his knees as I could only imagine him, the story on Lorelei's voice, "Like an old mule, Scrag." But at the memory of her telling of that thing, the thought was of Lorelei herself kneeling for him, her bitter words, "I knelt on bare boards . . ." Again I shouted at the darkness. "Old bastard! Old bastard!" My blubbering returned, and it was for Sylvester once more, Thou-Wert suddenly no longer the defiler of Lorelei but the good minister who stayed behind to be with Sylvester in his last hour, and to plead with Jack Pewter. Another picture, grimmer than any I had ever imagined, tried to force itself into my mind, but I shied away from it, protecting myself from it by the noise of my blubbering, and words thrown into the night.

I had let an unusual distance come between me and the wagon in front. As my emotions ebbed, I was aware again of failing to keep alert. For a while I peered about with exaggerated intensity, willing Daniel to appear. Occasionally shapes that seemed to be wagon covers stood vaguely against the background of thick woods on the right, becoming undergrowth as we passed. A pair of wild white horses walked toward us, whinnying, before bolting away. Then the minutest point of light, like a spark, stood at a distance for a few seconds, disappeared, returned, and disappeared. In the same moment that I called to Daniel, he called to me.

"Whoa," Axel bawled.

I dropped down and ran toward Daniel. He tapped his pipe on the wheel, a little spray of sparks falling around.

"I'll fetch some light," he said.

He went into the wagon and brought out a lantern, Henrietta coming behind him, pulling a shawl around herself. When we had told him of Sylvester's wish that we should leave Halo, he looked at the ground.

"That's settled, then." Looking up, he caught my eye for a moment, then put his head down again. "That's settled, then."

Axel gave the order to form the circle. We did that, then I went back to Lorelei and Justly. We stood in our own close circle of embrace for some time, unmindful of tears, saying nothing. Their small warm waists under my hands were token of a strange richness that had come into my life and that touched even these hours of misery with blessing. Momentarily I had a thought of such desolation faced without them, and saw Sylvester in his cell. "I would have liked that," he was saying. "I didn't know how good that was till I saw you with her." When Justly eased herself away and went to sink into the grass and cry alone, I stood with Lorelei for a while longer. We clasped so close, still, or swaying slightly, that when we broke apart it was to a feeling of incompleteness, and we locked together again, until Daniel came and said that the coffeepot was still warmish if we wanted it. Lorelei said she would get to bed with Justly. I said I would take coffee. Daniel smiled in the lantern light.

"Scrag's lucky. That looked some sweet lovin'."

"Daniel"—she turned close to him—"you're one good man."

Her arms went around his body, and almost as quickly his free arm went around her waist, the lantern held out toward me, wavering. I took it, and he held her like a young man holding a girl, his old face creased with astonishment and pleasure.

"Lulu-lulu," he said.

"I must go sleep." Lorelei let go. "You don't be talkin' all night, Scrag." She hurried toward the wagon while I turned with Daniel toward his.

"Lulu-lulu." Daniel took the lantern. He stopped to pee against his wheel, and I joined him. "Some lulu, Scrag. Lulu-lulu-lulu."

The coffee was cold. I drank it, trying not to show that it tasted bitter, while Daniel told me he was going back to Halo, that he had spoken to Traven and was borrowing Dick's little roan, that he could be there by first light if he started soon, and that he was taking his rifle. While he bent to unlace his boots and pull on riding boots, Henrietta pushed a penciled scrap of paper toward me on the table. "Tel him nut to go," I read, then, underlined, *"Plees."* She saw that I had read it, then pushed it in her apron pocket, nodding toward Daniel, to indicate that I should say something now.

"Reckon you should go, Daniel?"

"I reckon I should."

"You like me to come?"

"Hell, no."

"You take care?"

"I'll take care." He put his hand on my wrist. "Mornin', see you move on. Don't wait. Tell Axel I said that."

I looked at Henrietta, shrugged. Daniel took my hand, held it in his warm, rough grip.

"Now I'll give you some good advice. Go find her mattress, boy. You'll never have a better, Scrag. Do you know that?"

I said I knew that.

Lorelei had left the cover untied. I was not sure that she had expected me to come there, but I pushed my britches off without speaking, and she did not speak.

"Scrag's come," Justly said sleepily.

Lorelei was enfolding her. I slipped in behind and shaped close, surprised by the feel of her drawers against my thighs.

"Glad you come," she murmured, and pushed back a little into my lap.

I wanted to say that the spread of her haunches was beautiful, and that this was another first-time moment, for she was constantly new and surprising, but I said nothing.

"You got room?"

I said I had, but immediately wished I had said otherwise.

"Aw, Scrag." She pushed back farther. "Them things don't know no fittin'ness."

"What things?" Justly was almost asleep.

"An' nor do ours." Lorelei paused, and I thought she had drifted into sleep. "An' that's for sure."

"Daniel's goin'," I said.

"Goin' where?"

"Back."

"Back *Scrimshaw?*" She was wide awake, incredulous.

"Halo."

"Daniel goin' back Halo?" Justly roused. "But that ol' man, he just can't help Sylvester, Scrag — can he?"

"Listen." I could hear Henrietta's voice, its odd, muffled tone, then there was the soft tread of hooves and the creak of a saddle, passing, diminishing to silence.

"He'll help hisself t' Kingdom Come if he don't mind," said Lorelei. "Was there two horses, Scrag?"

I said it sounded like two, and that Daniel was taking his rifle. Lorelei asked if Axel knew what Daniel was doing. I told her that he had told Traven and me, and nobody else.

"How will Henrietta manage if he don't come back?"

I said he would come back. We lay thinking on that.

"What things?" Justly asked.

"What, girl?"

"What things don't know the fittin'ness?"

"Aw, sleep, child."

"What fittin'ness?"

Lorelei sighed sleepily.

"Time an' place." She shuddered, and after a moment shuddered again. I knew she was crying. Her words about fittingness had not been a rebuff to me, only a half-amused understanding, a kind of endearment. Now she was crying for Sylvester, and I wanted only to comfort her and find some comfort myself. I moved my hand from her waist to her breasts, gathering them gently in the loose cotton stuff, Justly's breasts so close that my fingers brushed by them.

"Aw, Mama, don't cry no more." Justly's fingers touched

my wrist, then moved on my hand. "Ain't she just somethin', Scrag?" I knew she needed no answer. She pressed herself close. "You mind I share?"

"You know what Daniel'd say?" Lorelei murmured.

"Lulu," I said. "Lulu-lulu."

"Somethin' like that."

I lay thinking of Daniel riding toward Halo. A few hard drops of rain smacked the canvas, then a quickening flurry of them crackled like kindling fire, and soon a downpour was battering above and around, as if it would rip the cover apart. Justly drew my hand closer to her breasts, but Lorelei took it back to hers, then mother and daughter pressed closer together, the dispute over, my hand willingly trapped there in comfort while my mind followed Daniel on the little roan, with the spare horse trailing, through the storm.

"Will it rain in the mornin'?" Justly sounded like a child with a foolish question.

"Why you askin', girl?"

"Maybe they don't hang people when it's rainin', Mama, do they?" Justly said.

"I just don't know about that, love. Right now I feel somehow I don't know nothin' no more, 'cept this hand here you're sharin', child."

I watched Daniel, bent low, moving through the torrent toward Halo.

54

We woke soon after dawn, to the sound of rain. A weak place in the cover, toward the opening, had begun to let water in, a steady drip pattering to the boards beyond our feet. Lorelei got up to set a bowl there, then peered out at the opening for a minute before coming back to bed. She eased in behind me and pushed me into the middle. I lay on my back, watching the drips gather and fall, wondering how many would fall before Sylvester died. Nobody spoke. We were dumb with apprehension and misery. If only this one thing were not to happen, I would never want to complain about anything in my life, I thought. How perfect life would be without this single happening. Was there just the slightest possibility that Thou-Wert could be rewarded for all those years spent on his knees, by having the power to persuade Jack Pewter? Was there more chance through Daniel's rifle? Or through the rain, as Justly had asked like a child in the night? For an instant I had the wish that I might fall asleep again, and wake in a couple of hours and know that by now it must be over, and only the misery left, without this terrible apprehension. Then I felt ashamed, suddenly started up, pushing away the blanket.

"I'm goin' t' Halo."

Lorelei grabbed my waist.

"You ain't, Scrag. You jest ain't." With a tremendous wrench, she flung me to my back and pressed over me. "You jest damn well ain't."

I bucked to throw her off. She told Justly to hold my hair. Together they held me down while I bucked and twisted.

"Boy, you could get up by hurtin' me. I can't hold you here, an' you know that. You'll have to hurt me, though. You want t' hurt me, Scrag?"

"He won't hurt you, Mama."

I knew that Justly was right. I went limp and lay looking at the canvas, my head tilted back by Justly's grip on my hair, my breath catching in deep spasms again. Lorelei's face was close to my throat. After a moment I felt hot tears falling near my mouth and running away toward my ears. She made no sound. I thought of that morning when her nipple had traced like a tickling finger around my face. I heard Justly whimpering quietly, and soon she let go of my hair. A tear fell at the corner of my mouth and trickled in, salty, followed by another.

"I didn't hurt you."

"Never," she said. I wondered what that meant. After a while she said, "You'll always know you would have gone, won't you?"

"I'll know that."

"An' why I stopped you?"

"Yeah."

After we had stayed awhile in silence, apart from an occasional quiet whimper from Justly, Lorelei said we should get up and help search for firewood. We were the first out. We walked about in the rain, looking for wood that might be dry enough to burn. Stopping by night, we had not noticed that Daniel had waited for us by the edge of a forest. There at the edge, where saplings were struggling to root, there was nothing to gather, so we went on into the gloom under the dripping leaves, breaking off sear bark from the underside of a fallen tree, finding cones among the rotting leaves underfoot. By the time we emerged, Axel was breaking sticks from the supply he always carried in the woodbox at the side of his wagon, and was about to start a fire.

We made four trips back into the forest, and when we came to the fire with the last load, there was a good blaze going, and most of the company had gathered. The rain had lessened, becoming little more than a drifting mist on a slight breeze as the sun rose. Everyone was standing still, and as we came near we heard Clement leading a prayer for Sylvester. We put down our wood and stood, too, a little way off. When I put my hands together, I noticed that one was bleeding, a small gout of crimson growing among the wet dirt. We were just too far away to hear clearly what Clement said, but Sylvester's name came several times, then Daniel's and Thou-Wert's.

"Amen," said Martha loudly, "amen, dear Lord, amen," and the company murmured "Amen" together and separately several times. I always felt embarrassed to do that, but made myself say the word aloud once, as did Lorelei and Justly, then said it once more to myself before we took up our wood and went forward.

There were a few wan smiles as people made conversation about small concerns and did helpful things for each other —

Clancy wiping a child's nose, Martha ladling out porridge, Dora tending Chosen Arthur while Emmy took food to Henrietta, who would not leave her wagon — but we all knew we were covering our true feelings, which were of desolation and agony.

"This ain't vet rain," Axel joked.

I wiped my hand in the grass, washing off dirt and blood. Axel scowled.

"But last night's rain, that vet aroun' that ol' man Daniel, Scrag. Vot good he tink he do? I like that ol' man, Scrag."

I told Axel that Daniel had said we should not wait for him. He shook his head.

"No, no. Ve vait. No ol' man he don't tell me vot to do. Ve vait for friggin' preacher, too." He turned to Lorelei, who had come up beside us. "Excuse my lankwidge, ma'am." His eyes went down the front of her dress, where there were marks from the wet wood. "Hey, there, you spoil your clothe." He unknotted his neckerchief and held it out. "You vipe that muck off, ma'am."

"Axel, I'll change. You keep that clean."

"Oh, it don't matter, I got a clean one back in there." He brushed at her dress, hardly touching it, suddenly looking foolish and clumsy. "I damn sorry 'bout Sylvester, Lorelei, you know. I real damn sorry 'bout that man."

We stood there spooning Martha's porridge, Axel's dry rain still falling. On the other side of the fire, Justly was with Jane and Clancy, Jane's arm around her shoulder. Slowly the company moved away, to sit disconsolate in the wagons or tend animals. I released Sylvester's chickens so they could peck around and threw a handful of grain from his bin. Justly said that Clancy was sure Sylvester was still alive, and she went into the wagon with Jane. Eventually I was left alone with Lorelei beside the fire, until Emmy came slowly toward us, a shawl over her head and shoulders, and Chosen Arthur almost hidden in it.

"I'll be with you," she said. "Excuse me, Scrag, this poor mite's ravenous."

"Emmy," said Lorelei, the first smile of the day breaking around her eyes, "Scrag don't exactly disapprove such things."

"I somehow thought not." Emmy looked at me, smiling.

"He ain't no stranger to a bosom, are you, Scrag?" said Lorelei.

"I guess I ain't." I looked at the smudges Axel's clumsy wiping had spread on her dress. "You said it, though."

"And I ain't shy of sayin' it."

"That's beautiful," Emmy said.

"I want to tell you somethin', tell you both," said Lorelei. "Last evenin' in Halo, in Sylvester's cell . . . somethin' he said. Justly had gone, and I stayed on five minutes more. We stood against a little window by the settin' sun — you seen it, Scrag. One at each side, we stood. He said he wanted . . . wanted to say . . . wanted . . . to say . . . good-bye . . . good-bye where light was catchin' . . . catchin' me. 'Would you believe,' he said, 'I've never touched a woman's breast?' I said, 'Touch mine.' He smiled. 'I'll store that up for Heaven,' he said." She looked past me, in the direction of Halo, her eyes brimming, then to Emmy. "Ain't that just somethin' to be said?"

Emmy put out a hand, took Lorelei's hand, and we walked slowly.

"I'm honored to be told that, Lorelei. That's somethin' to be said."

Later, in my wagon, while Lorelei boiled water for coffee

on the embers, I sat and thought of the strange intimacy between women, and of how I had been welcomed into it with
so little reserve — with mother and daughter, and now with
Emmy — as if revelations pleased them. With a touch of
unease, I wondered if it was because they still thought of me
as a boy. "Boy," Lorelei was always calling me, in spite of
saying I was a man. "It was a boy left Scrimshaw," she had
just said to Emmy, "but he slipped away some distance back
there on the trail." I knew that was not fully true. In some
ways I was still the boy who had strolled across her path in
Scrimshaw, doting on her glance and smile. I did not imagine
I could ever not be him. I would always be able to recall the
feelings of that boy. I would always know how it felt to be
him because I would always be him. He lay inside me on
Lorelei's wagon floor. He had watched from my eyes as she
dressed at morning and undressed at night. But not alone, I
thought. He had not watched alone because from the same
eyes someone else looked, who had known the strangeness of
her body in darkness and the sweetness of love coming from
her in word and touch. I wanted the hardness of a man — of
Axel, who had chosen me to shift rocks with him, stripped to
the waist, in a stream; of Daniel, who had driven his wagon
alone halfway across this continent, grieving; of all the men
of this company. But then I remembered Axel playing his
harmonica by his wagon at evening, a tender tune, of loneliness
and longing; then Sylvester telling of showing to Daniel his
photograph of Justly with her new way of putting up her hair,
and his surprised words: "And, do you know, that old man
cried." So, in the midst of hardness, there was tenderness, and
that was how I wanted it to be for me. In the midst of women's
tenderness, there could be hardness, too. I thought of Lorelei

bringing up Justly, and of the pair of them holding me in their grip on the wagon floor at daybreak. What a fierce and loving hardness in their tenderness there was. But, with that thought, the knowledge of what it was that had made me start up in determination to ride to Halo forced itself back from where it was being held at bay, and at the same time Lorelei was calling me for coffee.

She was serving coffee at the tailboard of Clancy's wagon. The rain was still falling lightly, a faintly golden blur in the sunshine, with a rainbow almost overhead. Justly was looking a little brighter. She had changed from her wet clothes into some offered by Jane, things saved from long ago, Jane said, a white blouse with puffed-up shoulders and tight waist, and a long pale yellow skirt. Justly said she would not come out of the wagon for fear of soiling the hem, but it was plain that something said by Jane or Clancy in their quiet wisdom had somewhat soothed her distress, if only for a while. I wished that something could soothe mine.

When I asked him for the time, Clancy looked first at the position of the sun, then took out his watch and said it was almost nine o'clock. A conviction, hard as a blow, struck me that this was the moment when Sylvester was being taken out to be hanged. I saw a throng of people gathered near the square in Halo, others hurrying toward it, Belle and Ruth hesitating at the corner, not certain whether they should follow, wide-eyed, curious, and fearful, thinking, "This is George's friend."

"You all right, Scrag?" Clancy was clambering down, the coffee spilled on the ground, Lorelei's arm around my waist. I felt weak and sick. A cup was being held to my lips, a box set behind my legs. I sat, and Lorelei tilted the cup.

"Take some brandy," said Jane.

The liquid stung my gums, flared on my tongue and against the sides of my mouth, then down my throat.

"Take it all," said Clancy.

I took it all.

"You'll soon feel better," said Jane.

"Sylvester," I said.

"Keep off them thoughts," said Clancy.

Jane said she and Justly would go visit Henrietta. Clancy helped them down, and they picked their way through the squelching grass, Justly holding her skirt high.

"Change your wet clothes, Mama," she called back. "And you, Scrag."

"I'd rather walk some more," Lorelei said to me. "They'll need more wood for noontime."

With even one person less, the forest seemed more eerie. It was not possible to go far in because of the thick undergrowth. Though the rain was now so light, the leaves had been so well drenched that droplets were pattering everywhere. We stood under a wide branch for shelter, holding together loosely, without speaking for a while, simply regarding each other. I tried to read her thoughts as her expressions changed slightly, and tried to tell what color her eyes were among these green shadows. I breathed the scent of her wet hair and the fainter scent of her skin.

"That's some adorin', Scrag."

"Is it?"

"It surely is. Enough to last a lifetime, boy."

We were quiet again, thinking on that.

"When you move on sometime, you just remember that."

She was looking me in the eyes, so she saw my protest coming before I could speak, and touched a finger to my lips. "No promises. Don't make me promises."

We gathered wood, emerging several times into misty rain. Occasionally we paused, to stand together, and once to sit on the fallen tree, careless of water soaking through skirt or britches. I wanted not to feel the comfort of dry clothes, thinking of Daniel riding through the night of torrents and wondering if Sylvester was hanging in the tree where Joe had been, this soft rain blurry around him.

Toward midday the little roan trotted into camp without Daniel.

We waited through the afternoon for Axel and Clancy to return. Leaving, Axel had handed me one of his shotguns, telling me to sit guard. I watched the horses disappearing into mist, envying Clancy for being the chosen companion. Restless, I walked the circle a few times, sporting the gun on my arm, then decided to sit on Daniel's barrel by his wagon, somewhat sheltered from the drift of rain.

My thoughts went back to Lorelei's story of standing in the cell with Sylvester. I realized why he had not touched her breast. He had not wanted to give her the deeper connection with him that such a touch would have made, and so the deeper anguish afterward. There was all of Sylvester in that story.

Rawhide, I thought, and Justly's voice came back: "He just ain't rawhide, Mama." Maybe, with his cultured manners and experience in far cities, he was not suited to a word that called up notions of the rougher places of the earth, but was there a better word for his strength? Not iron or rock, with no connection to life. Lorelei's word was nearer to Sylvester than Justly had imagined.

As I was sitting there, eating a cake that Henrietta had brought me, with wringing of hands and gestures in the direction Daniel had gone, I remembered the piece of folded paper Sylvester had handed me last evening, which I had dropped into my tin trunk. After leaving Sylvester, there had been the hurried preparations for departure, and I had thought no more of the paper since we had rumbled away in the dusk. Now I bolted to my wagon to fetch it, struck by the fact that the prospect of a few written words could excite me so much. How that would have pleased Sylvester, I thought, as I opened the lid.

Halo, 1859

Light falls on the square
Where high in a tree
The hanged man rides
His horse of air.

The last light goes
From the silent wood
Where the hanged girl dances
On pointed toes.

Ah, sweet girl, tomorrow
I'll dance with you there
And ride with your lover
His horse of air.

Dear Scrag,

   As you see, I've gone back to short lines, and an attempt at elegance.
   Art is an answer to ugliness and evil. Not the only answer, perhaps, but the one I know.

Yours, for as long . . .
Sylvester

The page blurred. I got up and put the paper back, then walked around the circle at a good pace, with the gun on my arm. The words were already in my head, and I said them over, keeping well away from the wagons. Then I went around again, this time with a few glances coming from under the covers, and I imagined comments that Scrag was taking his duties too seriously. If Clancy had been there, he would have made some joking remark.

I wondered what Clancy and Axel might find. Where was Thou-Wert? And where was Sylvester? The horror of the picture of Sylvester hanging in the tree, which I had managed to protect myself from last night by blubbering on the dark trail, now forced itself across my vision for a moment, then, strangely, I found that horror had turned to something that could be better borne, the anguish of pity, by a sense of Sylvester's poem running in my mind and, almost at once, breaking from my lips. As I walked on, it seemed that, in an unbelievable way, the words could ward off horror, as though they were a charm. Had they worked like that for Sylvester? Fervently I wished they had. Was that what he meant by art being an answer to ugliness and evil?

A moment later I thought I was deluding myself, or that the poem was deluding me. It did not alter the reality, which was that Sylvester was to be hanged in a tree at Jack Pewter's orders, and that this was his wagon I was passing, and he was not here, and never would be again. "Delusion," I blurted, "damned delusion." I coughed loudly, in case anyone had heard, and snapped open the breech of the shotgun, as if inspecting it, to cover my foolishness. I remembered Daniel crying "illusion" in the compound.

But as I sat on Daniel's barrel again, despondent and near to jabbering my anguish to Henrietta, who would not be able to hear it, the poem seemed to be asking to be considered again. I heard it on Sylvester's voice, quiet and measured. I went to my trunk, wanting to hold the paper, to see the words on the page and be back with him at the moment of writing, to savor this gift to me. As I returned to the barrel, Henrietta signaled that she would like some help to the ground. I set the barrel for her to step on, and she gave me her arm as she came down. She pulled my head forward and lightly kissed my cheek, before going off into a clump of bushes beyond the circle. When she came back, she indicated that she would stay on the ground awhile. I offered her the seat, but she shook her head. She stood near me, as if wishing for the conversation that was denied her, gently twisting her hands together, look-ing toward the horizon, occasionally glancing down on me. I thought she might be glancing at the paper, so I handed it to her, wondering what she would make of it. She must have noticed Sylvester's signature, for she spoke his muffled name. She looked at the paper for so long that I began to think she might be having some difficulty with a word — though, as the poem was so simple, I could not imagine which — or even have drifted into a dream, but slowly her eyes moistened, and a tear ran out from the inner corner of each. She lifted the hem of her apron and wiped beside her nose, holding the paper out to me. Then she indicated that she would like to go into the wagon. I set the barrel and helped her up. She motioned me to come up behind her. I went up and put the shotgun against the wagon side, expecting another cake or some such offering. But, instead of handing me anything, Henrietta lowered herself to her knees, holding the table edge to do so, and put her hands together for prayer, her elbows on the table. Then, nodding to me, she took her hands apart briefly to indicate that I should get down on the opposite side. Taken by surprise, I felt a flood of embarrassment, but knowing there was nobody to see, I went to my knees and put my hands together, grateful that at least Henrietta would not be expecting to hear me. She already had her eyes closed, and her lips were moving very slightly. As I looked, her eyes screwed up with feeling, her fingers, which had been pointed upward like a child's, now clasped tightly. I closed my eyes and tried to pray, but could not concentrate because I thought of Justly and Lorelei coming by, which was unlikely, and Justly saying, "Look at Scrag in there," and an odd smell was mingled with the smell of Daniel's smoking in the wagon. The wagon was very clean and tidy, but had a much-used smell to it, perhaps of much-used clothes and especially of Daniel's much-used boots, which were stout and ancient, and were standing beneath the table, where I had seen him put them as he pulled on his riding boots. I had, anyway, said all my prayers for Sylvester as I blubbered along the trail last night. But might not this one extra, made in this strange embarrassment, and yet in the presence of Henrietta's heartfelt prayers, be the one answered? "Dear Lord, let Sylvester be saved and Daniel be back before sundown," I asked, "and let there be a sign when I look outside the wagon in a moment that it shall be so." I did not know what the sign might be, but I would instantly recognize it. Then I was aware that Henrietta had stopped praying and was struggling to her feet, her knee joints cracking, and opened my eyes into hers, as she watched me with a sad, pleased look.

I stood up and looked out, but everything was as before, the rain somewhat heavier again, though still not much more than a mist. At least the prayer had not been useless because it had given Henrietta comfort. Nobody had come by and seen my head and praying hands, and now I thought I would not have cared much if they had. Henrietta had signed that I should wait a moment before stepping down, while she rummaged in a chest. She brought out a small box, showed me that it contained several clay pipes, some old and brownish, a pair white, unused. She held out the pair and wanted me to choose one, saying, "Daniel, Daniel," pointing to the pipes, then to me. I took one and mouthed my "Thank you" clearly. She indicated that I should wait again, and handed me a pouch of tobacco. I beamed my satisfaction. Henrietta smiled, then mimed Daniel smoking. Then her face went serious. She mimed her praying and said a word I could not recognize from her strange voice. She wanted me to understand and repeated it several times, then took a pencil and scrap of paper from the table drawer and wrote, "Re leef." I said, "Relief," nodding, and turned, then turned back, thanking her again for the pipe, putting it in my mouth, patting the pouch. She patted my back. I took the shotgun and jumped down.

I wanted to avoid upsetting Lorelei and Justly by showing

them Sylvester's poem. There would be a time for that. I took another turn around the circle, staying a long way out, pausing to light my pipe. The blur of rain stayed, little hisses coming from the pipe bowl as droplets went in. The smoke came thick and hot because of the short stem. I choked and gasped, glad I had stayed well enough away from the wagons not to be noticed in that. Soon the bowl itself was hot to my inexperienced fingers and I was feeling disappointed in my new badge of manhood. I could understand why Daniel's saliva ran like a stream when he smoked, gurgling at the bottom of the bowl — it was his mouth's way of protecting itself. Before I had completed the circle, my mouth was learning the trick, but by then the tobacco was burning through, the heat hellish, my tongue writhing for coolness. I opened to the rain, drawing it in like spring water.

I had put Sylvester's poem in my britches pocket, with Lorelei's. Now I stopped at my wagon to take them out, damp from my damp clothes. I put them on the table to dry, thinking how I had vowed to myself that I would carry Lorelei's always, and always in that same place. In my trunk I found the tiny leather-bound volume of religious thoughts that had been my grandmother's favorite book, so old and often held that the cover was becoming detached. Gently I helped it the last half inch and put the pages back in the trunk. For half an hour, while the poems dried, I worked leather soap into the pliable cover, restoring it to a shining nut brown. The title, *Devotions*, on the front and narrow spine in gold, seemed right for my two most valued possessions. I folded the poems again and put them between the covers, but, as I was slipping them into my pocket, I hesitated. To carry Sylvester's poem there always would be a daily reminder of pain, and I could not bear the thought of today's agony never absent. And I wanted the sense of joy that came from that other poem never to be lessened. I sensed Sylvester saying that the place for his poem was in the dictionary, to which so many of the lessons learned from him had taken me. I put it on the page that held "grace," and heard again the voice of that fellow in the sheriff's office as a tear splashed on the worn cover. One day soon I would soap that cover, too. *Webster's Dictionary* gleamed in gold on red momentarily, against brown leather as fresh as it had been in my grandmother's hands in 1829. I took my pipe and pouch, and went back to Daniel's barrel.

Henrietta looked out and mumbled her approval, nodding, gesturing toward Halo with a shrug and a motion of prayer. I mouthed, "Soon," and she smiled, putting a hand on her left bosom, patting above her heart. I lit the pipe and drew carefully, trying to please her. She murmured, nodded, and went in.

When that filling was smoked through, I sat as Daniel sat, with the spent pipe clenched at a corner, thumbs in belt, or held it in pursed lips, pressing the lower one down a bit, taking pleasure from the touch of it. A pair of rabbits, with a family of young, were nibbling on the crest of a small rise, gradually coming closer. I remembered that evening, several weeks back, when I had gone out with Daniel to set his snares. I had thought of the women skinning rabbit for supper, the creature becoming briefly like a human baby, newborn as Chosen Arthur was then. Something Daniel had said then came back, too: "Watch some poor creature strangle theirself, then think about the ways of humankind." With that, the horror of a scene back in Halo stood in my mind, and the sound of Jack Pewter's voice, and its barely believable words in that courtroom, came as they would come forever: "Hang him."

For a moment my eyes had turned from the rabbits on the slope. Now there was a sudden twang from somewhere to my left, and in an instant the buck took an arrow in his side, screamed, leaped a little way, trying to go with his bolting family, then, screaming still, began to whirl madly, tumbled forward, and whirled again. Shouts of delight had come from Dick and his brother as they ran from between the wagons, with bows in their hands. Now, in the face of the creature's agony, they stood daunted, until shortly the violent movements slowed, and the buck lay jerking, his legs stretched as if in leaping. They went forward, but with no hurry to take their prize, half turning to Traven, who followed them. They let him pass, followed closely, then shied back a little as a last effort at a leap was made when Traven took the hind legs and held the rabbit up for a sharp blow with the side of his hand on its neck. He pulled the arrow from the limp body, handed both to Dick, and they walked back.

"You see that, Scrag?" Dick called.

"Yeah. I saw."

I was thinking back to the day when Thou-Wert had larruped him for stealing Martha's rabbit pieces, and of the apology when he had found the punishment unjustly given. He had said that he could not take back the punishment, but doubtless the Lord would spare the boy chastisement for some future wickedness. I recalled Dick's blubbering and took some satisfaction from it. This was near enough to the kind of occasion Thou-Wert had in mind.

I lit my pipe and went to see Lorelei and Justly. They had been drawn to look out by the screaming.

"I'm tellin' Mama she don't need make no rabbit stew for me ever," Justly said.

"Hell, that's some dwarf's pipe you got there," said Lorelei.

As I was about to climb up with them a wagon appeared in the distance, with two figures on horseback alongside. I called that it was our party. As they neared, Axel came on ahead.

"Ve got ol' Daniel safe, but he ain't vell. You go tell Henrietta gentle, Scrag."

I wrote, "Daniel back — not well," on a scrap of paper and took it to Henrietta. She was undisturbed by all the commotion outside, knitting in her chair. I helped her down, and she clasped me against her bosom for a couple of seconds, gasping with anxiety at the sight of the company gathering around Thou-Wert's wagon. Axel and Thou-Wert were removing the tailboard. When it was ready, it was slid into the wagon and Daniel moved onto it. He was brought out and taken to his own wagon, Henrietta going alongside, jabbering, Daniel looking up at her. As they lifted him in, I thought his eyes caught mine. His look seemed to be saying, "Hell, look at me, boy," but I wondered if I was fooling myself.

55

"He said he'd shoot my ass off." Thou-Wert finished his story by coming back to its beginning, shaking his head slowly.

He had failed to find Pewter, but had been seen by John Sloan, who had given him an order to leave Halo within ten minutes. He had traveled slowly because for some miles outside the town his wheels had sunk in mud. A man had passed him, riding hard, with a spare horse alongside, some distance out, where the trail was wide, and he had not recognized Daniel, not expecting him to be there. But, a few miles on, he had come upon him, stretched face upward in a waterfilled rut, groaning, the horses gone. He had stripped him of his soaked clothes, wrapped him in blankets, put a board under him, and set about making a fire for coffee. He had never wished so much to have been a drinking man, carrying brandy. Then, as Daniel had been unable to drink, he had realized the old man had suffered a stroke. His right arm and leg seemed useless, his right cheek sagging somewhat. He was barely aware of what was happening. It was impossible to lift him into the wagon without help, so he had slid the board underneath for shelter, and sat there with him, hoping for passersby.

At one moment he had thought Daniel dead because he was so still, his groaning suddenly stopped, but he had gone into sleep, in which he stayed until Axel and Clancy arrived.

"Shoot my ass off," Thou-Wert said again.

I thought he seemed pleased to have been, briefly, more than a man of words. I wondered if John Sloan had taken some amusement in using a rough tongue to him, knowing that if he said ten minutes, Thou-Wert would be gone in five. To Thou-Wert it would seem that he had tested himself among ruffians, and failed only because of the threat of a gun. I fancied I heard John Sloan's laughter behind him. I fancied, too, that Thou-Wert was taking pleasure in putting his own tongue to words that seemed strange there.

Later, when I stood a little way off from the fire as the sun was going down, watching Lorelei and other women at their pots and pans, he put his hand on my shoulder, coming from behind.

"A sad and sorry business, Scrag."

"It's that."

"Two very fine men."

"They are."

"You're hopeful, still."

"I'm hopeful."

He pressed my shoulder, moved forward as if to go to someone else, then turned, holding his lapels.

"Sometimes I feel that I've been tethered to this garb too long."

I looked at him, saying nothing.

"Maybe someday I'll loose myself." He came close again. "What will you do in Oregon?"

"Find what there is. Look around for what suits me." On

an impulse that gave me no time for hesitation, a word that took me by surprise was on my lips. "Record things."

It was a keeping of faith with Sylvester, a promise now made again.

"Record, Scrag? You mean . . . ?"

"Things as they are."

"How, boy?"

"In words."

"You mean you'll write?" Thou-Wert seemed none too sure that it was the right undertaking for me. "What sort of writing, Scrag?"

That same impulse leaped again, more reckless than before.

"Poems, maybe." I had written a line that seemed full of grace, and one short poem that told something truly about my own experience, and had seemed good to Lorelei and Justly, who knew more about the experience than anyone else ever could. It was a small beginning, but it was a beginning. "I'd like to write poems," I said firmly.

"Poems?" Thou-Wert showed surprise. "Do you write poems, Scrag?"

I feared he might ask to see some.

"Not much just yet." That reckless impulse leaped: "I'm hopin' for the grace."

"Ah, *grace*." Thou-Wert studied my face. "You know, I hadn't thought of it like that. How true, boy, true. A grace. And you are seeking that grace, Scrag."

The impulse had shrunk back somewhere, leaving me to my own devices on a dreary plain at the edge of a forest, a campfire burning at dusk, a blur of rain still falling, with a doubting man I had once called spurious and still thought so.

"I'm hopin' for the grace," I said. Suddenly it was as if I

were no longer talking to this red-faced, bulky man in a black suit, on which the rain had revived the smell of horse dung he had knelt into in his crazy penances, but somehow past him to Sylvester. I'm hoping for that grace, I told him again, silently.

56

We traveled slowly, as if Sylvester might at any moment come riding out of the distance behind to catch up with us. I went in to Daniel whenever we rested, and sat watching him, gently rubbing his arm or holding his fingers, trying to make them grip on mine. Much of the time, he slept, restlessly, then woke with a look of puzzlement. Sometimes he tried to speak, struggling helplessly to form words and get them across the little space between us, chopping with his left arm, kicking with his left foot. A few times, Clancy took my place. After one visit he came out and put an arm across my shoulder, saying he had asked Daniel to nod if he was sure Sylvester was dead.

"We press on now, Scrag boy," he said.

A few days from Halo, we were back on the marked trail, trundling in well-worn ruts. A cheer went up from the company as we found it, and we waved back and forth to each other. I wondered how different our experiences might have been if we had not departed into unknown country on that day we found the dead Indian, or if we had soon rejoined the trail. There seemed a strange inevitability in the events of our

journey, as if Daniel's telling of the story of Halo had somehow
led us to the place; as if the finding of the dead Indian had
somehow led us to the saloon in Pewter's Palace; as if the
delightful hours with Sylvester in Lorelei's wagon, and the
sweetness I had found with Lorelei, had come from our weeks
of unmapped journeying that had led to Halo. The more I
thought in this way, the more quite small happenings seemed
to be significant, and to be part of a chain of events. I saw
Lorelei sitting in the grass on that long slope the day she was
made to walk behind the wagons, finding the rock with "Halo"
chipped into it. If she had not noticed it, would we have taken
the turn at the bottom of the slope, which brought us to Halo?
Certainly she would not have seen it if she had not been sitting
there, and she would not have been sitting there if there had
been no accusation against Thou-Wert, and no accusation if
he had not raped her, and no rape, perhaps, if he had not
found me with her, or if he had not touched her when she
was young, and he would not have done that if she had not
already been mother to Justly. So was Sylvester's fate in Halo
connected with Lorelei's innocent loving of a boy while she
was still a child? So my thoughts ran on under the oppressive
sun of mid-morning. I was glad to escape them temporarily
when we stopped to rest, and I could run to tell Daniel that
we were back on the trail, if Henrietta had not managed to
do so already.

Henrietta was already looking out for me, her face full of
consternation. I jumped up and clambered over the board, to
find Daniel agitatedly pushing off his blanket and trying to
get up. As I came in, Henrietta hurriedly tried to push the
blanket higher, because he was undressed except for his shirt.

Annoyed, he pushed it down again, and indicated that I should help him to a chair. With a guilty look at Henrietta, I pulled the chair close. With a great struggle, Daniel came to his knees and, after a rest, to the chair, grunting with satisfaction. He looked down at himself and tucked his shirt between his legs. He indicated his trousers, hanging by the front bow where they had dried, and Henrietta took them down.

"S—S—rag." With effort, he managed to get his tongue almost around my name and looked pleased with himself. He meant that I, not Henrietta, should help him on with his trousers. When he was sitting up, decently dressed and feeling that he looked something like himself again, he indicated that I should sit on a box. I sat waiting while he moved his lips and throat, breathing deeply, and pointing to his mouth to show that he was wanting to say something. When the first word came, it was distorted but unmistakable.

"Pew—uh."

He looked at me with satisfaction.

"Pewter," I repeated.

His eyes smiled. He extended his left arm, pointing, and squinted along it, in a gesture I immediately recognized. He struggled with his right arm, but it would not rise. I extended my own left arm, squinted, and curled my right forefinger in front of my chin. He gave a single slight nod.

"Dead." It seemed like the most triumphant word I had ever heard.

Daniel lowered his arm, but kept it held out toward me, opening his palm. I knew what he meant, and leaned forward, reaching out, letting him take my hand in his. He gripped tight.

"S — S — ves . . . S — S — ves . . . vestah."

He gripped tighter on my hand, shaking it slightly, looking at me earnestly.

At some point during the moments we sat there looking at each other, our hands gripped, I thought that silence can be better than speech. When I began to feel my calmness about to break, and would have gone outside somewhere, perhaps to run blindly along the trail for a while, the grip of the gnarled hand on mine tightened and held me there.

57

We measured the rest of the journey in campfires without Sylvester. It lay through forest and wind-sculpted desert, by gorge and cascade, through bare valley and fertile valley, in the sight of turning fruit, under stark sun or frequent soft rain. We made our fires by pearly dawns and vivid sunsets, by pearly sunsets and vivid dawns, always with the sense of an absence that did not lessen.

At this point, memory and imagination withdraw from a detailed reliving of days in which numbness beset every sense and was relieved only by the pleasures of companionship or the practical demands of guiding tired animals and battered wheels. A few moments stand clear across time and distance and attach themselves to the story.

One day Daniel asked me if I would ask Will to make him a small stepladder like the one Emmy and her children used. I went to Will, who said that George was already making one, and by next evening it was in position, Daniel able to take his normal ease.

His speech was returning. It was indistinct on some sounds, and slow, but there, and coherent. One night, as he sat on his barrel, smoking, he asked me to stop as I went by. I sat in the dampening grass at his feet.

"Pipe?"

He held out his pouch to me. I took out the little clay and filled. He struck a match for me, plainly delighted in showing that he could control both hands again. But the control was not as good as he had hoped, and the flame trembled and went out.

"Hell." He handed me the box. "I ain't in . . . proper shape yit, Scrag." He paused, the pipe gurgling. "I'm in better shape . . . than Pewter, though." He paused again, longer. "Did I do right?"

"What sort of question's that?" I thought I sounded like Lorelei.

The match flared. I thought of him looking at my face in the light of it.

"Jest say the answer, boy. You know the score."

"Yes, you did right." I flicked the match and struck another.

Daniel drew for a few seconds.

"I think I did. I hed no other choice . . . an' didn't want none, boy." He struggled for the next words. "Mebbe . . . best thing I ever done. Danced . . . they danced in the street."

"Too late," I said, but I thought he did not hear.

We sat together silently, smoking, refilling, smoking.

"Henrietta found you the pipe," he said absently.

"Yeah, thanks. But I ain't much hand at it."

My thoughts were a long way back on the trail. The grass was dewy. I had pulled a stalk, as Lorelei had then. Sylvester's voice was quoting Whitman: "The smallest sprout shows there is really no death . . ." I wanted to say something like that to Daniel.

"I was readin' a book," I said. "One of Sylvester's. It said about the grass: 'The smallest sprout shows there is really no death.' "

Daniel drew hard a few times, his face glowing, then dark again.

"There's death," he said.

For a while our route was along the bank of the Columbia. Then the day came for us to begin to part. After breakfast at the fire, Thou-Wert preached, saying that in spite of the vileness of Halo and the death of Sylvester, the company had journeyed under the hand of Providence. Even the disaster that had befallen us might be part of a design of which we could not know the purpose. Whether he spoke with the intention of deceiving others or was simply deceiving himself, I was still not sure. As he went on to say that today three wagons — Lorelei's, Scrag's, and Sylvester's — would depart on the trail to Oregon City, and soon the rest would separate, to Portland or Fort Vancouver, the company began to turn aside to each other and murmur. He said he could see that the time had come for personal farewells and that he would detain us but a moment longer. At this, he began to undress, taking off his coat and holding it at arm's length before dropping it on the ground, then unbuttoning his shirt, saying that he had learned on the journey that he needed no special clothing in which to do his Maker's work, that sin could be committed as easily in the religious garb as out of it, and that grace could be attained only with the greatest difficulty whatever the garb.

He stood in his gray undershirt and black trousers as the
company began to sing about meeting somewhere beyond the
mountain, Axel taking up the tune on his harmonica, and it
seemed that everybody was weeping, some openly, others hiding behind sniffs or averted heads. As the words finished, we
began embraces and words of farewell that lasted until Axel
banged two cooking pots together and called for wagons to
roll in twenty minutes.

After harnessing the horses, I went to see Daniel and
Henrietta. Since being able to use his stepladder, Daniel was
mending quickly, and had just managed his own harnessing.
He said he wanted to stay a few days in Portland, then press
on to the coast before the weather changed. Where he would
go after that, he was not sure. I said he would be able to
contact me through John Ogilvie. He said he would do that,
but as we stood there face to face and grasping hands, I think
it was in his mind, as it was in mine, that this was a huge
country and it was not at all certain that we would ever stand
like this again. Henrietta came and embraced me, her two
tearstains beside her nose, and put a tin of oatcakes into my
hand. Daniel gave me a jar of tobacco, saying I should smoke
it in Lorelei's pipe and, when I did so, think of how he had
said about its curving stem laid anywhere on her, and maybe
test sometime if what he said was true. I said maybe I would
do that, and tell Lorelei why. He said he guessed she would
say she thought well of the old man who suggested it. She
had just been and given him another of those "Lulu" kisses,
and Justly had made a fair imitation. We knew we were joking
to hold back emotion we could not try to shape into words,
and were quick to make our final embrace when Axel called
for Daniel to get up. I handed up his stepladder, and imme-

diately he slapped the reins, his old face set and flushed, with only one glance down as he raised a hand. I stood with Lorelei and Justly, waving and calling as the wagons went by, then silent as they headed away, old Tickler's "amazin'est balls" swinging as ever behind them.

58

I read the letter again, then dropped it back on the round table. It lay in the circle of lamplight with the others, Lorelei and Justly sitting there touching them, John Ogilvie standing over us, silent.

Dear Scrag,

> *So much we could have done, dear boy. See what you can do. Look after Lorelei. She is a benison.*

> *Sylvester*

I pushed it toward Lorelei, then she pushed hers to me. I took it up again.

Dear Lorelei,

> *I was quite wrong about apple pie: a lesson learned at your table in hours of such sweetness.*

> *Sylvester*

I held it back to her, and she passed on the letter that Justly was holding to me again.

Dear Justly,

    Heaven does not lie about us often, and in those moments it does we are fortunate indeed if we can recognize it. I did once, in watching you.

                                                    Sylvester

I turned and looked at John Ogilvie, who had gone to a lamp standing on his desk and was reading again his own letter, which had been waiting for him in a package with the others when he reached home a few hours earlier from a trip to Portland. With the news of Sylvester still fresh, he was distressed, wiping his spectacles, touching his hand to his balding head.

We had arrived in the early evening, the sky to the west a mass of small rose-gold clouds, its light glowing on the scatter of buildings of the small city, on the rocks above them in the background, and on the surface of the Willamette. John Ogilvie had provided a meal of cold turkey and insisted that if we would sleep in our wagons for one more night, he could provide us with beds for as long as we needed them. Fetching glasses and a bottle, he had said, "Sylvester says you all like rye whiskey and that Scrag likes it inordinately at times."

"Says": the word had fallen there so naturally.

"Said," John Ogilvie murmured, almost inaudibly. "Sylvester said."

"Inordinately": I sensed Sylvester smiling at the thought of the pages of my dictionary turning.

We drank, occasionally picked up a letter again, then moved to more comfortable chairs by the large fireplace filled with pinecones. A sweet fragrance came from them, lost as I drank more whiskey. We talked of Sylvester, recalling moments on the trail. Ogilvie wanted to know of Halo, but I sensed that Lorelei and Justly were unable to let their thoughts return there, and I asked him to talk of the distant past. A young Ogilvie and young Sylvester walked up dusty hillside roads in Italian sun, sat under noontime olive trees with wrinkled peasants in black, and beautiful shy girls stood, timid, in low doorways. Sylvester and his friend made drawings and poems, slept in rooms with families, and found small children and chickens walking over them at daybreak.

When Lorelei said that she and Justly should excuse themselves and go to bed, Ogilvie insisted on boiling milk for them to take to the wagon in a jug. As we walked out with them to the yard behind his house, he asked if I could take in some of Sylvester's photographs to look at over a final whiskey. I handed some boxes down to him and told him that I would follow him after securing the wagon for the night. Then I stood for a moment, listening to Lorelei and Justly talking indistinctly under their canvas. "This is the meal pleasantly set . . ." A sense of Sylvester's presence and of his voice, the voice in memory, but the presence more immediate, were there with me for an instant, and I said his name. Then I was standing alone in his desolate wagon, near to blubbering.

My glass was full again. John Ogilvie had opened a box and was looking at pictures under the lamp. He took one and held it at arm's length, close to the light.

"Tender, tender, my dear friend." He put the picture down. "Now tell me about Halo."

———

I slipped in beside Lorelei. She had been lying awake, waiting.

"Scrag, what's a benison?"

"A blessin'."

"And Sylvester thought I was that. Jesu!"

As I fell into sleep, I vaguely recalled something John Ogilvie had said to Lorelei in reply to a question I had not noticed: "The coast's only a hundred miles away — but it's getting late in the year."

I jolted awake at my own laughter, dreaming of Daniel asking me about Robinson Crusoe. It was a week since we had parted. I wondered where he was now. He had said he might go to the coast. I went into sleep again, thinking of how I used to try to imagine the ocean, from the close print of that other Daniel's pages.

59

Justly turned the small green pebble on her palm, holding it out for us to see.

"Is it jade?"

"Maybe," said Lorelei.

"Maybe," I said, with no idea.

The tips of Justly's fingers were wrinkled with the coldness of the water in the beach pool where she had found it. Her palm was a pearly pink, contrasting with the brown of the backs of her hands from the months of the trail. It seemed a kind of nakedness, and stirred me strangely, as if never seen before. I touched the pebble and turned it, almost nervous, though this girl had slept beside me for weeks.

"Pretty," I said.

I looked at her eyes. They seemed to return my look for the merest moment longer than ever before. It was the look that Lorelei had when she seemed to know what was in my mind. It was in Justly's eyes for the first time.

As I looked away, her toes, partly covered in sand, were pale, too, against the tan of the upper part of her foot and her ankle. I had noticed them in the water when she had been exclaiming at its coldness.

"Put it in your pocket for me, Scrag." She dropped it into my britches pocket. There was the same look in her eyes again, then she turned and ran back to the pool.

It was still being fed by the small running waves, water trickling over the ridge of an outcrop of rock. Beyond, the ocean was a vastness greater than anything I could have imagined, its far horizon merging with the sky in limitless pale blue haze.

"Go, then."

I glanced at Lorelei. She gave the look of knowing. As if to show that I should go with Justly, she dropped to the sand, clasping her arms around her knees, over the draping blue of her skirt.

"Go, Scrag."

I went to Justly. She looked up, waiting for me to come. I wondered what Lorelei was feeling. I felt I should not be walking away from her, but she had said I should go, knowing my impulse. She could have come back to the pool herself, but was choosing to stay alone.

Justly had tucked up her skirt and hoisted the legs of her drawers, though they were already wet. Her arms, too, were bare. As I pushed off my boots and socks, and rolled up the bottoms of my britches, she groped on the bed of the pool, taking up pebbles, examining them, dropping them back.

The shore was deserted, pale sand shimmering for miles, with occasional outcrops of rock. I scanned it for any sign of human life apart from ourselves, hoping for Daniel, but there was nobody. Nearby, a great tree trunk, bare and bleached,

with the remains of a pair of broken branches, lay alongside
the reaching surf. I guessed that it had tumbled from a shore
somewhere and spent years in the water before being thrown
up to sand and sun.

"Look, Scrag."

She was holding something to me again, water trickling
from her hand. I waded toward her, the pool surprisingly cold.
In her palm there was a small pink pebble, smooth, rounded,
but drawn somewhat to a point on one side, the color deeper
there.

"Titty," she said. She let it fall.

I thought she would put it in my pocket with the jade, but
she let it fall. I tried to catch it, but it plipped into the water.

"You got enough of them." She laughed.

"I'd like it."

We searched for a while. Each time she opened her palms,
I looked with her before the handful of commonplace stuff fell
back. Sometimes I was driven to touch her cold fingers momentarily, feeling, in the same instant, both foolishness and a
knocking of excitement that came each time undiminished. I
wanted the little pebble, and I wanted the strange excitement
that had come from nowhere I could have harbored it, as
surprising as the jade in her wet hand.

Justly said her feet were numb. She went out of the pool
and stretched on the sand behind the white tree. I searched
for a while longer, then sat on the tree, looking down on her.

I wanted the pebble, I thought, because it would stand in
my mind with feelings drawn to it from sweet experience. I
turned on the log and looked at the ocean. It seemed to swell
and lift slightly, stretching its surface like the bosom of a
woman in sleep. A sense of words stirring at the back of my

mind, toward the shape of something to be written, gathered as the blue surface moved, and I thought that I would want to write something like "The sea is the breast of the world," but I was not sure that the words were not foolish, and let them drift, as I stretched out on the tree and closed my eyes. I want words, I thought, as I want the little breast-pebble, to stand in my mind for the experience itself, "as it was."

As it was, I said over, silently. The trail seemed an immense distance behind. I looked toward Lorelei. She was getting up, brushing sand from her skirt. Without rising from the log, I watched her coming toward us. I thought how there were no words I could find to tell how that was — the simple action of her walking toward me, the feelings it aroused, the memories drawn around it.

"You tired of lookin' for jade?"

"For a while," said Justly.

"I was lookin' for somethin' else." I wanted to tell her about the pebble, but I thought I would search again and find it, to show her.

"What was that?"

"Oh, treasure."

"Buried treasure," said Justly. Then she was suddenly remembering, as I was, a day far back on the trail, when we watched Sylvester at work. She looked at me, tears welling. I wondered if she now understood his teasing. "I'm goin' wadin' in the sea."

"Justly was rememberin' Sylvester," I explained, but Lorelei was not curious.

"I thought when we got to the ocean I'd want to throw off my clothes and plunge out there — like it could wash off all that sorrowin'."

Justly screamed, running out of the water.

"It's ice! Enough to take yer feet off!" She went back in, yelling again, hopping from foot to foot.

"I'll just be satisfied with wadin'." Lorelei hitched her skirt. "You comin', Scrag?"

I said I would search in the pool again, the thought of showing her the pebble later, and hearing her talk of it, a sharp excitement. She went along the edge of the sea, hitching her drawers, her footprints erratic on the clean, hard sand.